damaged

DARK ROAD SERIES

KRYS FENNER

damaged

DARK ROAD SERIES #2

Published by

TWO REALMS PUBLISHING LLC

HTTPS://TWO-REALMS-PUBLISHING-LLC.COM/

Cover and Interior Design: We Got You Covered Book Design
Editor: Jamie Morris

Printed in the United States of America

I dedicate this novel to my mom. She has always been there for me and supported me when times were hard. This book would not have been possible without her.

I love you, Mom.

Tattoo design by Freaky Deaky Designs

http://freakydeakydesigns.wix.com/home

"Thou shalt also consider in thine heart, that, as a man chasteneth his son, so the Lord thy God chasteneth thee."

– Deuteronomy 8:5, King James Bible

"WHAT'S LEFT OF ME"

The filth just won't wash away;
I see what you left of me every day.
You can't begin to imagine the pain.
Hollowness has made its claim.

A small piece of my heart still remains,
But can I still give it away?
All the trust I had is gone.
Will I ever see a new dawn?

Written by: Bella Kynaston

prologue

The weight of the muscled body on top of hers overwhelmed all of her senses. No pain radiated from her shoulder down her arm. Her ribs no longer throbbed from the beating she received by her attackers. The broken bone she'd suffered no longer bothered her. She felt nothing, not even the tears that prickled her eyes.

She was numb. All she could focus on was the large body brutally pounding into her for the second time. Or the third. She'd lost track. How long had they been behind that rancid dumpster? How long before her body caved from all the damage and she died? The man rammed into her one final time and moaned as he finished. She cried out at the invasion.

Bella gasped and bolted upright. Frantically, she scanned her surroundings. Bed to her left, closet to her right. Okay. She was on the floor of her bedroom, exactly where she'd fallen asleep. It was just a nightmare. She tucked her knees against her chest. At least this time she didn't scream and wake her parents. Had they checked on her?

What time was it?

She peeked at her clock. It was only midnight. Meant she'd slept about two hours. Bella rubbed the sleep from her eyes. Her parents were likely in bed for the night. She could quietly slip out of her bedroom and enjoy some time sitting in the bay window. She'd pop a couple of hydrocodone, too. They wouldn't kick in right away, but eventually they would help with the pain.

1

Wait. Noises echoed down the hall.

Leaning against her door, she listened closely to the voices. Bella frowned. Her parents were yelling at each other. Sounded like they were in her father's office. Their words were too muffled for her make out. Gently, she cracked her door and tiptoed along the wall until she was close enough to hear.

"I don't care what you think is going on. I will not hospitalize our daughter and alienate her any more than she already has been alienated," her mother said.

Bella's father replied, "I don't believe it would cause more division in her life or in our family. It would be advantageous for all of us. She could get the care she needed."

"Was that not the point of getting her to the psychiatrist you recommended?"

Her father sighed, loudly. "It was, but I suspect her sessions go nowhere. If she doesn't cope with what has transpired, things will get worse."

"And if we send her to an institution, you don't think that will happen? Have you not considered what it would do to her if we took her away from her friends?"

"She doesn't spend time with them now!"

"Keep your voice down." Milena hissed. "I will not discuss this with you any further. Your idea may be mentioned at our meeting with Dr. Filmore, tomorrow. But do not discuss it with our daughter before then."

Shit! Bella slipped back into her bedroom, closed the door, and lay back on the floor. When her door opened and the light shone in, she pretended to be asleep until it shut again. Whew. Just in time. God, how could her parents even have that kind of conversation? Would they really have her committed? It wasn't like she was psychotic. But her father viewed her as unstable.

Maybe he was right. He was the one with a counseling degree. She loved her mother for her protection, but Bella had to wonder, would she be better off in a mental institution? She considered the option. They'd definitely make her stop taking the painkillers. And they'd probably monitor her every move. Make her talk about all the tragic events in her life. No, no, no. That would be awful. She'd have to convince her parents she was improving—and learn to hide the pain.

one

Swifty stared at the letter in his hands. He hadn't read it in quite some time. For his sixteenth birthday, he had been given the knowledge of his birth parents. The woman he had spent his life calling Madre was his caretaker, not his birth mother. The letter he'd received on his birthday that year indicated his mother had died when he was just a child. As for his father, that was a story unto itself. For his safety, he had been tendered unto the woman he knew as his mother to be cared for. Although that first and second letter held a lot of vital information, the third letter, the one he had received nearly two and a half years ago, was the one that mattered the most. It was so important that he held it in his hands now, and read through it again.

My Dearest Luis,

I understand you wish to meet. Though I would normally take this into consideration, I cannot agree. The risk is too great. You must understand. If certain individuals knew of our relationship, you would not be safe. I promised your mother long ago I would ensure your protection. It is my hope that one day I may return, and we can be a true family, as we once were. But today is not that day.

However, I believe there is a task of great importance I may ask of you. A girl, Maylin Kynaston, will be fourteen in a couple of months and starting Jackson Heights

3

in the fall. I need you to keep an eye on her.

There are rules you will need to follow. I cannot explain why, but it is imperative for your safety and hers that you do as I say. I have listed the rules below and included a few photographs of her and of those with whom she spends time.

1.   *Purchase a burner phone with cash.*

2.   *Learn the difference between her friends and enemies.*

3.   *Get close to each, discreetly.*

4.   *Discover her habits, from a distance.*

5.   *Do not approach her at any point.*

6.   *Do not interfere with her normal life.*

7.   *Do what you can to protect her from harm.*

8.   *Memorize these rules and her image from the photographs.*

9.   *And then destroy them all.*

That had been nearly two and half years ago. Swifty had followed every rule except one. A fire had been started in a large garbage can in his backyard. He'd stood before it with the letter and pictures in hand, but for a reason he had yet to fathom, he couldn't bear the thought of burning it all to ashes. Instead, he'd extinguished the fire and hidden the photos and letter.

Something familiar about the girl tugged at his heart. Those hazel eyes of hers haunted him every time he looked at the photographs. Her gaze invaded his dreams nightly. It was like she held a piece of him that was missing. In the past two years, he had learned all he could about her—but discovered nothing that explained why she meant so much to him.

Maylin used the nickname Bella. Victor, she had befriended as a child. Her friend Alex was a regular *cosa* fanatic and a weekly partier. Bella had been friends with Sarresh since camp, but that appeared to have ended. She had been hospitalized only once in her life—until recent events unfolded. And she had been adopted, but the records were sealed.

Could the adoption be the connection he felt they shared?

After Swifty started dating Heather, he'd asked her to learn what more she could find out about Bella. But, although he had hoped Heather's ability to obtain information would prove useful, she'd found out nothing he hadn't already known. Heather also happened to be one of Bella's enemies—although her enmity was nothing compared to that of the obsessed Gervasio Rodriguez. If only Gervasio hadn't met Bella at the Fourth of July party. A lot of heartache could've been prevented.

Swifty had thwarted many of Gervasio's plans, but he'd ultimately failed to keep Bella safe from that asshole. A couple of weeks after the party, he learned what Gervasio had done to Bella. He'd hoped when he shared his knowledge with Cristobal, the guy would do something to intervene and stop any attack on Bella. Except nothing happened. It was then that Swifty realized he was out of his league—and he'd done the only thing he could think of, contact his father.

Unfortunately, although he'd called the phone number his father provided in his letter multiple times and sent several text messages, no response from his father had been received.

At least Gervasio was in jail, Swifty thought, now. But for how long? The man had the money to post bail, but it seemed he was biding his time. He must have some kind of scheme. If only Swifty could discover what that scheme entailed, then maybe a plan could be devised to keep Bella safe. He would be damned if she had to face Gervasio alone, again.

If his father hadn't contacted him within the next twenty-four hours, well, he'd have to break another rule. Just as Swifty tucked the letter away, the burner phone he'd purchased two and half years ago vibrated. He flipped the phone open. "Finally."

Bella half-glanced at Alex. "You look fine."

"That's what you said about the last pair of jeans."

"They were fine, too."

"You're no help!" Alex exclaimed loudly and stomped back into the changing room.

It was cruel, but Alex's reaction when Bella failed to compliment her amused the hell out of Bella. She'd only agreed to the trip to the mall to escape her parents. They were back in the house, and although her parents had been eager to return, she was the one who had to go back to the room where it all started. But between the pills and her capacity to stay out of the house, she managed to hide her pain well. Even better than she had as a child.

"What about this?" Alex stepped out in a tight, black miniskirt. The black should've washed out her white legs; instead, her skin glowed with an ethereal beauty.

"Fine."

"Fine? Again?"

Bella snorted a tiny giggle and whipped a hand to her mouth to stifle a laugh.

Alex crossed her arms. "You're screwing with me."

"Maybe. Who're you trying to impress, anyway?"

"Raul's going to be at the party." Alex blushed.

"You must really like him."

"I do. He's, you know, different."

"I'll take your word for it." Bella grinned. "Try something else. You might give the poor boy a heart attack in that skirt."

Alex brushed the skirt down and glanced at her legs. Self-loathing flitted across her face. She nodded and disappeared back into the changing room.

Bella sighed. She hadn't meant the comment to come off as negative. It was supposed to be a compliment, but it appeared her friend didn't take it that way. "Alex."

"No, no. It's okay. You're right. I'll just change into something else."

How could she forget her friends had their own demons? Alex had never accepted she was beautiful. The girl was tall and thin, and her skin was flawless, but she could pinpoint everything that was wrong with her body. Now that Bella thought about it, she had never seen Alex in a skirt. Alex had often complained about her legs. They were too long, they were too pale, people could see her freckles.

Lord, she felt so stupid. Bella had enjoyed teasing her friend about all the jeans the girl had tried on, but hadn't thought twice when she commented on the skirt.

Someone brushed against Bella's back. She flinched and her whole body stiffened. She spun around and swung, and the palm of her hand smacked the face of the guy behind her.

"What the hell!?"

Oh. It was just some stranger. *Shit!* Bella shoved a hand through her hair and inched backwards. Surely, he hadn't done it on purpose, but that never mattered.

She panicked, now, at even the slightest hint of anybody's hands near her body.

"I ... I ... I'm sorry."

"Get a grip, would ya? Sheesh." The guy shook his head and walked away.

Bella eased her back against the wall, gripped her head, and slowly slid to the floor. This wasn't the first time she'd hit some random person. Her body was a time bomb triggered by the slightest touch. She'd talked to the freaking doctor her parents asked her to see. But nothing improved. It all just got worse with every day that passed.

That monster had invaded her life and stolen all she'd had, leaving a horrible world in its place. It seemed like everything would be better if she hadn't survived. The pain she carried in her chest wouldn't exist. The fear she faced every time she left her house would be gone. There would only be peace.

Peace. Not heaven. Just peace. Bella hiccupped, and her tears subsided.

She just wanted her old life back. The time she had had with Jeremiah— *Oh God!* No. She couldn't think about him. The hole he left in her heart magnified the pain she felt from the attack. Why? Why had this happened to her? She was a good person. Nothing about her life made sense anymore. Everything had spun out of control. Someone had to take the reins. She wasn't sure how much longer she could hold on.

"Shh. Hey it's okay. You're okay." Alex's strong and steady voice broke through the haze.

A relaxing voice. That was what she needed when the panic attacks occurred. Someone to comfort and calm her ... without trying to reassure her with touch. Just a voice to pull her out of her head.

Bella blinked unshed tears from her eyes. "Alex?"

"Yeah, B. Everything's okay. Come on. Take a deep breath with me."

Bella did as her friend directed, and the darkness reluctantly disappeared. "It happened again."

"I know, but it's okay. Can you stand? Good. Come on, stand up."

As instructed, Bella stood. She wiped at her face and sniffled. "I should go."

"Okay. Just let me change back into my clothes, and we'll leave."

"No. Stay and shop. You need something for the party tonight."

"Are you sure?"

"Yeah. But get the skirt. Raul won't be able to resist you."

Jamar glared at the thin case file on his desk. The intelligence from Juan Castell's missing person's report was minimal. According to the documentation, a neighbor had reported him missing. The house had been searched, and all that had been found was a hairbrush. That was how the man's DNA had been obtained.

A half-assed search had been conducted, but no other information had been gathered. It appeared that either people didn't care that the man was missing or they assumed he'd disappeared on purpose. As for the neighbor, she died of a heart attack two years ago. If they were going to find this guy, his detectives would have to start from the beginning.

Detective Russell's knock interrupted his train of thought.

"Sheriff, they're here."

"Send them in."

DeWei and Milena Kynaston stepped into his office, followed by Russell.

After taking a seat, Dr. Kynaston got down to business. "What have you discovered?"

Jamar removed a photograph from the file and laid it on his desk. "Have you ever seen this man before?"

Bella's parents studied the picture, and Mrs. Kynaston nodded. "Yes. Once. About two years before our wedding, I spent a weekend with Ileana. She introduced this man to me as a friend."

"But?"

Mrs. Kynaston sighed. "They both had a ring tattooed on their ring finger. Ileana never confirmed nor denied they were married, but I suspected they had done so in secret."

"Did this strike you as strange?"

"Yes. Ileana and I discussed everything when we were younger. I could not comprehend why she would hide such news from me."

He could. The woman had to have known what she'd gotten herself into.

"When she introduced him to you, Mrs. Kynaston, did she tell you his name?"

"Yes. Juan ... Juan Moreno, I believe."

"What does this have to do with our daughter?" Dr. Kynaston asked.

"This man's name is Juan Castell," Jamar said, stabbing the photo with his index finger. "He was the leader of the Grim Reapers. The man who took his place is the one we believe responsible for all the attacks on Bella. Mr. Castell, though, he's her biological father."

"What?" Mrs. Kynaston gasped.

"He was arrested with Ileana for drug possession in New York nineteen years ago. Just after she died, he left New York and reappeared here. Then, in 2003, he went missing."

Mrs. Kynaston fidgeted with the strap of her purse, then glanced at her husband. "I have to tell him."

"We agreed we would follow the documents."

"To hell with the documents! This is our daughter, and I will do whatever it takes to protect her."

Dr. Kynaston leaned back in his chair. "Very well."

"Tell me." Jamar glowered at the two of them. The last time he had spoken with them, he felt they had purposely left something out. He would have guaranteed it linked back to Juan Castell. They had withheld too much information for far too long.

"You must understand, we were instructed to keep all information regarding her parents, the adoption, everything to ourselves. We signed nondisclosure agreements before the adoption paperwork proceeded."

Interesting. Jamar suspected the secrecy served the purpose of protecting Bella's true identity, as well as that of her father. Children of powerful men in the drug trade were at great risk, simply by fact of their existence. "Go on."

"First, we had to change her name. Birth records were altered to make it seem that I was her biological mother and DeWei, her biological father. Second, a bank account was established in her new name. We were given shared control. After the rape, we decided to give Bella access. We provided her a debit card to use and told her it was money we had saved for her since she was born. All of her transactions are monitored."

"By you?"

"No."

No? Jamar frowned. He didn't like where this was going. "Then by who?"

"I don't know for certain. Possibly the lawyer. I just know we got a phone call a couple of weeks ago when she withdrew two hundred dollars each day for five days."

"Do you know what she spent it all on?"

"Clothes. She has been on a shopping spree these last few weeks."

Lord, let that be the God's honest truth, Jamar thought. With access to cash like that Bella could do a lot of things.

"Okay. I need to speak with her again. But, first, the two of you are going to sit down with her and tell her she's adopted. Don't tell her who her parents are. I'll be showing her photos, and I need her reaction to be unbiased."

Three days had passed since her parents revealed the awful truth. Milena told her that Ileana was her biological mother, but had refused to provide Bella with information about her biological father. The news that they'd kept the adoption from her infuriated Bella—and her "mother's" continued refusal to share all the important details angered her more. Her rage was the reason she sat in this stupid waiting room, once again prepared to spill her guts.

Bella glanced at her watch. How much longer would she have to wait? She despised the positive phrases carefully hung on the walls. Why couldn't her shrink's outer room be sterile, like any other doctor's office?

"Bella."

Finally! She stood and exchanged greetings with the short, stout, dark-haired woman who appeared in the doorway, then walked past her doctor and crossed to the window. She normally liked the view, but she was so on edge the familiar scene appeared rundown and grungy to her eyes.

"They lied to me."

"Why don't you sit on the couch? You seem quite anxious."

"I don't want to sit." Bella paced the length of the room. "How am I supposed to trust them? How am I supposed to accept that everything they did was in my best interest?"

"Is that what they've told you?"

"Yes. But I couldn't listen to them anymore, not once they told me I was adopted. They've tried explaining ... but I can only hear so much at a time."

During her last few sessions, the doctor had simply let Bella to rant—which she'd appreciated. Most of the time, Bella could find a slight hint of relief in talking, even if she shared nothing that seemed to be of real importance. But, truthfully, everything she talked about mattered to her—and her doctor said she was making progress. Now, though, they had a topic it was difficult to avoid.

"Trust is difficult to earn back once it has been damaged. It doesn't mean it is impossible."

"That's the thing. I don't care that I was adopted. I care that they didn't share that information willingly." Bella slumped onto the couch.

The doctor grabbed her notepad. "Do you think they purposely hid the truth?"

"Well, they obviously kept it from me." Not that DeWei or Milena ever explained why they'd hidden the truth—even though Bella asked. And there was so much more she needed to know. What was her mother like? Why wouldn't they talk about her father? How did her mother die? Did she have any siblings? But the people who called themselves her parents refused to answer any more questions.

"Many adoptive parents don't mention the adoption to the child because they think of the child as their own."

"That's the thing. They didn't give me any reason for having hidden the truth. Just that now they *had* to tell me because the sheriff thinks my biological parents are related to my attack."

"And you haven't seen the sheriff, yet?"

Of course, she hadn't visited him, yet. He'd called the house several times over the last two days, but Bella refused to talk to him. She would go to his office—but only when she was ready.

"What are you, inside my head, doc?"

"No. It makes sense. You're exasperated and confused by the situation. Sheriff Detrone implied that your biological parents have something to do with the rape, and you think it might be true. And that scares you. Why?"

As usual, the doctor nailed her feelings. Except it wasn't just the possibility of the horrible truth about her parents. It was more than that. Facing the man who attacked her freaked her out. What if he got released from jail? Would he come after her again? Try to kidnap her again? Her world had been shaken. This new information, it shattered what little of her old world she had left. She had nothing, now. She was emptiness personified. "Maybe I don't deserve the happiness I've had."

Swifty swallowed, grateful for the window between him and Gervasio. The man looked downright pissed. So the news he'd delivered hadn't been positive.

A few days ago, he accessed the court records and learned that Bella planned to testify. In his mind, this was good. He'd given the information to his father, who hadn't responded since the conversation they'd had last week.

Unfortunately, Gervasio didn't share the joy. The only thing that seemed to please him was the intel regarding the DNA. How had the man managed to plant somebody else's DNA? Of course, Gervasio had not explained. Even if they'd been talking in code, their conversations were still monitored.

"Should I check on her?" Swifty asked into the phone that allowed them to communicate.

Into the handset on his side of the glass, Gervasio replied, "Yes. She have great problem with health. Worry too much."

Swifty winced. The only problem Bella had with her health was sitting right in front of him. But he needed to keep up appearances—otherwise, he wouldn't have bothered with this visit. "I understand, sir. And expenses?"

"Whatever it take. Is that clear?"

"Yes, sir. I'll report back."

"Good." Gervasio scowled. "And Swifty?"

He hated that nickname. The Grim Reapers had given it to him after they appointed him messenger and learned about his ability to access certain information quickly, while remaining practically invisible. "Yes, sir?"

Gervasio's gaze homed in on Swifty, and a sinister smile spread across his lips, emphasizing the jagged scar on his face. Then his gaze bounced over to the guy who stood behind Swifty—and man Swifty knew looked like just another guard watching the room. "You should get small gift for your ... girlfriend."

"Yes, sir. I understand. Is there anything else?"

"No. That all. You may go."

Swifty returned the phone to its cradle. This would be one of those moments where serving as the underrated courier benefited him. He exchanged a handshake with the waiting guard and discreetly tucked away the folded envelope in the pocket of his pants.

Interesting. The guard's fingers looked similar to his own. Like Swifty, the man had no fingerprints. He suspected his father had something to do with the fact that all ten of his fingers had been badly burned when he was a child. Those unmarked fingertips had proved more useful to the Grim Reapers over the past two years than he liked to recall.

Trekking toward his car, Swifty tightened his grip on the envelope. He would open it when he reached his vehicle. Then he would see what Gervasio was scheming—and decide on his own course of action. Either way, he refused to contact his father again. Juan Castell had gone absent for the last time.

two

There it was. The hideous door marked New Mexico Rescate County Sheriff. This particular door had become the bane of her existence. It was supposed to offer comfort. But for her, it did the complete opposite. She walked to the half-open door and knocked.

"Sheriff Detrone?"

"Hey, Bella. Come on in. You know you can call me Jamar."

"I know, but it doesn't feel right." He had always been nice to her. But she saw Miah in his father's face—which made the sheriff a sad reminder of what she'd lost.

"Why is that?" the sheriff asked, as Detective Russell joined them.

"If I call you Jamar, then I have to think of you as Miah's dad and not just the sheriff."

"I take the two of you split up," Sheriff Detrone said.

"Did he tell you?"

"No, but you don't come around anymore and he doesn't go out as much. Not to mention that he quit the play."

"I see," Bella said. She knew about *Hamlet*. It would've been better if both Miah and David hadn't backed out of their respective parts. "Look, I don't want to talk about Miah. I was told you needed to see me."

"Sure. There are some things Detective Russell and I need to discuss with you about your case. Are you okay to be here for a little bit?"

"Yeah, I guess." How many times had she been to the police station since she'd been released from the hospital? More times than she dared count. Too many questions popped up. The police wanted her to remember every minute detail, and she wished to forget them all. Just pretend none of it had happened. She'd happily go back to when there was no bad stuff, she hadn't suffered any physical or mental damage, and she still believed her parents were her parents.

"August 27th, how many men attacked you?" Detective Russell asked.

Bella despised reliving her nightmare over and over, again. Her stomach clenched up at the regurgitated memory. Somehow, she managed to keep the bile down, and answered, "Two men. Just the one grabbed me from behind, then the second showed up a few minutes later."

"Had you ever seen them before?"

"No. And I only saw the one man's face. The other kept his face covered. Aren't they both in jail? Is this really necessary."

The sheriff nodded. "We wouldn't put you through this if it wasn't.

Detective Russell shifted toward her. "Now, I'm going to show you a photo array. Tell me if you recognize anyone." He presented a sheet of cardboard to her with six photographs stuck to it.

Bella pointed to the one of Jorge Smith. She could still taste his awfulness and feel his grimy paws on her body. "Him. He was the one who grabbed me from behind. He attacked me first."

"Good. What about the second man? Were there any distinguishing marks? Anything that stood out?"

"I think he had a scar on his face too, like the one Petar has. But he had gloves over his hands, a bandana over his face, and he kept his hoodie up. And he mostly stayed behind me. So, I'm not sure."

"What about smells? Any particular scent that stood out?"

Something about his question triggered a piece of memory stuck in the back of her mind. The alley had stunk. They had taken her near a dumpster. But there was more. Bella bit on her bottom lip and, despite her best efforts, faced a crossroads. If she allowed this memory access, she could never push it down again.

What was she thinking? There was only one way forward. She had no choice.

"His breath."

"What about it?"

"It ... he ... tasted like garbage." Tears rolled down her cheeks. She couldn't fight off the pain. This was what she had to endure. Her story had to be repeated until every possible detail was plucked from it.

Miah's father presented her a box of tissues, and she yanked one out.

"Take your time," Detective Russell said.

"I remember the stench, how awful it was when he ... he put his tongue in my mouth." Petar had tried to kiss her once. She couldn't remember the smell of his breath, then.

"Why does that matter if you said the DNA matched Petar?" Bella asked.

"We just want to make sure we have all the details. That no stone gets left unturned. Okay?" With a look of sympathy eerily like Miah's, the sheriff held the box of tissues out again.

Bella refused another tissue. "Okay."

"Good. Let's go back to your first attacker, Jorge Smith. Do you remember if he used a condom at all?"

Revisiting that day was so hard, but she had to. She recalled nearly everything that happened until she passed out. She hadn't seen him put anything on, but her mind hadn't really been focused on anything other than survival. "No. I don't know. I just wanted to escape, see another day."

"Did he say anything to you?"

"He called me his honey bear and kept telling me to be a good girl. Then he claimed me as his."

Sheriff Detrone scanned his notes. "What about at the Fall Harvest Festival? Did he say anything to you, then?"

Weeks had gone by between her rape and the Festival, but the two events were linked by a never-ending nightmare. All the damage she'd suffered in the attack had healed by the Fall Festival. At least the physical damage. The mental and psychological damage? It had just been getting started.

After the attack, Bella'd been determined to return to normal and refused to relinquish her position as director of the Halloween event her church put on every year. But her strategy hadn't worked the way she'd hoped. While all the people in town enjoyed the festivities, Smith showed up, attempted to kidnap her, and shot Miah.

The sheriff and Detective Russell were eyeing her. She brought herself back to the present. "He said he wanted me to go with him. He planned to take me away. Said I belonged to him. Something about collecting on a promise my father made."

"Did he tell you what the promise was?" Detective Russell asked.

"No."

"And you had never met Jorge Smith prior to the rape or the Festival?"

"No."

"Have you ever been to the Detention Center where your father works?"

"You mean my adopted father? DeWei? A few times, yes."

"Do you remember the exact dates?"

Bella leaned on the chair arm and tucked her chin in her hand. "Not really," she concluded, after thinking about it for a moment. "But the guards should have it in their logs."

"Good. I'll have those checked out. Have you ever attended a party in Desemper Ridge?"

"Yes. I went to a Fourth of July party with Alex this past summer." Hmm. No one'd asked about the party before. Or the times she'd gone to visit DeWei at work.

"What happened at the party?"

Bella blinked. She hardly remembered the party. The only thing she really recalled was what she wore. Something Alex had picked out. Something much more revealing than her usual clothes. She may have danced with someone, but the rest of the night remained a blur.

"Not a lot of anything. Not that I remember."

"Is it possible you and Jorge Smith could have met at that party?"

"I ... I don't know. Maybe? I got dressed at Alex's house. When we got to the party, things were already in full swing. She wasn't supposed to leave my side, but we got separated. At some point, I got a drink. But I don't remember how I got it. The rest of the night is a blur."

"Why didn't you mention this before?" Detective Russell asked.

"It didn't seem relevant."

"Okay. So, you could have met Smith at the party, but you don't remember. And if you had met at the party, it could be the reason he claimed you as his— and branded you."

Of all the things to bring up, it had to be that. Bella glared at the two men in front of her. A pair of crisscrossed scythes had been the only thing to link the crimes to a gang called the Grim Reapers. She stood and rubbed her neck. The last thing she intended to discuss was the scar branded into her neck, visible for everyone to see. She'd never been so glad for long hair in her life.

But Sheriff Detrone's questions still hadn't touched on the topic of her birth parents. And she wanted answers more than she desired to leave.

"I don't know," Bella said, and sat back down.

The visit to the police station took longer than she'd anticipated, running into the early evening. Initially, she planned to go straight home, but she needed space after the information she'd discovered about the type of people her birth parents were. Not to mention the disclosure of Jorge Smith's claims. According to him, they'd met at that Fourth of July party, where she introduced herself as Giovanna. He told the police they'd "had a good time"—that she didn't remember and which made her, somehow, feel she deserved the attack. Smith also said she dodged calls he'd made to her, after.

Space wasn't the only thing she required, though. She also needed to be reminded that happiness actually existed. That she hadn't imagined the happiness she'd once had. So, Bella drove her new VW bug, a gift from her parents—or a bribe—to the place she remembered feeling that happiness, the only place she'd ever found true peace. Miah lived on the outskirts of Nautica Valley, about twenty minutes from her house. She had spent one night at the Detrone's residence, the night her own home had been vandalized. Unable to sleep, she'd slipped out Mandy Detrone's room and settled in their living room—where, after a couple of hours, Miah found her curled up on the couch. He took her to his bed for safekeeping and slept on the floor beside her. That was the first and only night she could recall actually sleeping peacefully, without nightmares. A peace she lost the day he walked out of her life.

"It's my job to protect you." Miah paused. "We need to talk ... about us."

Standing at the end of his hospital bed, Bella's eyes locked on Miah's. She'd heard girls talk about how those words signaled death hovering near a soon-to-be rotting corpse.

"What ... what about us?"

"I don't think this is going to work."

With that, she felt a stab in her heart. A hole opened up. She was wounded in a way she hadn't known existed. "I don't understand. Why would you think that?"

"Look at us. Look at where we are." Miah gestured to the hospital bed he'd been laid up in. "Yeah, so I'm going home. But how long before one of us ends up back in here. Or worse. We've been fooling ourselves this whole time."

Bella looked to him. She was utterly confused. He couldn't mean that. "How? By caring about each other? By trying to protect one another? How does that make us fools?"

"Because we aren't protecting each other. We're the problem. Not the solution."

"I don't believe that. Everything with us makes sense. Please don't tell me this is your honest-to-God response to all that has happened."

"This is what's right. We can't be together. It's over." Jeremiah's face was pinched tight and his voice, harsh.

Her heart shattered. He might as well have reached in and pulled the thing out. Because at that very moment, whatever beat beneath her chest become nothing more than an organic mechanism. Tears rolled down her cheeks. "Why? Why are you doing this?"

"Because I don't want you."

"You said you'd never leave me," Bella whispered.

"I lied."

Those two words hurt more than the damage done by her attackers. Sobbing, Bella grabbed her purse and ran out the door.

She'd broken down in a way she'd never done before. Nothing could've prepared her for the immensity of the heartache she'd felt with him gone. The emptiness consumed her. Prior to that night, Miah hadn't ever seemed disturbed by their relationship. It only proved he was as good an actor as she was.

At that point, Bella didn't deny she needed to see a shrink—but she wasn't eager to go, either. She hadn't mentioned the break-up to anyone, not even her friends, but her parents knew she wasn't recovering emotionally from the attack, even if they didn't know about the rift with Miah. What convinced her to talk to the psychiatrist was the conversation she'd overheard a couple weeks after the break-up—her parents discussing the possibility of having her committed.

Maybe they'd overreacted, but things were not returning to normal. No denying that. And normal only existed with Miah.

Now, Bella gasped when the man running a marathon in her brain walked around the corner of the house holding a bag of trash. Last chore of the evening. Part of her hoped Miah saw her, and part of her demanded she remain hidden. This tug-of-war was more than her heart could handle.

three

Whistling, Jeremiah walked barefoot around the side of the house and dumped the trash in the bin. He turned around and started back, but paused mid-step. That black VW Beetle. Was someone sitting in it? Who? Why? He walked toward the car cautiously. Suddenly, its headlights flooded the street, and the black bug sped off. He'd only caught a glimpse of the driver. A dark-haired girl. He'd heard through the grapevine Bella had gotten a car, but not the make or color. Had it been her?

He missed Bell like crazy. He'd destroyed one of the best things in his life. Even though he did it for her own protection. He still checked up on her as best he could. Without her knowing. And he'd seen, over recent weeks, how the storm behind her hazel eyes had worsened.

Stepping back into the house, he turned to one of the two people he could ask for information about his angel. Jeremiah stopped in front of Amanda's door and knocked. "Hey, sis, you decent?"

"Whatever you think you need can wait."

No, it couldn't. He opened the door and poked his head in. "Come on. I need to talk to you. It's important."

Amanda lifted her eyes and glared at her brother. "Can't you see I'm busy?"

"Just a minute? Please, Mandy." Jeremiah folded his hands together as if he was praying. It might just do the trick.

Amanda slammed her book shut and spun around in her chair. "Christ, you're annoying. Go 'head. Come in."

Jeremiah arranged himself on the bed across from her. "Look, I know you and Vick are tired of me asking questions."

"Yet, you always have more." She tucked her feet under her butt. "I'll listen, but you need to stop coming to us. You need to talk to her. Even if she brushes you off, you should try."

"I can't."

"Why?"

He hadn't told anyone about the break-up. Though they figured it out, obviously, no one except him and Bell knew the details. "I broke up with her."

"I know, but that still doesn't explain why you can't talk to her."

"Didn't she tell you?"

"No. She doesn't talk about you at all when we hang out."

So, his sister didn't know how he pushed Bell away, like he was disgusted by her and no longer hungered for her. Thank God. And he wasn't about to tell her.

Instead, he asked what he came to find out. "What kind of car does she drive?"

"A black Volkswagen Beetle. Why?"

So, it was her. "She was here."

"What?"

"Just a minute ago, when I was taking out the trash. She was just sitting in her car. I wasn't sure it was her because I couldn't see her clearly, and I didn't know what car she drove. She took off when I started toward her."

A warm smile stretched across Amanda's face. "Then maybe it's time you return the favor and go get your girlfriend back."

Jeremiah hung his head. It sounded so simple when Mandy said it. But he couldn't.

"Okay," she said. "What did you do?"

"I pushed her away." He jumped to his feet. The words had to come out. "I really screwed up, Mandy. I said things I didn't mean. I thought I was doing what had to be done. I could've gotten her killed. But I didn't think she'd just accept it if I told her I wanted to break up because I was trying to keep her safe."

"What're you talking about?" His sister stood in front of him and squeezed his shoulders, kindly. "What did you say?"

"I said I didn't want her."

Sarresh stoked the fire. "Shh. Takina's sleeping."

"You're always shushing me. Baby made you no fun," Bella said.

The girl had drunk enough for the two of them, Sarresh thought. Over the past couple of weeks, she'd noticed Bella had started enjoying a drink or two, but nothing like this. "You don't normally drink this much. What's going on with you?"

"My life. I hate it. All of it."

"I thought you were dealing with everything."

"Talk, talk, talk. I talk, but not about the right stuff. Not like I could know I was adopted." Bella put the bottle of wine to her mouth and took another long swig.

"Adopted? When did you find that out?"

"Last week ..." Bella hiccupped. "... end. Sheriff made my ... I don't even know what to call them. Parents, Dr. and Mrs. Kynaston, doodoo heads ..." Bella giggled.

"How about calling them Mom and Dad? Like always."

"Noooo. Booo. Cuz my mom is dead, and my dad ... welp, he's a drug king. Bastard."

"What?"

"Yep. And, and, and he ran the same gang as the guy who raped me." Bella gulped down some more wine and hiccupped again.

Bella had never once used the word "rape," even though Sarresh knew that was what happened to her. But Sarresh had no idea the rapist belonged to a gang. And that Bella's biological father had run a gang—the same gang! No wonder Bella had been all inside her head earlier. At least until David made an appearance. Somehow, he pulled Bella from wherever she had been. There had been such a difference afterward.

Sarresh worried about that. She didn't trust David at all. And them going to the tattoo parlor tomorrow? That seemed like a really bad idea.

Uncharacteristically, Bella kept talking. "Then there's Petar Jacobs. He was one of them. He's with the gang, too. Never saw that coming. Just too much, too much. Too, too much."

"Petar? The police think he raped you? You can't be serious."

Bella swallowed another gulp from the bottle. "Yep. His DNA. Sweet Petar. He was so nice freshmen year. We were in book club and the thing ... you know, the thing."

"Tutor group?"

"Yeah, that. Always so nice. Even tried to kiss me."

"What?" Bella and Sarresh were still friends freshmen year, and yet the girl had never divulged that juicy tidbit? Petar had been a junior, and they both adored him. He protected them from the usual jokes upper classmen play on freshmen. The guy was popular, but genuine.

"Yep. He tried, but I saved that first kiss. Gave it to the butthead."

"I thought you still liked Jeremiah." When Sarresh had learned about Bella and Jeremiah's break-up, Bella had nearly flooded the couch with her tears. Not only liked—still loved him, Sarresh thought.

"Yes, no, yes." Bella gulped some more wine. "I drove to his house."

"Oh? Did you guys finally talk?"

"No, no, no, no. Will never talk to him again." Bella's whole body trembled and tears rolled down her cheeks. "It hurt so bad. I love him and he says that to me? Who tells someone they don't want them? No, I can never talk to him again."

She inspected the wine bottle and frowned. "Empty." Grumbling under her breath, she set the bottle with the other two on the coffee table and stood up. "Whoa. Room's spinnin'."

"Sit back down." At this point, Bella needed water. Sarresh headed to the kitchen and poured a glass of ice water for her friend, thinking about all the beans she'd just spilled: adoption, gang affiliations, drugging biological parents, Petar Jacobs a rapist, and Jeremiah Detrone a cold-hearted bastard.

Sarresh set the glass of water on the coffee table. Bella had passed out. Good. Rest was a good thing. She trekked across the foyer and headed to a room tucked behind the staircase, knocking lightly and opening the door. "Mike ..."

He held a finger up. "No, that's excellent ... Okay. Keep me posted." Mike returned the phone to its cradle and glanced at Sarresh. "What can I do for you?"

"Did Takina wake up?"

"No. Is that all?"

"B passed out. Can you carry her upstairs?"

Mike followed her to the living room and looked at Bella on the couch. "I don't like her being like this around Takina."

"Don't start that again."

"I have every intention of protecting our daughter to the best of my ability." He scooped Bella in his arms and headed for the staircase.

"And, what? I don't? You know what, don't answer that. I'm not incompetent. I know what you're trying to do, and given our situation, I get it, but I'm being the friend I haven't been to B. The least you can do is—"

"She's lost weight," he said, looking at Bella's sleeping face.

Sarresh frowned. Was he attempting to change the subject? To avoid the fight that often followed any mention of their "situation"? No. Mike truly appeared concerned.

"I know she's going through a lot, but I don't like this. Have Mrs. Adams make waffles, eggs, and bacon for her in the morning."

Sarresh smiled a tiny smile as Mike carefully settled Bella on the bed. She hadn't seen his caring side in so long she'd nearly forgotten what it looked like. Maybe they needed her friend as much as she needed them. "I'll get her into nightclothes, check on Takina, and then call Mandy."

"Make sure Bella has some aspirin and water. She'll need them when she wakes up."

"Thank you, Mike. I'll do that."

With one ear out for Jeremiah's arrival, Amanda continued her phone conversation with Sarresh. "I got bits and pieces. He bolted before I could get a lot out of him."

"Wish I could say I was surprised," Sarresh said. I just don't know what to do with them. They really need to talk. Both of them love each other. Too bad they can't see it."

Amanda grinned. "You said it, Z. You know what we need to do, lock them in a room together. Then they'll have to talk."

"I'm in. Just say when and where, I'll help make it happen."

The front door opened. "Call you later." Amanda quickly hung up and texted two words to her boyfriend: *He's home.* Then, stepping into the living room, she greeted her brother.

"Hey. Where'd you go?"

Without answering, Jeremiah walked to the fireplace, grabbed a poker, and stoked the fire—then just stared at the bright flames as they popped and cracked.

Worried by his silence, Amanda placed a hand on his shoulder. "Jeremiah, you okay?"

Jeremiah shook his head. "She went out with Sarresh. I followed them to the mall. Seemed like a good idea. Watch from a distance."

This obviously wasn't going to end well. Amanda plopped down on the couch. Her phone beeped, but she ignored it. "And you saw something?"

"You going to get that?"

"Later. Tell me what happened."

"She was trying this outfit on. I didn't want to take a chance of her spotting me, so I didn't go in. I just watched from outside. The clothes were so ... different. Sort of sexy. Nothing like what she used to wear, but she looked good." He sighed, dragged his hand through his hair and slumped in the chair. "I hoped ..."

Amanda waited, but he never finished his statement. Not that he really had to. Bella, who always wore modest skirts before the rape, had taken to wearing jeans since her house was vandalized, not long after the attack. According to what her younger brother had just seen, the girl was still making herself over. But if Jeremiah'd hoped Bella would go back to her old self ... Well, the girl had changed, which wasn't necessarily a bad thing. At least in Amanda's opinion. "Some change is to be expected. Bella can't be the same after what she's had to deal with. Doesn't mean you should think less of her."

"I don't."

"Then what's making you act like you lost the love of your life?"

"David showed up."

"Oh." Sarresh'd mentioned they'd run into David in the store. And there had been a rumor going around school about David being seen around town with Bella over the past few weeks. Amanda, Alex, and Sarresh had all pestered Bella about it, but the only thing she'd admitted to was hanging out with him. As friends. Nothing more.

"It wasn't just that he was there. It was the way she lit up. Like he was the only one in the room."

"You know she doesn't see him that way."

"Then why does it feel like I've been punched in the gut?"

How to answer that? Her phone beeped again. Amanda scanned the text and responded. *Still talking. Call soon.* She tucked her phone away.

"Because you love her. Any possibility she's moved on, no matter how slim, is going to hurt. I promise you though, she still cares about you."

"I don't deserve her love." Jeremiah sat up and swiped at the tears streaming down his face. "I don't know if I can forgive myself for what I said to her."

Amanda frowned. "I don't get it. Then why did you end things?"

"I didn't want to, not really. But all I could hear was Dad telling me how reckless I had been. I could've gotten us both killed."

"But the charges against you were dropped."

Jeremiah shook his head and stood. "Not the point. Thanks for listening, but I think I'm going to crash."

"Yeah, sure. 'Night."

Amanda was puzzled. Jeremiah seemed to have no idea the reason the charges were dropped was because Bella insisted to the police and the district attorney that Jorge Smith had every intention of killing her, and that if Jeremiah hadn't intervened, she wouldn't have made it out alive.

She sighed. Getting them to talk really wasn't going to be easy.

four

Bella filled a small paper cup with water from the bathroom tap, then picked up the unlabeled bottle and stared at it for a moment before shaking out a couple of pills and popping them in her mouth. Most of her prescriptions ran out weeks ago. The doctor insisted on weaning her off them to prevent addiction ... but she couldn't function without them. That's where Tommy came in.

She slipped on her watch, picked up her brush, and pulled her hair into a ponytail, then looked at her reflection carefully. She was wearing a pair of ultra-low rise destroyed skinny jeans and a short-sleeved croptop. Her make-up didn't cover the scar as well as she hoped, though.

Quickly, she removed the hair tie. Her hair would hide the worst of it. Then she grabbed the pill bottle, dropped it in her purse, and headed out of the guest suite.

"Hey. I was just coming to check on you." Sarresh paused at the top of the staircase. "Don't you look bright-eyed and bushy-tailed. I figured you might have a hangover after last night."

Great. It had been one of *those* nights. On the weekends she'd stayed with Sarresh and Mike, Bella usually had a drink or two. But yesterday had been a bad day. Between the police station and her parents, the day had pretty much been ruined. It got better when she ran into David at the mall, but she still carried all the problems back to the house. Drinking had been in order. "I didn't say anything stupid, did I?"

"You don't remember?"

"No." She did recall the first bottle of wine though, and what happened about four hours ago, when she woke up with an enormous headache. Like someone pounded a nail in her skull. The pain ebbed slowly after she spent a half hour hovered over the toilet and then drank the water and took the aspirin on her nightstand.

"Good. And no ... nothing stupid."

"Great. Now, can we go downstairs for breakfast?"

"Yeah. There's waffles, eggs, and bacon."

Hangover food. Not Mrs. Adams' usual. The woman tended more toward grapefruit and soymilk.

Bella loved Sarresh and Mike's place. The house was huge. Two dining halls (formal and informal), kitchen, den, living room, and office occupied the first floor. Second level housed guest and private quarters, and the third was for staff. On the two-acre grounds were a tennis court, indoor pool, basketball court, a greenhouse, and a track—a recent addition.

And it was a great hiding place. A stone wall surrounded the property, and the main entrance was protected by monitored iron gates. Like her own little fortress, Bella was safely sealed in at night. It would've been damn near perfect if it only stopped the nightmares, too.

As Bella and Sarresh entered the dining room, Mike glanced up from his newspaper.

"Good morning."

"Good morning."

That would probably be the extent of their conversation. The man wasn't much of a talker—at least to her. Come to think of it, he hardly said anything to Sarresh, either. If the two talked, it was about day-to-day stuff. The only relationship they seemed to have dealt with their daughter.

Ladylike, Bella slid a napkin across her lap while she waited to be served. A minute later Sarresh walked in with the baby and settled into a seat to Mike's right. A nanny took care of the baby while Sarresh was at school and Mike worked. On the weekends, Mike tended to her. The relationship he'd established with Takina reminded Bella of what she once had with her own adoptive father. It was depressing to think she might never have that back, but she had no idea how to trust him. Not after all the lies and hidden truths.

Bella decided to focus on David Warren. Three years ago, David's family—including his twin sister, Heather—moved to Amorte Cliffstone Estates. Bella had tutored him in geometry for almost two years. Although he had been smitten with her, he hung out with the popular crowd. Not someplace she was comfortable. During last night's shopping trip, she and Sarresh ran into him and his friend Tyler, and she told the guys she wanted to get a tattoo. David insisted his tattoo artist was great, and she agreed to go to him.

Then David and Tyler ended up spending the rest of the evening with Bella and Sarresh—and it gave Bella a chance to get to know him better. He showed her he was thoughtful, kind, funny, and genuine. He answered all her questions honestly, even if they were personal. If he hadn't, she would never have considered him as more than a friend.

Emerging from her thoughts, she saw Sarresh hand Mike an envelope.

"What's that?"

"I don't know. Uncle Jamar asked me to give it to Mike when I was at the house the other day."

"Oh." The rest was none of her business. "Is your brother visiting soon?"

"He's coming up after fall semester is over."

"Is he going to see your mom while he's here?" It was a loaded question, but for giggles, Bella asked.

"No one's going to see that bitch."

Mike dropped the newspaper on the table. "Language!"

"For crying out loud, she's not even two months old. Like she's going to know what I'm saying." Sarresh glanced at Bella. "I'm sure he'll want to see you again. He used to tell me you were like a second sister—annoying."

Bella tore off a piece of waffle, and threw it at her friend. "I think I'm offended."

Sarresh grinned and threw a bit of toast back at Bella.

Mike interjected as if he were the only adult present. In fact, he was literally the only adult there. "Ladies, ladies. Food is meant for eating, not playing."

Bella and Sarresh exchanged a look and simultaneously threw pieces of bacon at him.

"Oh, come on!"

Bella laughed. Then the front gate buzzer sounded. "Must be our ride. You ready?"

David insisted he pick them up today so he could show them his new car. As Bella and Sarresh stepped outside, David rounded the driveway. Bella whistled low. His car, a sleek, black, two-door BMW convertible, was beautiful. When it came to a halt, Sarresh climbed into the backseat with Tyler, and Bella took the passenger seat up front. Although it was winter, the weather was perfect for riding with the top down.

"What do you think?" David asked proudly.

"It's beautiful. Really. But your parents let you blow, what, fifty grand on a car?"

"More like a hundred grand, and there is a reason." David grinned at her.

Tyler snickered. "Birthday present from dear old Mommy and Daddy."

"It's your birthday? Today?" Bella's eyes widened. "How old are you?"

"Shut up, Ty. Yes, today is my eighteenth birthday."

"David Matthew Warren, I'm utterly shocked you withheld the fact of this momentous birthday from me." Bella crossed her arms and feigned disappointment.

Tyler and Sarresh both laughed.

David shook his head. "I can't believe you know my middle name."

"I've been tutoring you for almost three years. I know more than you think." Her feigned disappointment dropped. Curiosity replaced it. "Seriously. How come you didn't say it was your birthday?"

"Because it's not a big deal. My parents travel a lot. As long as I spend their money on something nice, they consider it a good birthday. Heather and I used to celebrate together, but we've kind of drifted. Besides, I can't imagine a better way to spend my birthday than with you."

"I'll have you know, flattery won't work with me."

David reached into his back pocket. "How about bribery?"

"Is that my tattoo design?"

While introducing Bella to his tattoo artist, Bobby, David wrapped his hand around her waist. She flinched. What had she been thinking wearing this top? She leaned forward and shook the artist's hand, relieved to break the contact with

David. "Nice to meet you."

"Likewise," Bobby said. "Is it just you? Or the two of you?"

David peered at Bella for a moment before he spoke. "Both of us. We'll go back together, but do her first, then me. Sarresh, are you wanting something too?"

"Yeah, but you guys go first."

"Is that cool with you, Ty?" David asked.

"Yeah. Gives me a chance to figure out what I want," Tyler said.

Bobby nodded. "Cool. Come on back and we'll start."

This time David offered his hand to Bella, which she accepted. Had he noticed her reaction? He squeezed her hand, gently. A small smile tugged at the corner of her lips. He must've realized the contact was difficult for her. It made her trust him a little more.

A huge mirror took up half the back wall. Glancing at herself, Bella readjusted her hair so the scar was covered. God, would she really be able to watch as Bobby used the assortment of colored ink bottles on her body? Or handle staring at herself from that long chair? She inched a step back.

"Do you have something in mind?"

Bobby's question snapped her out of the downward spiral. She nodded and handed him the design. A skull and crossbones with a tattered pirate flag. "Deuteronomy" was scrawled in Old English font between the tips of the dagger-shaped bones, as if it was the name of a ship. The 8 and 5 filled the eye sockets.

"This. On my lower back."

"Okay. Do you want a sugar skull? It's a bit more feminine."

"I don't know what that is, but no. I want that exact design."

"Okay. Let me get this scaled down." Bobby disappeared into a back room.

Her eyes settled on the mirror again. The girl who stared back at her had dead hazel eyes, not the vibrant brown they used to be; the skin had faded to caramel, rather than its natural mocha; the hair was a flat black, not its full, rich midnight. She was nothing compared to the beautiful man who stood beside her holding the thin hand in his own.

Her gaze drifted to David. Tall, well-toned, shiny blue-black hair and piercing blue eyes. What the hell could he see in her? Nothing but damage.

She needed to distract herself, otherwise she'd never go through with the tattoo. And it was something she had to do. "I'm surprised you've got a tattoo," she said to David."

"Two, actually. Why are you surprised?"

"I guess I just didn't peg you for someone who would mar his body."

"I don't see it that way. It's a form of art. Besides, if it's defiling, then why are you doing it?"

Oh, he really wouldn't like her answers. Because it matched her darkened soul. Because she desperately needed to feel something besides the emotional pain that weighed her down. Not that she ever intended to admit those truths to anyone. How could she answer him without actually answering him?

"What? I don't look like the type of person who would get a tattoo?"

"No, but looks can be deceiving."

"That they can." Bella muttered.

"You okay? You seem a little on edge since we got back here."

Thankfully, Bobby picked that moment to walk back into the room. He patted the chair. "Ready?"

"Um, yeah. So, uh, how do I ... sit in this thing?"

"For the low back, you're going to straddle it."

Which meant facing the mirror. Of course. But there was no way she could stare at her reflection for however long this would take. She fidgeted with the hem of her shirt.

Bobby looked at Bella. "All your information is stored. If you're not ready today, you can always come back."

"No. I want to get it done, I just ..." The law said she couldn't get a tattoo because of her age. Sarresh had helped her with a fake ID. For today, she was eighteen. She had to get it done. There was no room to chicken out.

"Will some adjustments help?" David asked.

How did he know? "Yes. Can we turn the chair away from the mirror? And, Bobby, can you put a smaller mirror behind me, just where you'll be working and give me a handheld one? I have to be able to watch."

Bobby made quick work of her requests. "Will this do?"

"Yes, thank you." Bella inhaled a deep breath and swept one leg over the armless chair. She glanced in the handheld mirror as Bobby tucked a sheet of paper into her pants and swiped a wet, cold wipe along her low-back. Watching made the touch easier to handle. It was still awkward, but her nerves had settled more than she could've imagined.

David smiled. "If you need a hand, I'm here."

"Just talk to me. Yeah, that'll be good."

"Okay. I'll transfer the design, get the colors together, and then we'll get started. Let me know if you need a break at all," Bobby said.

"Do you think I'll need one?"

"It depends on your pain tolerance. This is a fleshy area, so it's a good place for a tattoo."

Pain tolerance? She'd taken painkillers that morning. Would she even feel the sting of the needle as it danced across her skin? Maybe she shouldn't have taken the pills. No, that would've been dangerous and unpredictable. Besides, maybe she would still feel some delicious lick of pain. The whirring noise pulled her back into reality.

David leaned back against the wall. "What would you like to talk about?"

"Tell me about the tattoos you have."

Bobby was cleaning up David's new tattoo. How much longer did she have to wait to see the damn thing? She was getting antsy. Oh, wait, he was done.

"Yeah, let me take a look." David got up from the chair and walked over to the mirror to study the piece. He glanced at Bobby. "Exactly what I wanted."

"Cool. Let me get it covered, and you guys are set."

David had told Bella about his other tattoos, the Arc de Triomphe in ruins on his back and an intricate band of thorns that incorporated a cross on his left bicep. But when she inquired about the one he planned to get, she'd been shut down. She'd even had to sit so she couldn't see what was being done. Now, he really needed to show her what the hell he got.

Bella folded her arms across her chest. "Let me see it!"

He showed her.

Oh. My. God! What was he thinking? His tattoo matched hers—except instead of "Deuteronomy," he had her named scrawled between the blades in the Old English font. *Insane! Holy shit!* With no way to hide her shock, she simply stepped back, while Bobby put lotion on the tattoo and taped plastic gauze over it.

David was monumentally stupid. Okay, she was attracted to him, but they weren't dating. Why would he put her name on his body? Even *if* they dated—and it was a big "if"—who could say they would last? Big risk on his part.

Bella refused the hand he offered as they made their way toward the front. He had to know she'd be bothered by his lack of consideration of her feelings. She could hardly look at Sarresh and Tyler when they passed by each other. Sarresh was going to get her daughter's name tattooed. And that made sense; she was a mother for life. She had no idea what Tyler was going to get, but it wouldn't be a girl's name? Right?

But David? He was crazy for getting Bella's name permanently embedded in his skin. An explanation was well overdue. Bella dropped on the couch and glared at him.

"Why? Why would you do something so asinine?"

five

David gripped the back of his neck. Bella really was upset with him. He expected her to be slightly bothered. But enough to call his action dumb? Not so much. He hadn't told her earlier because he suspected she'd try and talk him out of it. And since this was Bella, she would have succeeded. He had no resistance to anything she requested.

Now, though, he was reluctant to give her what she wanted—an explanation. Only because he feared her reaction. She'd just begun to let him in, and he longed for that more than anything in the world.

"Despite all the warnings blaring in my head, I'm going to be honest."

"That's good, because I can't deal with any more lies right now."

Bells clanged loudly in his head. David ignored them. There were some things he'd just have to think about later. For now ... David sighed. "I've never known anyone like you. I felt it from the first time I saw you. It was October, and I had an English paper due. I went to the library and spotted you tucked in a corner reading. You were so focused that nothing could've gotten your attention."

Bella crossed her arms and sulked. "I'm not that bad."

He grinned, despite himself. "No. Of course you're not. The point is, I hadn't drawn your attention. I'm not used to that. Girls usually throw themselves at me. Okay, maybe that's a bit of an exaggeration. But you were the first girl I'd met in a while who didn't even notice me. So, I asked around."

Now that he thought about it, it was around that time that Heather started bullying Bella. Had his sister known he was intrigued by the girl? Surely, she had. They were twins—and his sister was nosey as hell.

"Okay. Still doesn't explain the tattoo."

David held up a hand. "Patience. I'm getting there."

"Get there sooner."

"I discovered you were in the tutoring group. I learned what subjects you tutored and purposely failed my next couple of math tests and quizzes. I knew if my grade dropped below C, coach would make me get help."

Bella walked over to the window and stared outside. "You mean you flunked on purpose and used unnecessary tutor time? Unbelievable."

"I know that sounds bad, but … when I finally met you, you changed my life. Made me see things I hadn't fully appreciated. You once asked me if it was your dad that convinced me Christ existed. It wasn't. Honestly, it was you. Maybe that sounds like a line, but I promise you it isn't. I became a better person. So. The tattoo. I wanted to be reminded of how far I've come. Something to commemorate my growth."

"Why couldn't you have told me earlier? I mean, I know life is all about our experiences, but you're the one who did the work. It would've made more sense if you got a tattoo that reflected your own journey, not mine."

"The thing is, I don't believe I would've taken the journey if not for you." Man, he'd said a lot. He'd never defined his path the way he'd just done with her. Hopefully, she would understand why the tattoo had been a necessity.

"I get it. Sort of. Just … give me some time to adjust." Bella sat back down. "Can I ask you something?"

"Anything."

"Is that why you stopped getting tutored?"

Heat spread across his cheeks. "How'd you know?"

"Vick keeps me apprised."

That made sense. The guy had been assigned the lead tutor position until Bella was ready to take back over. "To answer your question … yes and no. Yes, it was the only way I could spend time with you. But when you reassigned me, I stayed because I had to prove to myself it wasn't all about you. He teaches differently than you, though. And truthfully, I don't like him."

"Don't worry. The feeling is mutual." Bella snickered.

"You're laughing at my misery."

"A little bit, yeah."

"At least I entertain you."

"Your sister is more entertaining."

"That's because lately she has a tendency to get knocked on her ass."

Bella laughed. "Touché."

Her laugh was intoxicating. He could drink it up for hours. Man, he had it bad for her. But he knew he'd have to give her time. The rape changed her in ways he didn't fully comprehend. Surely, the only people who could understand are those who've been through the same thing.

David shook the thoughts free. "You know, I almost wonder what Heather will do next time someone else punches the shit out of her."

"I'm surprised she hasn't done something awful to Mandy."

"I know. It's like she's given up being evil." Or her sudden sense of restraint had to do with the ammo he had stowed away. The last time David discussed Bella with his sister, he reminded his twin of the damaging photos he possessed—Heather before fat camp. Something she much preferred not to have shown to the entire school.

"Enough about your sister. What are we going to do to celebrate your birthday?"

"I told you. We don't have to do anything."

Bella playfully shoved David in the arm. The one without the new tattoo. "Nonsense. I don't care what you've done in the past. We're living in the present, and I deem that we will go out for your birthday."

"All right. You don't get told no, do you?"

"Not often. So, I'll ask again. What are we doing tonight?" Bella smiled.

"Are you seeing warning signs?" the doctor asked.

Milena glanced at him. He would speak for them both. "Not for a few weeks now, but she spends less time at home. Have you noticed anything amiss?"

"You know I can't disclose the specifics of my sessions with Bella. If I believed she was a harm to herself or others, I would certainly take the appropriate actions."

"Dr. Filmore, we must have some reassurance our daughter can move past this ... trust issue that has been created."

Next to him, Milena fidgeted, twisting her fingers together.

"I understand. The trust can be regained, but you will have to answer all of her questions regarding the adoption."

"It is more than the lack of trust Bella has displayed toward her mother and me. We are also finding difficulty in trusting her. Two days ago, she arrived home with another three hundred dollars' worth of clothes."

"You understand the shopping is a way for her to lash out. She is only beginning to cope with the trauma she suffered. Dealing with PTSD is a struggle, but Bella is doing well." The doctor scanned her calendar. "Though perhaps we should schedule another family session. I have time available Monday afternoon."

"I do not think this family therapy is assisting in any manner. I think we should have her committed." DeWei frowned. He had mentioned the idea a couple of times before to his wife, both in private and with the doctor.

His wife stood, squared her shoulders, and glowered at him. "No! I have stated it time and time again. I will not have my daughter put in one of those places."

"I am in agreement with your wife," Dr. Filmore said. "I understand your concern, but I believe institutionalizing Bella will only hinder the progress we've made. She's socializing and keeping her appointments. She's even returned to school, and that seems to be going well."

"Yes." Defeated again by these women. His wife was emotional. Her reasons for defending Bella from his suggestion made sense. But Dr. Filmore was a professional. A renowned psychiatrist. That was why he had sent Bella to her. But he had yet to see the change in his daughter he expected. As a counselor, he understood therapy was not a fix-all, nor were positive foundations built overnight. Still, he suspected things were not what they appeared when it came to his daughter.

Dr. Filmore tapped her chin. "I understand your concern. If it will make you feel more comfortable, I will schedule a meeting with her principal and teachers. They can help watch her. Perhaps with more eyes, any hidden issues can be identified."

His wife crossed her arms. "I find this approach acceptable. As well, I would like to establish the session for Monday."

"What about you, Dr. Kynaston? Does this plan work for you?"

"Yes." It would be something, at any rate. Another safeguard. Among the obstacles he'd anticipated Bella would face on her road to recovery, his daughter getting in her own way was not one of them. He suspected something badly amiss—but could not say what it was. And the psychiatrist and his wife were turning a blind eye to the possibility. God, he needed someone on his side. Someone who understood the inner workings of his daughter. There had to be somebody who could get through to Bella.

"What do you think about going to T2 tonight?" Bella munched on another French fry.

"I'm in. You know how long it's been since I've been to a club?" Sarresh said.

"Um, I'm going to say about ten months." Bella'd actually never been to a club. Not one of her friends ever dragged her along, not even Sarresh or Alex. She knew a couple of clubs downtown had teen nights, but none catered specifically to teenagers like T2. What would it be like?

"More like six months, but who's counting?"

"For shame. I can't believe you went dancing while you were pregnant with Takina." In a repeat of the display at breakfast, Bella threw a French fry at Sarresh.

Sarresh's jaw dropped, and she tossed a fry back at Bella. The two went back and forth, pegging one another with the greasy, salted fries.

"Hey! You guys are making a mess," David protested.

Bella glanced from Sarresh to David and redirected a fry in his direction. Tyler joined in the fun, and it quickly escalated to all four tossing fries at each other.

Maybe they would get kicked out, but fun was buried so far back in her memory she'd nearly forgotten what it was supposed to be like. Hanging out with friends and enjoying life. Bella hardly noticed the touch until it was skin on skin. The hands were rough. No, no, no, no, no! She jumped off the bench.

"B? You okay?"

The words slipped through, but didn't stop the rush of thoughts. His hands. They had been rough and certain hands. Like these. They were always like his. Every touch belonged to him, even if the face belonged to someone else. How was she supposed to be okay, when people couldn't comprehend how touch freaked her out?

Who touched her? Who put their hands on her filthy body? She shook her head. There was no telling who committed the awful deed.

She walked away mumbling, "No, no, no. I can't." She couldn't let them look at her. They'd see it, all of it, all the dirt. It was always with her. Under her skin. Her skin used to be beautiful. A lovely mocha. Now it was tainted. So pale, and marred by the stench those men left on her.

Bella walked out of the restaurant and to the car and began circling it. How could David have let her get in his exquisite car? Certainly, she'd ruined his seats. Where her skin had met with the leather. Bella tugged at the belly shirt she'd worn. Why had she worn this thing? Stupid, stupid, stupid, stupid.

"It's just me." David held up his hands as he approached and stopped a few feet from her.

She was a mess, a full-blown mess. Bella raked her fingers through her hair.

"No, no, no, no."

"I'm sorry. I shouldn't have touched you. Can we talk?"

Bella paused mid-stride. David's words seeped through the garbage in her head. He'd apologized. No one had ever done that when she'd had an attack. Bella sat down on the lip of the sidewalk and peered up, as David unlocked his car and reached into the glove compartment. He moved toward her, but only close enough to hand her a pack of tissues. "Here, take these."

"Thank you."

"Welcome. Can I sit?"

He'd asked, but hadn't moved. He was waiting for her permission. She blew her nose. As long as he maintained a safe distance, she'd be good. "Um, okay. Okay."

He sat several feet from her. "Did you flinch earlier at the tattoo parlor when I grabbed your waist?"

"Yes."

"And again when I tried to tickle you?"

"Yes." His questions seemed simple enough, but they acknowledged the damage she carried everywhere she went. As far as she knew, she'd successfully managed to hide the depth of her despair from her parents. Not so much from her friends. Her shrink? She had no clue.

"But you were okay when we held hands?"

David had given her honesty; the least she could do was reciprocate. "I struggled. It was minor, but part of me demanded I pull away, while the other part insisted I not let go. The latter won out for a short time."

"Okay."

"You're not upset?"

"No. You've survived a great deal. I know that kind of trauma isn't dealt with easily. I just need you to do one thing for me."

"What's that?"

"Tell me when you're uncomfortable. I like spending time with you. If the most I get to do is hold your hand, then I'll accept that."

The way he made his request said a lot. David desired more than just holding her hand. Would he really settle for less than he coveted? She'd like to see where it could go, but he was likely unprepared for how damaged she was. Bella bit the inside of her cheek. There was no way to tell, but maybe, just maybe ... for him ... for herself ... she could try.

Swifty tapped the wheel of his car. Stupid policeman took forever. He'd recognized the guy from his photo. If he was at the juvenile detention center, it could only be for one reason: to question Cristobal. While this probably would be a good time to go in and tell the officer all he knew, that would create its own complications. He'd probably end up charged with accessory after the fact, since he knew everything that had happened and had done nothing to stop Gervasio. Hell, technically, he'd hindered the investigation by keeping his trap shut. Which was exactly why he needed to talk to Cristobal.

The light-skinned jackass walked out the door and headed toward his unmarked. But the man hadn't been inside for as long as Swifty had expected. Must mean Cristobal'd kept his trap shut, too. Great. Just what he didn't need. Cristobal had to sing like a canary.

Swifty ducked down in his seat as the unmarked drove past him. Then, Luis, aka Swifty, climbed out of his vehicle and stepped inside. Based on his coded conversation with Gervasio, he had less than a week to get Cristobal on their side and make sure his brother never got released. What would it take to convince Cristobal to work with him?

Luis knew the letter that had been dropped off at the girl's house was only the beginning. He'd spent the better part of the previous night trying to get someone's prints on the damn thing before it ended up in her mailbox. Heather, that stupid bitch, hadn't fallen for any of his tricks. She'd typed out Bella's name on the envelope, used a sponge to seal it, and wore gloves as she worked. If nothing came from this conversation with Cristobal, he'd have to figure something else out.

At check-in, he presented the fake ID that labeled him as Luis Hernandez, then walked to the corner table Cristobal usually occupied. The visit was unplanned, so he had to wait for the detainee to arrive.

"Swifty? I am surprised to see you. Does my brother know you are here?"

Luis stood and clapped hands with Cristobal. "No. He would not be happy if he did."

"Is everything okay? *Mi madre?*"

"*Sí.* Your mother is fine. I spoke to her this morning. I came because I need you to do something for me."

"I am not sure I understand," Cristobal said, as he and Luis sat.

Where to begin? There were things he dared not mention: his father, for one, or how he had attempted to protect the girl in question. "Your brother, he is worse than before. Obsessed, even. He says he only wishes to be free of this ... burden, but I do not believe he will stop there."

"What are you saying?"

Luis leaned in close and whispered. "I believe he plans to end the issue ... *permanentemente.*" Permanently.

"I cannot help. This ... issue ... is not the only one threatened."

How could he have forgotten? Gervasio had made certain the entire gang knew he'd assigned Bronco to deliver a message to Cristobal. The man hadn't cared if the two were related by blood. What would stop him from having Cristobal, his own brother, killed? Even in jail, Gervasio had connections.

Luis frowned and rubbed his chin. There had to be a way around the death threat. Hmm ... maybe. "What if I could get you released sooner rather than later?"

"I am not concerned for myself. I worry for *mi madre.*"

"You cannot think—" Would Gervasio actually have his own mother murdered?

"I do." Cristobal leaned back and crossed his arms.

That changed the game. His only way to convince Cristobal to help was to protect the woman. "I will get her moved somewhere safe."

"Is there such a place?"

"Yes." It was just a matter of how to get her there.

six

Bella sped across town like her life depended on it. A horrible reminder of the attack had awaited her at her house. There was only one thing she could do with the item. Screeching to a halt in the driveway, she ran up the walkway and pounded on Miah's front door.

When Amanda answered, Bella shoved past her. "Where's your dad?"

"In the kitchen."

Stomping to the kitchen, she shouted, "I thought you said he couldn't get to me!"

Miah's father turned around. "Well, hello to you, too."

"You said he couldn't get to me!" Bella yanked the letter free from her back pocket and threw it on the kitchen island. Unable to contain herself any longer, she sobbed. It was easier than throwing things.

Miah's dad held up his hands and urged Bella to relax. "Calm down and take a deep breath for me.

When she did as he asked, he scooped up the letter. His face remained frozen as he scanned the lines the first time. But the second time through, Bella saw hatred filling the sheriff's brown eyes.

She knew what he was reading. The lines rattled in her brain.

My slick and sweet honey bear,
How I wish I was there.
Your innocence so hot and pure
Is my only hope of a cure.
To feel your lips on mine
And taste your strong, lovely wine
When we're chest to chest,
Bare breast to breast.
There is a song beating in my heart,
That reminds me we'll never part.

The dam in her mind burst and the memories poured forth. Every bruise he left, every bone he broke, every piece of her soul he took. The rancid smell of rotting meat, the reek of his sweat, the stench of cigarettes on his breath, his rough voice whispering, "honey bear," in her ear … Bella dropped to the floor of Miah's kitchen and rocked back and forth as she relived the pain she had endured at that monster's hands. "Don't touch me!"

Three words and they shattered another piece of his heart. The girl he loved sat on his kitchen floor and sobbed—and Jeremiah stood in the hall, helpless to comfort her. The privilege no longer belonged to him. God, help him. But he couldn't stand by and do nothing, as his father, crouching beside Bell, failed to pull her back to the present.

"Dad? I might be able to calm her down."

"You sure?" His father stood.

Not as much as he'd like to be. Before all confidence completely departed his body, though, Jeremiah nodded and padded over to Bell. Slowly, he sat beside her. Hoping she wouldn't bolt, he hesitantly rested a hand on her back. Her shirt rode up and a strip of plastic gauze played peek-a-boo from her low-riding pants. He dared not think on it too much, otherwise he would lose his focus.

When Bell flinched, Jeremiah snapped his hand away. He waited a moment and eased his hand to her back again. Then, she stilled, and he started making gentle circles on her upper back.

Finally, her tears subsided. "Why? Why did he do this?"

His father answered her. "It's called a psych-out. Your identification and testimony are the only things that puts Smith in that alleyway. If he can keep you from testifying, or scare you into recanting, then the rape charge goes away."

"I can't do this. I can't face him. I can't testify." The shaking returned and more tears rolled down Bell's reddened cheeks.

Jeremiah didn't lift his hand from her back, when his father crouched in front of Bell again. "Of course, you can. I'll be there to support you the whole time. Your parents will be, too."

"Oh, God!" Bell hiccupped a sob. "No, no, no. I can't ... not with them there. They can't hear it. I don't want them to hear it."

"Okay. I'll talk to the prosecutor. He can petition for a closed courtroom."

"Closed courtroom?" As if a weight had been lifted, Jeremiah felt the tension in her shoulders ease.

"Yes. Most trials are open to the public, but some can be closed so only those with a direct interest in the case are allowed in."

A bit more relaxed, Bell said, "Yeah, I'd be okay with that."

Jeremiah stood. With his presence no longer required, he backed out the doorway and headed to his room. Surely, she'd noticed he was there, but she hadn't spoken one word to him.

"Hey. You all right?" Amanda sat on the bed beside him.

"I'll survive. Is she still talking to Dad?"

"Yeah. How come you didn't stay?"

Jeremiah rubbed his head. "I would've just been in the way."

"But you calmed her down. You know how hard that is?"

He shook his head. Calming her down wasn't a huge deal.

"I should smack you. Why the hell can't you see how much she needs you? This is your chance to get off your ass and make things right. Go talk to her."

Need him? His sister had to be blind. Bell hadn't needed him. She'd just needed a soft, comforting hand. "No. I'm not going to go talk to her. She's happier without me causing problems. I should've seen it before, but I hadn't."

Despite Amanda's glare, Jeremiah, continued right on with the truth that constricted his heart. "Trouble's always around when we're together. It's best that I stay away from her. Better we go our separate paths now before one of us really gets hurt. I probably should've ended things sooner than I did."

Bella stood perfectly still in the doorway to Jeremiah's bedroom. She wanted to thank him for the moment of peace he gave her in the kitchen. But what she thought could be the opening to a second chance turned into a slap in the face. *I probably should've ended things sooner than I did.* That's what he said.

Amanda saw her. "Hey, B."

"Bell!" Miah's gaze snapped in her direction.

"I ... um ... figured I'd say bye. Yeah. Bye." What else could she say? Nothing. She had nothing. Nothing that could fill the hole in her heart.

Feet pounded down the hall after her. "Bell, wait! I—"

"Said enough." Tears threatened to spill down her cheeks again. She had to get out of here. His words burned like a thousand bee stings.

"I'm sorry. I didn't know you were there."

She spun around. "What? And that would've made what you said less true?"

"No. But I don't think you understood what I meant."

"Then what did you mean?"

Miah offered no answer. He opened his mouth, but seemed to struggle to come up with the right words. With a sigh, he gripped the back of his head. "Can we not do this here?"

"What is there to do? We're not together. What else is there to do? You know what, I'm over it. Have a nice life." Bella stormed out the front door.

"Wait! How are you over it?"

"Why do you care? You're the one that walked away, remember? I sure as hell do."

He chased her outside and ran in front of her, his body blocking her way to the car.

"That doesn't mean I don't want you to be happy."

"Little late for that, don't you think?" She was beyond frustrated with him. He could release all the tension in her body as if he loved her one minute and push her away with gut-wrenching words the next. Miah played her like a fiddle, and she was tired of his inability to explain himself.

"That's all I've ever wanted."

"I don't believe you. Please move."

Miah hung his head and groaned. He stepped aside and allowed her to pass him. "Is it David?"

"Not that it's any of your business, but, yes."

"Did you hear that?" Amanda pressed the cell phone to her ear and shut her bedroom door. "I can see how she'd think it sounded bad, but Jeremiah was referring to himself as the problem, not her. You know he loves her."

Vick groaned. "Which is why I'm trying to suppress the urge to beat the crap out of him."

"He chased after her. Maybe he'll be able to explain what's going on in his head coherently. Then we won't have to lock them up together," she said to her boyfriend.

"Yeah. Because I'm not exactly thrilled with the idea. Can't you and Sarresh come up with another plan?"

Amanda rolled her eyes. "We don't— Wait ... hold on." Amanda cracked her door and peered down the hallway. *Shit.*

"What's going on?"

"He's back. Hold on." Amanda opened her door all the way and held the phone behind her back. "Everything copacetic?"

Jeremiah scratched the back of his head. "I think I've lost her for good."

"What?"

"She's seeing David."

Wait, what? Sarresh only said they'd hung out. There had been no mention of the two of them dating. Amanda frowned. "Are you sure?"

"Bella said so herself. Look, I'm going to—"

"Jeremiah, was I seeing things or was there a bandage on Bella's back?" Their father interrupted whatever her brother had begun to say.

"No, Dad. You weren't seeing things. I noticed it, too."

"A tattoo, I presume."

Amanda winced. She hadn't mentioned this particular detail to Vick. Sarresh had admitted they were going to get tattoos. Easy for her since, she'd been emancipated. Not so much for Bella. Well, at least until Sarresh spilled the beans about how they'd engineered a permission slip ... Should it matter that it was Mandy herself who suggested the fake ID? "Hey, Dad. I know you'll want to say something to B's parents, but maybe you can keep this to yourself? B has been through such ... a rough patch."

"I know she's had a difficult time, but the only way she could've gotten a tattoo is if they gave their consent. While I'd like to assume they did, I can't take that chance. To answer your question, Mandy, no, I will not keep this to myself."

"Okay, Dad. I've got some stuff to do. 'Scuse me." Amanda closed her door and returned the phone to her ear.

"Did you know?" Vick asked loudly.

She pulled the phone away from her ear and allowed him a moment to calm the hell down. "Yes, I did, but I can explain."

"Bella's calling, but we'll discuss this later."

"Sure. Later." Amanda hung up. Vick was going to explode when she explained to him how she knew. How she'd shared her experience and given them the idea of the fake ID. It was how she'd gotten hers. Thankfully, the only person who knew about her tattoo was her boyfriend. What fun that conversation would be.

seven

Vick's parents' summer house was quiet this time of year. Bella had fallen asleep on the hammock in the backyard, by the lake. Stupid phone woke her up. She'd ignored the god-awful high-pitched sound for an hour, now. The exquisite sunset claimed all of her attention. Unfortunately, the phone proclaimed loudly it required a response. She reached into her back pocket, which caused the hammock to swing a little, and brought the thing to her ear.

"Hello?"

"Where the hell are you?"

"What?" Bella moved too fast, flipping the hammock and landing face first on the ground. With a groan, she rolled over. "What time is it?"

"It's eight o'clock. You've been gone six hours."

"Oh shit! I'm on my way back, now. I'll be there in an hour."

"Where the hell did you end up?"

Bella brushed off her clothes and headed toward the house. "Not important. I just needed to get away. I'm hanging up. I'll be there in an hour."

"Fine. You just better be able to get dressed quick. You know I hate running late."

"Z, it's a club. There's no such thing as running late."

"Whatever. And call your mom. I'm tired of her calling me."

"All—" *That bitch.* Had Sarresh really hung up on her? Shaking off her annoyance, Bella dialed home while heading for the car.

"Hello?"

"Hey, Mom. Sarresh—"

"Thank goodness you are alive! I've been calling for hours. Why didn't you pick up?"

She hadn't checked to see who'd called, just ignored her phone. After her conversation with Vick earlier, some quiet had been in order. Not something she'd get at Sarresh's or at home, so she drove to the one place she knew would be unoccupied. "I'm sorry. I'm fine. I didn't mean to worry you."

"You can't disappear without telling us where you are going. Now, where are you?"

"I'm heading back to Sarresh's. We made plans tonight."

"I need you to come home, Bella. We need to talk."

Great, Miah's father had sworn he'd keep the contents of the letter to himself unless something was found—but obviously he hadn't.

"I can't. We're taking David out to celebrate his birthday."

"Bella, this is important."

"And so is this. I'll come home tomorrow night, and we can talk about the note then."

"Note? What note?"

Shit! Miah's father had kept his word. But then why was her mother demanding she return home that instant?

"The note? Nothing. Not a big deal."

"Well, I will still expect an explanation about that. For now, I want to discuss my concerns regarding the tattoo I was questioned about."

Oh, no. She'd really hoped to keep the tattoo a secret from her parents, but she should've seen this coming. "Can we please discuss this all tomorrow night? It's David's eighteenth, and I really want to take him out."

Her mother sighed in frustration. "Very well. I expect you home no later than five o'clock. You will sit down and eat dinner with me and your father. Do you understand?"

"Yes, ma'am."

"Good. Drive safe, and we will speak with you tomorrow."

Bella was thrilled by the crowd's reaction to their performance. She took an exhilarated breath as she stepped outside with David onto T2's wooden porch, which sat high enough that it overlooked most of the city.

"That was so much fun. And you were good. I've heard you sing, but not like that."

"Thanks, but you were better. I'll never get tired of hearing your voice."

The song selection was David's choice. Of all the songs in the world, he picked "Meet Me Halfway," by the Black Eyed Peas. A song about two people in love and meeting in the middle to resolve their issues. Bella liked the song, but David seemed more passionate about it than she had. Regardless, she enjoyed being on stage with him.

"We definitely have to do that again."

"I'm sure I can arrange that."

They stopped at the edge of the balcony. Bella's hair was down. It was the only option that covered the mark on her neck, the crisscrossed scythes that had been seared into her flesh. She leaned on the balcony rail and glanced at David. "That'd be nice."

"You okay? You seem a little distracted."

"Yeah. I just had a hard afternoon." More like wretched. The only nice part had been her long sleep. Those pills blissfully knocked her out, allowing the world to fade to black quite peacefully.

"If you want to go, I'll understand."

There was a whole lot of *I'm sorry* in that comment. And it was unnecessary. Her gaze snapped up to meet his. "Go? Why would I want to do that? I'm having fun, and after the day I've had, I need it."

Raising an eyebrow, David reached a hand up and tenderly tucked a loose hair behind her ear. "Do you want to talk about it?"

He genuinely wanted to know, but … no, it was too much. Bella stared out over the city. There had to be something she could tell him. "I'm supposed to testify at the trial. It's difficult to deal with the memories, when all I want to do is forget. Go on with my life."

"I'm not sure there is a way to forget. But I have faith you can move forward. There are a lot of people who care about you and support you."

Bella grimaced. There was a way to forget. But it would be a forever kind of forgetting. The kind where the only thing that lived on would be her memory, carried by those who remembered her.

"I'll always be there for you," David added.

"Thanks, I appreciate it. Still ..."

"Can I ask you something?" He lifted his gaze from Bella to the view of the town.

"Sure."

"Exactly how long ago did you and Jeremiah split?"

Bella closed her eyes. "About a month ago." People at school had noticed, and a few had asked her directly. Now, she wondered if anyone knew she'd been spending time with David? If someone talked to David about it, would he mention it to her? Probably not. Maybe their time together was a well-kept secret.

Bella bit the inside of her cheek. She wondered something else, too. In Miah's kitchen, she'd been in the eye of the storm and had found a rare moment of peace in a way she'd learned to accept since the attack. Would she ever be able to find that again? She wouldn't know until she made the attempt.

"Can I try something with you?"

"I guess." David faced her.

"Don't sound so confident."

"You asking like that makes me a little nervous."

A small smile crept onto Bella's lips. "I promise it won't hurt you."

"Okay. Tell me what you want me to do."

"Stand still. I don't know if this'll work, but if you move, I can guarantee it won't." Bella stepped closer and cautiously splayed her fingers on his chest. His heart pounded beneath her touch. She lifted her gaze to his piercing blue eyes, then hesitated. His eyes shone brightly. In the night, they were exquisite.

"I'm okay. Are you?"

Softly, she nodded and moved closer—but still left space between the them. Her body tingled and chills crawled up her spine. Bella inhaled deeply and focused on the place her hand rested. Hoping she wouldn't freak out, she pressed her cheek against her hand. Reassuring herself with David's steady breath and heartbeat, she carefully extracted her hand, and allowed her cheek to touch the cotton of his shirt.

"Still okay?" David's voice vibrated in his chest.

"Say something else."

"Okay. Um, I'm extremely comfortable with you against me like this."

Bella giggled at his sarcasm. "I'm sorry, but it tickles."

"I like the sound of your laugh. If I've got to stand like a statue, then I can hold the pose for a few more minutes."

She allowed her eyes to close, but then he shifted. Bella snapped back. "You moved."

"Sorry. Thought I could stand still longer than that."

"Thank you."

"I'm glad I could help. Now, why don't we head back inside and sing some more?" He held out his hand.

She gripped his hand with her own and nodded. "What do you think I should sing?"

"Some Lady Gaga."

The night before had been great. David had been quite patient with her. They hadn't repeated their experiment, but he had discovered ways around her problems with touch. When she'd considered the dance floor, David searched for a vacant spot and placed his body so that it protected her from any possible space invaders.

But now she was at her own house—and something altogether different awaited her. She might not like it, but she had to deal with her parents sooner or later. A quick deep breath and she headed inside. "I'm home."

"You're late." Her mother looked up from her watch. But Bella's father wasn't there.

"Well, not really. I've been standing outside for five minutes."

"Why would you wait?"

"I know you guys are upset with me and I didn't want to face it." Well, to be accurate, she assumed they were upset, based on the brief phone conversation she'd had with her mother the evening before.

Her mother sighed. "Not both of us. Your father and I feel differently about this."

"Is that why he isn't here?"

"Yes. Bella, put your things away, then come and sit."

This was strange. Her parents rarely scolded her, but usually, if they had to punish her for something she'd done, they worked together. Now, she sat in the chair across from her mother and laced her fingers together, worrying. Could she explain herself to the woman truthfully? Or had she completely forgotten how to be honest with her parents?

"I should've told you I wanted the tattoo, but I thought you'd say no."

"I agree. You should have spoken with me first. You are also correct that I would have said no. Although it may appear hypocritical because, as you know, I have a tattoo, which I got when I was eighteen. So, while I could lecture you on the reasons you shouldn't have obtained a tattoo, it would be hypocritical."

"So, you're not upset?"

"On the contrary, I am very upset. Simply not for the reason you suspect. If you absolutely felt you needed to receive a tattoo, I would have taken you myself. I am upset because you went behind my back."

Bella clasped her fingers in her lap, then steepled them. Her mother's response was so unexpected. She'd anticipated listening to her parents berate her about how stupid her actions had been. Instead, her mother threw her for a loop with her understanding.

"Then is Bàba pissed?"

"Your father is ... worried. He believes your rebellion goes deeper than just a tattoo. To a degree, I agree. You have changed, and that is to be expected. Everything you do, now, is rooted in your rape. But this tragedy has occurred, and we are all learning how to cope."

Cope. No. She had failed cope. She hadn't faced any part of her attack. Bad just piled on bad. And her parents had noticed ... something. But they remained clueless about how far her resistance to coping—hell, to life—had taken her. But at least she could talk about the tattoo with her mother.

"I wanted a reminder. I never intend to forget how quickly good can be washed away and replaced by bad."

Her mother nodded. "Yes, Bella, bad can happen at any second. That does not mean it has to run your life."

Bella looked down. "I'm trying to take control. Just in a new way."

"Promise you will come to me going forward?" Her mother grasped her hand and squeezed.

"I'll do my best."

"Good. Now, tell me about this note you received."

Jamar reread the letter left at the Kynaston residence. The fingerprints on it were unidentifiable, except for Bella's, but since Bella's parents had both handled it, they were stopping by to be printed, just on the off chance any of the prints belonged to someone else—someone involved in Bella's attack. Ignoring the prints, a couple of things about the letter set off alarms. The wording was rather sophisticated. And it wasn't stamped, which meant someone hand delivered it to the house.

Jamar bent to his intercom. "Russell, my office."

When Russell appeared, Jamar said, "Get Ali to scan this letter and envelope. See if there is anything embedded. If not, I want to know where they came from." Jamar handed the bagged evidence to the detective.

Russell took the bag between his thumb and forefinger. "Okay. And I'll go back through the prison logs and see if our guy's had any other visitors."

"We ever find this Luis Smith?"

"I checked out the address on his driver's license. According to the super, he hasn't lived there in over a year and there's no forwarding address. He's not anywhere in the system. Couldn't even find a work location for him."

"Great." Jamar leaned back in his chair. "Go talk with the Kynaston's neighbors. See if anyone noticed anything out of the ordinary. I want to know how that letter ended up at their house. I'm going to schedule a car to do random patrols of that area. This might only be the beginning."

eight

Four o'clock Monday afternoon and Bella sat on that stinking couch. When her parents purchased her car, it was on the condition that she attended regular therapy sessions, individual or family. The agreement made her parents happy. So what if she wanted to drive her little VW off a cliff. She'd need the car to do that, so she kept her end of the bargain—but their little family sessions were the worst.

"I am worried about you. Your behavior is atrocious. First, you begin going on spending sprees. Second, you are consistently away from the house. Now, the tattoo. Bella, what is going on with you?"

"I'm coping, Bàba. Dr. Filmore, I thought you explained all this to them." The doctor probably used some psychological term to justify her actions. But however the doctor had presented Bella's behavior, she didn't know the truth. Neither did Bella's parents. Only one other person knew she returned the clothes she made such a display of—and how she used the cash she got when she took the items back.

"I have explained, Bella, but your parents need your reassurance, too. They can't simply hear my words. They must see that in your actions."

How could she provide the information they needed without releasing all her secrets. If they delved too deep, they'd uncover the black hole that consumed her soul. Bella took a deep breath. "Okay. You want me to explain things, and I want you to explain things. So, you tell me something about my birth parents, and I'll tell you what's going on. Deal?"

Her father glanced at her mother. "Did you have something to do with this suggestion?"

"I beg your pardon!" Her mother crossed her arms and glared at her father. "I did not. I can't believe you would insinuate such a thing."

"She had nothing to do with it, Bàba. I've wanted to know some things since you told me about the adoption. You just haven't answered my questions. I figure, tit-for-tat. You share something, I'll share something."

Dr. Filmore scribbled a note on her pad. "This will be a good trust exercise for all of you. You must accept that what is spoken is absolute truth. Are you in agreement?"

Bella nodded, and her parents followed suit.

"Good. Shall we proceed?"

"I'll go first," Bella said. "When did you find out my mother was pregnant with me?"

"At our wedding. Ileana was about six months along at the time," her father replied. "Our turn. Why have you been spending money as if it has no value?"

Good question. She had to give her father credit. She would try to skirt the real reason, of course, but still tell something of the truth. "I needed an outlet. The schoolwork I do only holds so much of my focus. Shopping for clothes makes me think more than you'd imagine." There. Got past that one. "My turn. How long did you know my mother?"

"Ileana and I were childhood friends." Her mother paused. "Why do you stay away from the house for so long?"

Her parents were well prepared. They sought answers to the problems she created. Like hers, their questions must have been multiplying. "Home is another reminder of this whole nightmare. It's easier when I'm not there."

"I apologize, Bella. I had not considered the difficulty you would face when we returned to the house," her father said.

An apology from her father was unusual and unforeseen. Unlike the shock she got when she was standing in Miah's doorway, this was a positive surprise. Bella swallowed and collected herself. "Thank you, Bàba. Um, how did my mother die?"

"I don't know any way to soften this answer." Bella saw her mother squeeze her father's hand. "She committed suicide."

Bella tried to keep all expression from her face. How ironic, she thought. Her biological mother died in a manner she herself had contemplated for weeks. After taking a moment, she lifted her gaze to her parents' faces, ready for their next question.

"What caused you to need an outlet?" her father asked.

"It was … because Miah broke up with me." The words poured out of her mouth before she had the opportunity to stop them. She had successfully hidden the break-up from her parents. She knew they had been relying on Miah's support in her recovery, and the fact of her spending so much time at Sarresh's had helped in the deception. But now … The information of her biological mother's death must've hit closer to home than she'd realized.

"What? Why didn't you say anything of this before?"

Tears rolled down her cheeks. "Because I thought you would worry even more about me. And …" She choked a little on her tears. "… I had convinced you he was … a good guy. I stood up for him. I didn't want you to know I was wrong and you were right."

"My Bella, I would never have suggested anything of the sort. You cared for him. And he cared for you. Your mother and I saw this quite clearly."

"Yeah, well, he doesn't feel the same way—at least not now. I can't … I'm done talking about this." Bella stood and left the office.

Bella held no illusions that anything would be normal, again. Not even lunch. Which was a good thing, because first, there was Alex, who barely uttered a word throughout the meal. Bella worried the girl was mad at her. Had she unintentionally ignored her since their last shopping trip? Had she missed a call from her? She didn't remember. The last week had been exhausting. She was lucky she remembered her own name.

Then, there were Amanda and Vick, who sat beside one another and whispered as if they existed in their own little bubble. Could they be dating on the down-low? If so, why hide it from everyone? Or was she the only one who didn't know. With about ten minutes left, they excused themselves, leaving her and Sarresh at the table alone.

"What do you think we should do this weekend?" Bella asked.

"Mandy and I are going to a movie Friday night. You should join us."

"No, thank you."

"Why?"

Bella picked at the blueberry muffin in front of her. "I don't know. Things are just different between me and Mandy since the break-up. And Alex. Different there, too."

"Then why do you sit with them at lunch?"

"Would you join me if I moved to another table?"

"No."

"That's why. I don't want to ask my friends to choose sides." Although maybe they already had. Alex, Amanda, and Vick had sat there, but hardly said two words to her. The only person who talked to her at all had been Sarresh.

"I got you."

Sarresh looked up. "We've got company."

David had stopped in front of their table. "Can I talk to you alone?" he asked.

"Yeah. I was getting ready to leave, anyway. You can walk me to my locker." Bella glanced at Sarresh and stood.

He shoved his hands in his pockets. "Thanks. I'm not big on an audience."

"You didn't seem to mind on Saturday."

"That was different. We weren't talking."

"Makes perfect sense to me." Bella smiled and pushed through the cafeteria door.

David followed, and the door shut behind them. "You have plans, Friday?"

"No."

"Will you go out to dinner with me?"

"Yes."

Bella raised an eyebrow when his apparent nervousness didn't settle after she answered. What was up?

"There's just one catch."

"Which is?"

"There's a dress code."

Dress code? Oh, no. Since the house had been vandalized, her wardrobe consisted of jeans, shorts, blouses, and t-shirts. She had worn two dresses since then, and they had been for— Nope, she couldn't go there. Bella took a deep breath.

"Meaning?"

"Will you wear a dress? We could go somewhere else. I just want to take you someplace nice."

As she expected. But he'd given her an opportunity to change venues. Maybe she should give him the benefit of a doubt. "No. We'll go where you have planned. I trust you."

"I'm glad, because I would never let anything happen to you."

Bella disregarded the second part of his comment. She'd heard that before. From someone else. "What time are you picking me up?"

"Seven."

"I look forward to it."

"Me, too." David left Bella at her locker.

The bell rang, and as Bella gathered the books she needed for her next class, Sarresh skidded to a stop beside her.

"Did he ask you out?"

"What'd you do, run?"

"No, but I had to know what happened."

"Yes, he asked me out. And we need to go shopping. For a dress." Bella sighed. The idea less than thrilled her. Her weight had dropped over the past few weeks. Some of the clothes that had fit snugly when she bought them hung on her, now. All in all, searching for dresses, not something she cherished.

Sarresh opened her mouth and snapped it shut. She must've decided better on whatever she intended to say. "Okay. How about you come over this afternoon? I've got some dresses I haven't ever worn, and if you don't find anything, we can still go shopping."

"Yeah. Okay. Oh, God. I've got to tell my parents about my date."

"Are you really going to?"

"Yes. I'm trying to make an effort." The progress was slow, but communication was a start. If she wanted them to tell her more about her biological parents, she had to continue to share things from her own life with them.

"There better be a good reason you're here." Gervasio snarled into the phone at the dark-haired whore who smiled at him through the window. She was his *Mamá Gallina*, his mother hen, so to speak. She was the first whore he broke in in Rescate County. Now, she was the enforcer for his working girls. Nearly as invisible as the messenger. Except for one mark. Wisely, her shirt had been draped to cover the stamp he branded all his working girls with.

"Now, *papi*, is that any way to speak to your dove?"

"Why are you here? Tell me."

Mamá Gallina rested a hand over her heart. "I have a problem at home. *Mi madre*, she has disappeared. I searched all across town, but I cannot find her. I am unsure what to do."

"When?" He spat the question out. The fake concern tasted awful in his mouth. His mother never went anywhere. The woman had busied herself preparing for the return of her wonderful son, his useless brother. Should've had the little shit killed when he arranged the beating. Bronco would've loved to get his dirty hands even dirtier.

"I last saw her two days ago. What should I do?"

His mother was nothing more than a pest. He'd only kept her around in case Cristobal became a liability. Too many dead bodies presented a problem, especially if there was no safe place to bury them. Luckily, he had a safe place. "Get the others to help you search. Find out where she went. Is there anything else?"

"Just one more thing, *papi*. I was supposed to get some gifts from *mi novio*, but he seems to have forgotten all about me."

"Not possible. You're too special." The messenger had been commanded to deliver presents to his woman. But Swifty had opened the envelope, as Gervasio suspected he would. A letter and explicit instructions had been included. If the kid couldn't do as he'd been told, he would have to go.

Unfortunately, Gervasio had lost control after his associate had attempted to rape Bella. Bella was his, not for anyone else's touch. Pure, unadulterated rage had pulsed through Gervasio's body as he claimed her a third time. Then beat her nearly to death and stripped her. Afterward, he drove his associate to that safe zone, the one he'd long ago taken as his own—and buried him six feet underground. That man would never think of his girl again.

"It's true. I'm beginning to think I need to get my gifts for myself."

"Don't worry. This will be taken care of. Now go."

"Of course, *papi*." *Mamá Gallina* hung up the receiver and stood.

"Do you continue to believe she is using drugs?"

DeWei looked up from his computer. The woman he'd married was as fiery and protective as ever. She'd defend a wolf if she was convinced it hadn't eaten the sheep. And, honestly, it was a good question. He'd counted the pills in the prescription bottle daily, and Bella hardly used any. She kept up with her schoolwork and maintained her regular chores. He still didn't entirely believe they were out of the woods—but now, after the family counseling session … "I am less inclined toward my drug theory."

"I had hoped for more," Milena said, "but I can accept this for the time being. As long as the issue of hospitalization has been settled."

"Yes, my dear. It has." He stepped around his desk and placed a chaste kiss on his wife's forehead.

"Good. I am grateful to hear this."

The knock on the office door turned their attention from one another to their daughter. "I'm not interrupting, am I?"

"Of course, not my darling. What may we do for you?"

"Can I talk to Bàba alone for a minute?"

It was a rare request. The relationship he once held with his daughter had been battered. Over the last week, also, she seemed to bond more with her mother. DeWei glanced to his wife. "Of course."

His wife squeezed his hand and hugged their daughter on her way out the door.

DeWei gestured to a leather chair and sat in the one opposite. They hadn't had a quiet conversation between the two of them in some time. "Is everything all right?"

Bella arranged herself comfortably in her chair. "This is just weird. I want to keep the lines of communication open, like we said, but I'm having this sense of déjà vu. I mean the last time we really talked … Well, you agreed to let me date Miah. And this kind of has to do with a guy, too."

"I see." He paused. "I have pondered the things you shared with me and your mother on Monday. I don't wish you to ever feel as if you can't speak to either one of us. I know we've structured your life with rules. Perhaps at times they may have seemed quite strict, especially as it applied to boys."

"I get why you did it. I mean, Mãe has told me more about Ileana, and you were afraid I'd become like her. But I'm not. I'm me."

He had indeed feared Bella would become a drug addict like her biological mother. There was no logical basis for the fear. If the woman had done any drugs while pregnant with Bella, symptoms would've developed in childhood.

DeWei sighed. "It is not so much I believed you would become like Ileana. I simply want the best for you. My daughter deserves nothing less. You must understand, no matter when you disclosed the end of your relationship with Jeremiah, I would have told you it is his loss."

"You really mean that?"

"Yes."

"Xièxie, Bàba." Bella hugged him.

The thank you was unnecessary. His faith in her never waned, even if his instincts forced him to consider all the roads she might have taken. This moment was good. It reminded him of how things used to be.

DeWei returned the hug, pressed a kiss to his daughter's forehead, and reminded her that he loved her. "Wǒ ài nǐ, Maylin."

"Wǒ yě ài nǐ, Bàba." Bella sniffled.

"Why do you cry?"

"It's just ... he broke my heart. And I feel like it's my fault."

The depth of her sadness showed in her wide, faded hazel eyes.

"Nonsense. I am certain the wrong was on his part, not yours."

His daughter shook her head. "Anyway, I'm not here to talk about Miah. I wanted to talk to you about David."

DeWei studied Bella for a moment. Her face had gone from sorrow to what appeared to be joy in less than a second. "I recall the young man. He participated in the Festival, correct?"

"Yes. He asked me on a date for Friday, and I said I'd go."

nine

Jeremiah rubbed his brow. He had read the same line in his history book ten times. He slammed the book shut. The plan had been to get some schoolwork in before he left for Vick's, but it wasn't happening. Bell had been running a marathon in his head all week long.

Speculation about their breakup had gone on for weeks. Between that, the rape, and the shooting, the rumor mill had been burning the midnight oil. Now, all everyone talked about was Bell and David. The two were spotted cuddling by her locker. They had been seen whispering quietly in the lunchroom and holding hands in the hall.

Jeremiah shook his head, got to his feet, and headed down the hall. Female voices in the kitchen halted him.

"They're actually going out?" Amanda asked their cousin.

"Yes," Sarresh said.

"I don't like this. Not one bit."

Sarresh snickered. "You aren't the only one."

"I thought you were okay with the guy."

"No. I tolerate him for Bella. She likes him, but I'm worried about his temper."

"Temper?"

"He went off on this guy last year. Beat the hell out of him. Not to mention the fight he got into earlier this year when Alex told him about Mike."

"I remember that. Vick convinced me to leave before it got out of hand."

"It's not just that, though. He's done some things that make me think he has stalker potential. I don't trust him," Sarresh said.

"Like what?"

"Well, there's Bella's tattoo."

"Yeah. You said he talked her out of the tombstone she wanted. By the way, Vick chewed me out for not telling him. He thinks he could've talked her out of the tattoo, period."

"I dunno. Besides, it'd be kind of hypocritical, seeing as he doesn't mind yours. Not the point though. The point is that David got the same tattoo as Bella." Sarresh paused. "But his doesn't say 'Deuteronomy.' His has her name."

Jeremiah buried his face in his hands to stifle the groan that wanted to escape. This guy really was crazy. A freaking lunatic with a temper."

"I just wish Bella was more freaked by it," Sarresh said.

"Are you saying she isn't?"

"She told me she understood. Some stupid shit about how she changed his life, and he wanted to celebrate the journey."

"Did he tell her that before or after?"

"After. Guy's too smart to do it before."

"Damn. If I didn't want to kick his ass before, I really do now."

"Too bad you agreed not to." Sarresh laughed.

"Yeah, me and my big mouth. Maybe Alex would do it for me."

"Except he might break her."

"I hate when you talk about Alex like that. She's a good person," Amanda said.

"Who, for some reason, doesn't like me."

"I know, I know. At least all three of us agree about David."

"I'd like to believe he's good for Bella, but I'm not sure I can. He may've helped with her touch issues, though," Sarresh responded.

"You mean she isn't jumping up swinging every time somebody touches her?"

"Not as much. She's taking less time to calm down, too."

"I'd like to be impressed, but how do we know it's him? I mean, she was here last weekend, and it took a minute, but she let Jeremiah touch her," Amanda said.

"I get it Mandy. He's your brother, but ..."

He refused to listen any longer. Sarresh had only recently popped back into their lives. Anything she had to say about him would likely be negative. She had been around the house a lot the last month and Amanda was the only person she got along with. But if what Sarresh said was true, and David had eased Bell's pain, then the best thing he could do was keep his distance. Jeremiah collected his wallet and keys from his room. This time, when he stepped out, he purposely closed his door loudly enough that the girls could hear it.

"They're good together. Too bad neither of them can see it right now." Frustrated by the stupidity shared by her sibling and his ex-girlfriend, Amanda sighed. Jeremiah and Bella were so damn hard-headed.

Jeremiah stepped into the kitchen and politely nodded to Amanda and Sarresh as he snatched a bottle of water out of the refrigerator. "Ladies."

Amanda scrutinized her brother. "Where you off to?"

"Vick and I are going to the movies. See you later Mandy. Sarresh."

"Hey, Jeremiah."

Amanda glared at her cousin. Couldn't she keep her trap shut? Maybe Jeremiah would just keep going.

But no. He turned to Sarresh. "What can I do for you?"

Sarresh glanced from Jeremiah to Amanda and caught Mandy's glare. "Never mind. Have a good night."

"Sure. You too." Jeremiah left.

Amanda exhaled. *Thank you, Jesus!* She unfolded her arms. "Good job, coz."

"Yeah, well, it seemed pointless to tell him how much of an ass he's being."

"He beats himself up enough over Bella. Jeremiah doesn't need the added punches."

"Yeah, yeah. Too bad Vick won't let us lock them in that summer house his parents have." Sarresh frowned and forked another bite of noodles.

"I told you, he thinks we've meddled enough." Using a pair of chopsticks, Amanda picked up a piece of orange chicken.

"And I think we've only scratched the surface."

Amanda chuckled. "We'll give them time, see if they come together on their own."

"And if they don't?"

"Then we plan B it."

After dinner, David and Bella walked a couple blocks to a club he'd heard about. She'd visited Carlsbad a couple of times, but knew nothing of the city's nightlife. It'd never really been her scene. The club, Fresco's, wasn't like T2. There were fewer bodies and it was very upscale. David fit in perfectly, but she, on the other hand, was nothing but a poser, made up to look the part, but with no training to act the part. Somehow, he'd convinced her to stay.

She stared at her reflection in the bathroom mirror. Like her homecoming dress, this one had a single shoulder strap and its silky material hugged her curves. Yet this dress was sexier, somehow. Could it be the honey color? The lack of ruffle to break up the way it clung to her body? Sarresh said it looked amazing on her, still she felt ... awkward. Like a fake, caramel-skinned doll. She'd hardly accepted the compliments David had given her all night. Bella tugged at the dress. Not like she could do anything about it now.

She headed for the booth where David waited. The smile that spread across his face when she came into view was exquisite, and she just had to stare at his lips for a moment. What would it be like if he kissed her? Would his lips be soft? Her cheeks flushed. She feigned an innocent smile and returned her gaze to his beautiful, cobalt blue eyes.

David offered his hand. "Up for another dance?"

"Yes." Bella eased her hand into his, and together they walked onto the dance floor, just as the song changed. All the previous songs had been fast-paced, but this was a slow one. Slow songs were intended for close contact. Her comfort with touch had progressed, but was she ready for this? She inhaled deeply as they headed to the center of the dance floor.

"You okay?" David kissed the inside of her palm and slid a hand to her waist. Even with her heels, he still had a good eight inches on her.

A few inches of space remained between the two of them. She grabbed one of his shoulders and exhaled. She'd been closer to him last weekend when she pressed her ear to his chest. Maybe that was the solution. She leaned against his chest and focused on his heartbeat.

"I'm okay."

"Good."

Slowly, they started to sway to the music. The longer she listened to the steady thump of his heart, the easier she moved. Bella gazed into David's exquisite blue eyes and something sparked. Her heart raced, her cheeks burned, and tingles crawled up her spine. Her eyes dropped to his lips, then returned to his gaze.

David followed her gaze and eyed her lips in return. He leaned down toward her slowly ... and then held perfectly still.

Bella pressed forward and met him halfway. His lips *were* soft. Heat licked up her legs and abdomen. What started as innocent and sweet became desperate and hungry. The kiss deepened—and a memory triggered.

The club became an alleyway of dumpsters and David's arms transformed into her monster's arms. Panicked, Bella yanked free and ran. Outside, the air was stagnant. Halfway down the sidewalk, Bella stopped and yanked off her shoes. Behind her, feet were pounding up the pavement, and a male voice was calling out her name. She had to keep running ... she had to escape.

Bella wrenched open the door of the first taxi in line at the curb. "Please drive!"

"Where to?" The cabbie asked.

"I don't care, just drive!"

"I need an address."

"Just drive!" Bella yelled. She rocked back and forth, crying. Finally, the cabbie pulled onto the road, just as her name was shouted again. She pressed her head against her knees and tried to stop trembling. She had to calm down. Pull it together. She reached into her purse. "You got something to drink?"

"Yeah." The cabbie passed her back an unopened bottle of water, and Bella popped the pills in her mouth. Bliss was just around the corner, she thought.

ten

If Bella's parents noticed a cab dropping her off instead of David, they didn't mention it. She'd managed to say goodnight, get to her room, out of the dress, and fall dead asleep. She woke up shortly after her parents left for their weekend getaway—in her bed. The pills must have completely numbed her out, because, up until that point, the memories associated with her bed had been so overwhelming she had been sleeping in her bedroom chair or on the floor.

When the realization of where she'd ended up sank in, she'd immediately jumped up, vomited, and took her first shower of the day. Since then, she'd taken three more showers and changed four times. Now, Bella gazed at the clock on her nightstand. Five p.m. She could wait forever and it wouldn't make what she had to do any easier. Bella left her room, stopped in the kitchen, grabbed a bottle of water, and took off for David's place.

Forty minutes later, she pulled down David's driveway, which circled around a gorgeous fountain in front of the huge, stately house. Refusing to be intimidated, she parked, headed up the stairs to the door, and rang the bell.

David's ice-queen sister answered. "What do you want?"

Bella tucked her hands in her jean pockets. "Is your brother here?"

"Yep."

Then why didn't the girl step aside?

"Can I come in?"

"What for?"

Holy hell, she was *so* not in the mood. "Let's get something straight, Heather. If I start dating your brother, I plan to be around here a lot. Now, you have two choices: get used to the shit or get shoved on your ass every time I have to walk over you like a goddamn rug."

"There a problem?" David asked, appearing behind his twin.

Bella took advantage of the girl's momentary shock to address David. "None at all. Somewhere we can talk?"

"Yeah. We can go to the library."

Bella nodded and followed him. Once there, David closed the door, and she paced the large room, trying to get a hold of her nerves. David leaned against the huge oak desk and waited. Finally, she sat down on the chaise lounge. "I'm sorry about last night. I panicked."

"I'm concerned about what prompted it so we don't go there again."

Nervous, Bella stood again and resumed her pacing. "I was okay when the kiss was gentle. Then it changed, and everything beautiful about it got devoured, lost in my memories of the attack. All I could think was that I had to get away. I had to run."

Two hands wrapped around her arms to stop her from pacing further. "Bella ..."

She gasped at the touch, then apologized. "Sorry."

David turned her to him. "You could've told me. I'm in no hurry for whatever is happening between us. I'll wait as long as I need for you to be okay with any kind of intimacy." He placed a finger under her chin and lifted her eyes to his.

She'd managed to contain her tears through all the pacing and talking, but now, after what he said, the floodgates opened. How could she express her gratitude? He was so understanding. There was only one thing she could think of. Bella wrapped her arms around David's neck, placed a tender kiss on his lips, and snuggled against his chest. "Your heartbeat, it reminds of where I am."

"That's the best thank you I've ever gotten. We'll go as slow as you need to. I'm just glad I get to spend time with you."

He deserved better than her, but God knew she needed him. Bella sniffled.

"You need a tissue?"

"Yes, please."

"Okay." David kissed her forehead and started for the door. "You eat dinner, yet?"

Bella wiped her face with the back of her hand. She hadn't eaten since dinner last night. Not that she dared mention that. "No."

"If you'd like to stay, I'll have the chef whip up something."

"That sounds good."

"Okay. I'll be back in a minute." David closed the door behind him.

What the hell was she doing with this guy? Yeah, Miah'd broken up with her weeks ago. Yeah, he'd hurt her in ways she'd never imagined, but she still had feelings for him. And here she was encouraging David toward something he would never really have from her. She sat back in the chaise lounge. But the empty ache in her heart was getting to her. Maybe he could fill part of the void, and she wouldn't be so alone.

Whoa! The room began to spin. Bella gripped the back of the chaise lounge and waited for the dizzy spell to pass. With all the pills she'd taken that day, she probably should've eaten. She'd had a couple of spells like this, and they went away after a few minutes. But this one seemed to last longer. She leaned back and closed her eyes. Nausea climbed up the back of her dry throat.

God, she was going to throw up. She hopped off the chaise lounge and grabbed the desk to keep from falling over. Bella covered her mouth and stumbled to the door. If she was going to throw up, she'd do it in the bathroom.

She struggled to get enough control to grip the knob and turn it. Finally, she got the door open and looked out to see two people standing in the foyer. The last thing she remembered was calling David's name before her muscles gave out and she collapsed to the floor.

Slowly, Bella's senses returned. Something was clamped on her left forefinger. There was a steady beeping off to her side, and two prongs were stuck in her nose. As everything started to make sense, her eyes fluttered open. She was in the hospital—again.

"Welcome back." Miah's father smiled.

"Where's David?" Bella croaked out.

"Waiting outside."

"What happened?"

Miah's father rubbed his brow as if he was thinking about how to say what he needed to say. "As far as I know, you passed out at David's. He brought you in. When I got here, he was yelling at the nurses and doctors because they wouldn't let him see you. He calmed down while I assessed the situation and the doctors ran tests to see why you fainted."

"But why are you here?"

"Christine and I are listed as your emergency contacts if your parents can't be reached. So you could be treated without their consent. Where are your parents? They should be here for you."

"They're out of town, but I don't want them here. Can you just get David?" It was dumb to use David as a crutch, but she had to lean on someone she could trust.

"I think you should talk to the doctor first. When you're done, I'll send David in." Miah's father left before she had the opportunity to argue.

Next thing she knew, there was a knock on the door and a doctor entered. "I'm Dr. Gaither. How's my patient?"

"Confused. I know I passed out, but what happened?"

The short-haired woman sat with Bella's medical chart in her hands. "Yes, you fainted. There are a number of things that can cause a person to lose consciousness. When you were brought in, you had low blood pressure. Given your age, this raised some flags. I ran several tests to determine any underlying causes of the syncope."

"So, why'd I pass out?" It was unnecessary for the doctor to explain, but she asked anyway. Might as well face the music. If they ran blood tests, they would've already discovered the hydrocodone in her system.

"I suspect the amount of opiates in your system contributed to the event. Are you taking the medication as it was prescribed?"

"No. Sometimes I have a lot of pain. I take enough to help."

The doctor nodded. "I'm going to recommend a counselor for you."

"I already have a psychiatrist. I'm sure she can handle this." Like hell she'd go talk her brain out to another damn quack. One was more than enough.

"Okay. Talk to your psychiatrist and your doctor. If they haven't already, they should explain the risks associated with taking the pills during pregnancy."

"Pregnancy? What are you talking about?"

Dr. Gaither closed Bella's chart. "You're pregnant. About thirteen weeks."

No, no, no, no. Her gaze trailed down her body to her flat belly. She had dreamed of having children, later, after college. When she met Miah, she was positive he would be their father. This was nowhere near what she had planned. Another product of her attack. Bella glanced at the doctor. "I can't be pregnant."

"I'm sorry, dear, but you are. If the doctor who prescribed the hydrocodone is unaware of the fact, they must be notified. I saw from your records you were brutally raped a few months ago. Any residual pain should've subsided. Unless your doctor sees fit for you to be on the pills, you should discontinue their use. Your doctor and psychiatrist can work in conjunction to make sure that happens."

"I, um, yeah. I'll do that."

"Good. I'll sign off on your discharge, but I want you to eat something before you leave. Sheriff Detrone said you wanted to see your boyfriend. I'll send him in." Dr. Gaither stood and left.

Boyfriend? Good Lord, there were too many words being thrown around for her to deal with that one. *Deep breath, just take a deep breath.* "Thanks."

Less than a minute later, the door flew open, and David practically ran across the room to her side. "Are you okay?"

Bella managed a half-hearted smile. How the hell was she supposed to be okay when the doctor just told her that monster had knocked her up? And if Miah's dad was her emergency contact, he probably knew everything the doctor told her. But she wasn't going to tell David any of that. "I'm fine," was all she said.

Settling into the chair by her bed, he took her hand and sighed in relief. "I've been so worried. They wouldn't tell me anything. They wouldn't let me see you."

"Did you really yell at the doctors?"

"Yes. Maybe it was a little much, but they were pissing me off. The sheriff told me if I didn't calm down he would have me escorted from the building and I wouldn't see you until you got released. Bella, are you okay? You're looking a little pale."

"Yeah, fine." She squeezed his hand in reassurance. Suddenly, suicide appealed more to her than it had before. Could she really be that selfish? The baby growing inside her didn't ask to be here. But abortion was out of the question. It's why she declined the morning after pill when she was given the chance. What options were left for her? No way could she keep the baby. Only one other choice.

A knock on the door interrupted Bella's thoughts. Miah's father poked his head in. "Can I talk to you for a minute?"

"I guess."

"I'll just go get you something to eat." David kissed Bella on the forehead and left.

"He seems like a decent guy."

She hoped the sheriff would address any topic other than her love life. "He is. I take it the doctor told you everything?"

"Yes. She said you're going to talk to your psychiatrist and doctor about the pills and pregnancy."

"I will. And before you say anything, I'll tell my parents. Just ... give me time."

"I knew from the day I met you how smart you are. I never expected you'd have a drug problem. It's like seeing it in one of my own children. I want to believe that smart, strong girl is in there somewhere, and she'll do what's right. Not just for your own sake, but for the sake of your unborn child."

At that, the tears rolled down Bella's cheeks. He had to go and say something like that. He had to show he cared. The ugly was easier to believe. Who could possibly love her now? Sixteen and pregnant with her attacker's child. "I can't keep this baby."

"Hey. It's okay. Take some time to figure things out."

"Yeah." Bella sniffled. She almost wished the doctor planned to keep her overnight. An empty house sounded painfully lonely.

"Maybe you shouldn't be alone tonight. You can stay at our house if you'd like."

"Thanks, but no thanks. Being around Miah isn't exactly high on my priority list."

"Understandable. Listen, this may not be the best time, but I'd like your consent to do a paternity test. It could help with your case. It's just a blood test. And if you're okay with it, I'll get the prosecutor to drum up a court order."

"Why would you need a court thing if I agree?" Bella asked as she accepted the tissues he offered.

"Makes it legal and usable as evidence."

"Right. Yeah, I'll consent." Bella wiped the last of the tears away.

David glanced at the clock on his nightstand. It was late. He had no desire for Bella to feel as if he'd taken advantage of the situation. She may have insisted on sleeping in his room, but he lay on the floor, curled up against a beanbag, while she got the bed.

"After one a.m. Can't sleep?"

"No."

"Why don't I go downstairs and get you some warm milk? That might help."

"And maybe some cookies?"

"Okay."

They'd left the hospital nearly three hours ago. David had stopped by her house on the way back to his place. Given the tension between his sister and Bella, he hadn't thought it was good idea Bella spend the night. Bella already seemed stressed. In the end, he conceded.

He rubbed the sleep from his eyes. Odd, the kitchen light was on. David pushed on the swinging door and stepped into the kitchen.

Heather glanced up from her laptop. "Can't sleep, either?"

"Not until Bella falls asleep."

"Gag me. I don't even know why you brought her here."

"Can we not start? It's been a long-ass day." His sister, diva extraordinaire. They'd been pretty close as kids, then she failed her freshman year of high school at their last school. That was the summer she went to fat camp, lost a whole bunch of weight, and returned home as the world's bitchiest slut. After that everything changed.

"All I'm saying is you're too good for her."

David warmed up a mug of milk in the microwave. One of his twin's many rants, and it worked in his favor to ignore her. He searched out cookies for Bella.

She hadn't said much on the drive over. He had no clue what the doctor told her, but obviously the information bothered her. Maybe if he pushed her a bit more, she'd rest easier with the weight lifted. He'd try again when he got back upstairs.

"That's great. Ignore me. You know, while she's here, I should really discuss some things with her." Heather slid off the barstool.

"What could you possibly have to talk about?"

"Oh, I don't know. Maybe how her current boyfriend sabotaged her relationship with her ex-boyfriend. I'm sure she'd find that little tidbit interesting."

"What, and admit your own involvement? You're too self-centered to do something so idiotic." David turned toward his sister and crossed his arms.

"Here's the thing. She already hates me. But if I told her everything I know, she'd despise you."

With two strides, he closed the distance between them and shoved a finger in her face. "Utter one word to her, and I swear to God, I'll go to the police. Tell them everything about your little boy toy. Yeah, I know about him. I know more than you think."

"You wouldn't"

"Try me." David grabbed the bag of cookies and the mug of warm milk, strode past his twin sister, and headed back upstairs.

How dare she threaten him? Like she should really be surprised he knew all about her boy toy, Luis. Yeah, he knew all right, and he protected Heather by saying nothing. The police had the guys who raped Bella in custody. It wasn't like they were going anywhere.

He disappeared into his room and slammed the door shut.

Bella sat up. "Everything okay?"

"Yeah. Sorry. Just another wonderful moment with my sister."

"Oh."

"What about you? You feeling okay?" He sat on the bed beside Bella, handed her the mug and set the bag of cookies down.

"As good as I can be. Thank you."

He kissed her forehead. "I'm here for whatever you need."

"Then can I ask you to do something for me?"

"Shoot."

"Please lay next to me. The crap in my life keeps piling on. What I really need is ... I just ... with you all the way over there, I feel more alone." Bella sipped at the milk and bit into a cookie.

David gripped the back of his neck. Did he trust himself enough not to curl up to her? Because man, he wanted to hold and comfort her and never let go.

"Okay, but I need you to tell me what happened back in the hospital. What did the doctor tell you that has you so freaked out?"

"I'm pregnant."

"What?" He stopped halfway around the bed. Had he heard her correctly?

"Funny. I said the same thing when she told me. Couldn't believe it myself, either."

"Is one of your rapists ...?"

"Yep."

Were they truly having this conversation? Of all the things that could've caused her to pass out, this was the last thing he imagined. "Christ. I'm so sorry Bella."

"Not like I can change what happened. I just ... I'll let the police do their paternity test and then figure it out from there."

She finished the mug of milk and placed it on the nightstand.

"That why the sheriff wanted to talk to you?" Collecting himself, David rearranged the pillows on the bed and created a barrier. This way there'd be no chance of him inadvertently cuddling with Bella.

"What're you doing?"

"I think you'll be more comfortable this way. You know because of the whole touch thing." It seemed like a good idea a few minutes ago, but the way her face pinched together told him otherwise. "I can take it down if you'd like."

"No. You're right," Bella said. "Can we go to bed now? I'm kind of exhausted."

"Course." David adjusted the last of the pillows and climbed under the covers. He wanted her to feel safe. He didn't expect her to reach across the barrier and grab his hand. But she did—and he cautiously laced their fingers together. Her whole body stiffened for a minute. Then he felt her slowly relax into the bed.

He pressed a tender kiss to her hand and flipped off the light.

eleven

Bella stared at her locker. She had stacked and re-stacked her books four times, already. No matter how she fixed them, they didn't look right. The last bell rung, and the halls filled with students. She gathered the books and notebooks she needed and then shut the thing. She'd been back at school a month, and people still whispered "slut" and "whore." Some commented how she'd lost weight, and others called her "Pudgy the Pig." Peace belonged to anyone but her. Lost in her own thoughts, she turned to leave—and there stood her best friend.

"Crikey. Alex, you scared the shit out of me."

"Sorry, B. Can we talk for a sec?"

"Yeah, I guess." What was today? Tuesday? Was she supposed to go somewhere after school? An appointment? Right, the shrink. Whatever. She'd spare a few minutes for her friend.

"The police showed up at my house last night. They asked me about that Fourth of July party we went to this year."

"Yeah. One of my attackers said he met me there. I thought I told you."

Alex pushed the door to the parking lot open. "No, but I won't hold that against you. Listen, I told them what I remembered. Like about that guy you danced with."

"What guy?"

"The Latino guy. I'd never really seen you that interested in anyone before."

"What?" She'd never danced with anyone until she'd met Miah. She was a klutz, who tripped over her own two feet. Dancing wasn't her forte. Had she even talked to Alex the next morning about the party?

"Don't you remember? We talked about it when we got home. You told me you tried some funny tasting drink. Even babbled on about the guy and how cute he was. And how he called you a name you hadn't heard in a long time. B, you okay? You look like you just saw a ghost."

Ghost didn't come close. The trust she had in one of her best friends crumbled before her eyes. "Did you describe him to the police?"

"Yeah. I picked him out of the group of pictures they showed me."

"I got to go." Bella took off for her car.

"B? Did I do something wrong? B?"

Stupid shrink. What the hell was with all the adults needing to be on the same page? She'd described what happened four days ago, when her world turned upside down, a billion times—and now she needed to do it yet again. Bella unlocked the front door. *Tell my parents. Confide in them. Sure, and while I'm at it, I'll just tell them how miserable I am, and that I'd like to kill myself.*

"Mãe, I'm home."

"Come in the kitchen. I thought you would have been back an hour ago."

"Sorry. I had to go by the police station after my doctor's appointment." Bella sat at the kitchen island. The scent of onions, peppers, and coconut milk wafted across. "Your *moqueca* is making my mouth water," she said, and her stomach grumbled its confirmation.

"Good to know your appetite has returned. A package arrived this afternoon for you. I placed it on the table."

Bella headed over to the dining room table and stared at the large white box. No label on the front, nothing that indicated who it was from.

"It was delivered about an hour ago. I am certain a card must be included. Open and see," her mother called.

Bella hesitated. Unidentified presents had played a frightening part in the recent horrible events of her life. If David sent something, he would've made certain she knew it was from him. Warily, Bella lifted the lid. The box contained a dozen long-stemmed, red roses— and a card with *Congratulations!* scrawled across it. Tears prickled the corners of her eyes. It had to have come from him—Jorge Smith. He knew. She dropped the card and backed away from the table. "No, no, no, no."

"Bella! What is the problem?" Her mother rushed to her side.

Ignoring her mother, she dug out her cell phone and dialed the number Detective Russell had given her over a month ago. When he answered, she stammered, "I got something else ... roses with a note ... please come." At the detective's instant assurance he would come immediately—and his quickly blurted instructions—she hung up, crying.

"My darling, what is the matter? Why have you contacted the police over roses? They look lovely." Her mother reached for the box.

"No! Detective Russell said not to touch anything."

Her father stepped into the kitchen. "What is with the commotion?"

"Bella received beautiful roses, but she has contacted the police. She has not yet explained why."

Her father frowned. "Does it not say on the card from whom they came?"

"I'm pregnant, and only one person would send them." Bella blurted out the truth. That wasn't exactly how she intended to tell them. But now she had. Then the box shuffled across the table. Her gaze shifted from the shock on her parents' faces to the box.

Was something hidden inside?

Jamar sat in the breakfast nook, waiting. He set his cup of coffee on the table when the phone rang. It was Russell, calling to fill him in on the Kynaston situation. He'd stayed up to find out what happened.

"Was there anything beside the roses?"

"Couple of rats. Animal control picked them up. Don't think they were dangerous, but they were sent to lab anyway."

Jamar lifted his mug and sipped. "Who signed for the delivery?"

"Mrs. Kynaston, but she didn't remember a whole lot about the flower shop.

Box had a logo in the corner, so I'll check it out in the morning."

"All right. Go home and get some sleep."

Jamar dropped his phone on the table. It had been a long night. Taking his wife's advice, he hadn't asked whether Bella had mentioned her hospital visit to her parents. Drugs in her system? Hard to believe. Sure, she'd been given painkillers, but that was nearly three months ago. Was there any reason she still required them? He had to trust Bella had discussed the problem with her parents.

"Dad?" Amanda paused in the entranceway to the kitchen.

"What are you still doing up?"

"I heard Bella got some weird package. Is she okay?"

He leaned on the table. "She's fine. There's nothing to worry about. We've got it handled."

"I kind of wanted to talk to you about something." She slid into the nook across from him. "Is it true Bella's pregnant?"

Jamar frowned. How did his daughter know? "Why do you ask?"

"I heard a rumor at school."

"I suppose I shouldn't be surprised." It sure as hell wasn't what that poor girl needed. Jamar inwardly groaned. Must have been the Warren kids who started it.

"I figured if it was true … I don't know. That maybe Mom could talk to her. Seeing as she's been there."

His daughter's words caught him completely off guard. He and Christine had gone to great lengths to protect Amanda from the truth. She couldn't possibly know.

"I know, Dad. I've known for a few years."

"How?"

Amanda interlocked her fingers and slumped back. "You remember that trip I took with Grandma to Mexico? I needed a passport. I went looking for my birth certificate, and I found the original and the amended versions together."

"Oh, Mandy. You've known and kept quiet all this time. Why?"

"Because you never treated me like I'm not your daughter. And now, B needs someone to talk to. So does Jeremiah. He's devastated. Keeps blaming himself. Like he could've prevented all of this from happening."

Bella slammed the book shut. Two days had passed since she told her parents she was pregnant. As expected, they'd freaked out. Then, they'd sort of accepted it. Although her father had been angrier than usual. Though she suspected that had more to do with the flower delivery than her unborn baby.

And when her parents weren't around to fret over her condition, David hovered. He'd barely left her by herself since Saturday night. Good thing a trial date had finally been set. Gave her a reason to escape from both him and her parents. She'd met with the prosecutor a few hours ago to go over her statement. It was difficult to retell her nightmare. And she hadn't called anyone when the meeting ended early.

Now, she was home alone and had no clue what to do with herself. Homework didn't take her mind off things. It was just one boring subject after another. She had never been this antsy. Sighing, she got up from the dining room table and headed to the refrigerator, grabbed a bottle of water, then padded to her room.

She had energy to burn with no way to expend it. Maybe she could clean.

She surveyed her room. Where to start? Her body made a decision before her brain caught up. She turned to the bookcase. She had a lot of books, and she had read them all at least twice—and sometimes more. She smiled as she glanced at the titles. A lot of good memories.

Then her hand landed on the Bible. Slowly, she pulled it out. Funny, it used to be an object that contained words of great importance. Spoke of how much God loved his children. How had the verse gone? *For God so loved the world, that he gave his only begotten Son, that whosoever believeth in him should not perish, but have everlasting life.*

God loved his kids, but he punished them, too. Killed a whole lot of them in the flood. Bella stared at the thing. The words she'd learned as a child now meant nothing. With all God had put her through, no way he loved any part of her.

Weirdly, the Bible had also been the one thing in her bedroom the criminals who vandalized the house left untouched.

Suddenly, all the rage she'd repressed blew to the surface. She ripped pages out of the Bible and threw it across the room, and then she tore every book out of her bookcase, flinging them at the wall. She stalked to the closet, yanked clothes from their hangers, and tore at them until all her anger, frustration, and sadness had been expended. Then Bella dropped against the wall and slid to the floor. Calming her breath, she scanned the room and laughed until she cried. She had made a mess. It matched her life.

Sheriff Detrone stopped in front of Detective Russell's desk. "Tell me we know who sent those flowers."

Russell held out an evidence bag with an order form inside. "Went by the shop this morning. No video surveillance, but the store owner handed over the order form. Look at the signature."

"Luis Smith. Great. Facial recognition ever come back with something?"

"No, sir. But there's more going on than we thought." Russell walked over to the board they used to keep track of evidential findings.

Sheriff Detrone frowned at the new face added to the board. "Who's this?"

"Meet Jocelyn Smith. Name sound familiar?"

The woman Petar Jacobs had sworn up and down would alibi him for the time of Bella's rape. Not to mention the last name stood out. It was highly unlikely there would be three people with the last name "Smith" unless they were all connected, somehow. Jamar gestured for Russell to continue.

"She visited Jorge Smith twice in the last week. Her driver's license is fake, too. Made me wonder how these guards didn't recognize a bogus ID."

"In my office." The conversation had turned to something Jamar suspected a couple months ago, when the investigation first started. He couldn't confirm he had a dirty cop on his force, so he hadn't involved appropriate authorities. Now, though? Things appeared to have gone deeper than he'd suspected.

Russell entered behind him and closed the door. "I ran background checks, and something interesting popped. One of the prison guards is related to Detective Simms. Rodney Harrison is his brother-in-law. I put the file on your desk."

"What about the conversation between the girl and Jorge Smith?"

"They seem to be talking in code. She mentioned the disappearance of her mother and something about gifts her boyfriend was supposed to get her."

"Okay. Let's not tip our hand, yet. Talk to the warden. See if he can tell the IDs aren't real. I don't want this Harrison guy spoken with, yet. Word could get back to Jorge Smith. We need to let these people in to figure what he's up to. And bring Cristobal in. I think it's time we talked to him on our turf."

They suspected Jorge Smith was really Gervasio Rodriguez, but had yet to prove it. And Cristobal Rodriguez hadn't given anything up. It was time that changed.

"Yes, sir. And I'm going to try to figure out who this Luis Smith really is, too. And I'll do some more digging on the aliases for known Grim Reaper members. No way the last name Smith between these three is a coincidence."

"Good. Keep me apprised of updates."

"Yes, sir."

"How's she doing?" Luis asked Cristobal. The guy had spent about ten minutes talking to his mother.

"Good. Safe, thanks to you. How'd you manage it?"

Excellent question. Not that he ever intended to reveal that information. "Let's just say I've befriended the right people."

"No matter. She is away from this storm my brother has created. I will keep my word."

"I don't think it's that simple, anymore."

"Why not?" Cristobal crossed his arms and eyed the wall of Luis's room.

Luis had collected a few movie posters in his eighteen years, from *The Matrix, The Girl with the Dragon Tattoo,* and *Code 2600.* What he preferred, though, were the books tucked neatly in his bookcase. Most were beautiful books on code.

Luis glanced up from his laptop. "Why? Because your reticence has the police believing you're colluding with Jorge Smith—who they still haven't identified as your brother."

"I would not work with him as he is now. He has darkened so much."

"Which is why we need something you can take with you as proof of your disloyalty."

"Like what?" Cristobal perched on the edge of Luis's bed and looked at him hopefully.

"Like his book of secrets. Except I haven't been able to find the damn thing. And I've run out of places to look."

Cristobal tapped his chin. "I might have a few ideas."

twelve

The Friday afternoon bell had rung. David tossed one last book in his backpack and slung it over his shoulder. A heavy hand landed on his shoulder. One of his friends from the soccer team, Keith Reynolds.

"Tell me we're partying this weekend."

"Can't. I'm taking Bella to the Electric Light Parade in Roswell tomorrow night."

"You've gone soft, man." Keith shook his head.

David laughed. "I like her."

"You must. Too bad you can't get others to follow suit."

"What're you talking about?"

"Come on. Don't tell me you haven't heard the rumors." Keith raised an eyebrow.

"I don't pay attention to that shit. And neither should you."

"I'm not saying I shared any of them, but they're out there."

"Well, none of its true," David snarled. His friends should know better than to listen to rumors. Even if they were based on truth, they were usually transformed into big, ugly lies.

Keith stepped back. "Which part's not true? The rape? I know there's disagreement over whether or not that really happened. Or how she caused a shooting? Cuz I heard a lot of police were around when that went down. Or how her ex knocked her up?"

"Sounds to me like you've heard a bunch of bullshit." David's muscles tensed. The guy needed to shut the hell up—or risk losing a couple of teeth.

"All I'm saying is darkness surrounds this girl. Be careful or she could bring you down with her. I gotta jet. Catch you later." Keith bolted down the hallway.

David spun around. Good thing his friend took off. He'd been prepared to pound on the guy—but he'd spouted some truth. That made David curious. How the hell had anyone found out—? Oh, hell. He glanced down the hall toward his twin's locker. Heather. He'd bet anything she opened her trap. David cracked his neck. He'd speak with his sister later. He slammed his locker shut and stalked toward the other side of the school, where his girl awaited … and stepped around the corner. *Son of a bitch.* Jeremiah was approaching Bella from the other end of the hall. There was one way to ensure the jackass knew who she belonged to. Without a thought about her anxiety, David walked up to Bella and staked his claim loud and clear, slipping a hand around her waist and kissing her lovingly and deeply.

At first the kiss was a nice surprise—until it went from a kiss to a *kiss*. Sharing a moment of bliss had gotten easier over the last few days, but this wasn't blissful. Bella's back tensed and her eyes flipped open. The sight of David's blue-black hair kept her grounded. She pulled out of David's grip and saw him staring at something behind her. She followed his gaze.

It was Miah, walking away down the hall.

"Why'd you kiss me?" Bella folded her arms across her chest.

"I always kiss you."

"Not like that. You're too conscientious of my issues."

"I don't know what you're getting at. I simply wanted to, um, appreciate you for a moment."

"Sure you weren't trying to rub our relationship in Miah's face?"

David gripped the back of his neck. "Maybe. I got a little jealous of the way he looked at you. And I thought he wanted to talk to you."

Bella closed her locker and slung her backpack over her shoulder. She hadn't noticed Miah waiting for her. "So what? I'm not your property to claim."

"You're right. I'm sorry, Bella."

"I'm not the one you should apologize to."

"You can't be serious."

"Deadly." She stomped off toward the parking lot. David had picked her up for school that morning. They planned for her to spend the night at his house and tell her parents she intended to stay with Sarresh. He chased after her. "Come on, Bella. I'll do anything, except that."

"Do you think this is some sort of game? He's a person with feelings, as much as I am, and I expect you to act accordingly."

"But he doesn't have anything to do with us. You said so yourself."

"I can't believe you just said that." Bella climbed into the BMW, buckled up, and crossed her arms. If this was how he was going to be, he was not the boyfriend for her. She stared out the window as he got in the car and the engine purred to life.

"Come on, you—"

"Do not say one more word to me. Just drive."

Bella and David lay on his king-size bed. They hadn't discussed Miah, again. She'd managed to calm down and just added it to the multitude of problems gathering on the backburner. Now, she dug her hand into the bowl of popcorn between them and arched an eyebrow skeptically at the two teenagers on the sixty-inch flat-screen HD television. How was this supposed to be believable?

According to David, he picked something his sister claimed girls liked and he was fairly certain she'd never seen—which included practically everything. The first movies she'd ever really been exposed to were those she'd seen with Miah. But this was much stranger than anything of those. Okay, the talking fish were a little weird, but she loved *Finding Nemo*. Oh, and the short, brown alien, too— but she'd liked *E.T.*

This one, though, *Twilight?* Bella had heard of it, but now that she was watching it herself, she couldn't grasp the hype. The fantasy books she read were better than this crap. She gave David a sidelong glance. "Never let your sister pick out a movie again."

"What? You don't like it?"

"I just don't get the point. And this Edward guy. Is he supposed to be hot?" Sure, he was cute, with his mussy hair, but she was attracted to guys who were more clean cut. "Honestly, did you pick this out for me or yourself?"

David's cheeks flushed. "Truthfully, I think Kristen Stewart's hot."

"Excuse me?"

"Don't worry, you're the hotter Bella!" David laughed and kissed her forehead.

"Do not associate me with her. Maybe you should call me something different. Christa? Maylin? Or what about Nadalia? I have two middle names, you know."

"No way! Bella's sexy. I like how it rolls off my tongue." With a wide grin, David waggled his brows.Banter over the movie eased the tension she hadn't realized had settled in her shoulders. Helped remind her of the good times they shared. She munched on some more popcorn, then said, "Edward doesn't know how to talk to girls, does he?"

"Well, he's supposed to be like a hundred years old."

"Eww. That's kind of gross."

"Yeah, but he's permanently seventeen."

"I don't know if I'd like that."

"I could see it. Lot of chances to fix your mistakes." David leaned on an elbow, and his bright blue eyes stared into hers.

Bella knew his words referred to more than the movie. The Miah situation. David hadn't conceded to her request, and she refused to back down. She glanced at the screen and directed the conversation back to the film. "You know, I really don't get her. Twenty seconds ago, he walks away and she's still drooling over him."

"You going to comment through the whole movie?" David snatched a couple pieces of popcorn from her hand.

"I make no promises."

He glanced at the clock on the nightstand. "Duly noted."

"Who blurts things out like that?"

"You lasted less than three minutes."

"How can you expect me not to comment about a movie with sparkly vampires?" *Oops!* Bella shoved a handful of popcorn in her mouth.

"I thought you hadn't seen this."

She shrugged. She hadn't. But seeing as how the story starred her namesake, she knew more about the movie than she did about most movies she hadn't seen. "I haven't."

"Then how do you know something that hasn't been revealed yet?"

"Really? Do you not know my name? Have you not met the other teenagers we go to school with? Are you seriously not seeing an association?"

"Okay. I get it. But you do have to pay attention to know what's going on." David grinned and snagged some more popcorn.

Bella groaned. "Fine."

Bella stared in the mirror, her hands pressed against the cool marble of the sink. The pill bottle sat on the counter in front of her. After she and David finished watching the movie, she'd excused herself. She'd brushed her teeth and washed her face. And she had opened and closed the pill bottle twice.

She couldn't sleep tonight without the pills. David would know if she never fell asleep. With a heavy sigh, she reached for the bottle again. Taking a deep breath, Bella twisted the cap. Her gaze lifted from the bottle to the mirror again, and she glared at her reflection. Then the bathroom door swung open, bumping her and causing her to spill the pills.

"Bella?" Heather asked.

She frantically scooped pills from the counter and the sink.

"What're you doing?" Heather grabbed Bella's arm.

She yanked away and kept picking up pills. Not a single one could be lost down the drain! She glanced all around. Satisfied she had retrieved every last pill, Bella turned her attention to Heather and gave the girl a weak smile. "Need the bathroom?"

Heather crossed her arms. "You've got to be joking. I'm not blind. I thought the doctor said you shouldn't take those with the baby?"

"She said to get with my doctor. I've got an appointment next week. And how did you know about the pregnancy?" She'd heard the rumors around school and figured where the leak had come from. She assumed Heather overheard her tell David.

The cell phone Heather had in her grip announced itself loudly. She scanned the caller ID and huffed in annoyance. "You're lucky I have to take this."

Heather brought the phone to her ear and spun away from Bella and started down the hall. "Hey, babe."

Bella closed the door and filled a glass with water. With steady hands, she shook out one pill and knocked it back. Not what she'd taken lately, but it would suffice.

David rolled over. His arm landed against the mattress. He patted around and opened his eyes. Where was Bella? He switched the light on and climbed out of bed. Rubbing the sleep out of his eyes, he paused in the doorway. Soft sounds of the piano echoed through the house. He followed the musical notes. The piano had been moved to the library a few weeks back, after his sister'd gotten tired of hearing him play. Something he'd done more since the Festival.

Bella had an exquisite voice. She was the most melodic creature he'd ever met. David stopped halfway to the library and listened to her sing. It was eerily beautiful. As she rounded into the second verse, he recognized the song: "Behind These Hazel Eyes," by Kelly Clarkson.

Bella poured so much passion into the words. He'd never heard her sing with such devotion—as if she alone could properly express the significance of the lyrics. She was really singing a break-up song, but it couldn't be about him and her. Could it?

As the last of the song filled the air, his heart sank at the loneliness, heartbreak, and emptiness she conveyed with the words. In all his attempts to show her his love, he'd overlooked her pain. As much as he hated to admit it, her ex-boyfriend had been significant in her life.

"Bella?"

She yanked her hands off the piano and jumped slightly. "David. You scared me."

He walked over and sat on the bench beside her. "I love hearing you sing."

"I was just messing around. Couldn't really sleep."

"I feel like that's my fault."

"What? Why would you think that?" Bella's eyebrows rose with curiosity.

"Because I let us go to bed upset with one another. I should've just listened to you."

"I get it. You don't trust him. Just wish you trusted me."

Where the hell had she gotten the idea he found her untrustworthy? David grimaced. He was an idiot. By staking a claim with a kiss the way he had, he'd acted like he had no trust in her. Of course, he trusted her. More than anyone he knew. Bella was the only person who'd ever been honest with him. She'd always been truthful. "I'm sorry. I've acted like a jerk. Can you ever forgive me?"

"Only if you can forgive me. Miah's part of my past, and I haven't exactly been forthcoming about how our relationship ended. I should've told you."

"I don't need to know the details. I flipped out because we haven't formalized our relationship, yet. And you're right, I should apologize to him. I can take the high road." David smiled and tucked some of her hair behind her ear.

"You mean that?"

"I do."

Bella leaned up and pressed a tender kiss to his lips. "Thank you."

"Anything for you. Now, what do you say we play one more song on this thing?"

"I'd like that."

After what she'd just sung, they needed something with more hope. David smiled and lightly stroked the piano keys. He opened his mouth and sang, "All of Me," by John Legend. Yeah, it was a sappy love song, but Bella deserved to know how much he cared.

thirteen

They'd been in downtown Roswell for at least an hour now and still no sign of Bella. This was such a shitty idea, Amanda thought. But she'd gone along with it anyway. Jeremiah stopped and stared through a shop window. Something had caught his eye.

Amanda looped her arm through her brother's. "Come on. Let's go inside."

Once they entered the shop, Amanda stepped away from Jeremiah. Yes, she'd spent the night scheming with Sarresh about how to get Jeremiah and Bella talking, but she also had a boyfriend to shop for. There were only eighteen days until Christmas. She was a horrible girlfriend. She looked around for a few minutes, but nothing she saw screamed Vick.

Amanda pivoted and headed for the door. Seeing that her brother found something, she joined him in line. "What's that?"

"Something for Bell. It's probably stupid, but I don't know."

"Not stupid, but I don't get the Christmas ornament." It was a teacher bent over a child, who was sitting at a desk with a book open.

"What's not to get?" Jeremiah asked. "She wants to teach. One time she told me how she helped Vick out with a math problem. The feeling she described afterward, one with purpose. Kind of symbolizes that don't you think?"

Amanda smiled. He understood his ex-girlfriend better than he knew. "It's perfect." She wished she could pick out something that perfect for Vick. She sighed. Things with him were different than with any other guy she'd ever dated—but shopping for him?

"I'll just be outside," she told Jeremiah. Stepping through the door, she scanned the sidewalk across the way. There she was! Bella stood across the street with that douche new boyfriend of hers. *Shit!* She told Sarresh this was a bad idea.

The bell in the door behind her dinged, announcing Jeremiah's exit, just as David ushered Bella into the shop they'd stood in front of. Amanda gave her brother a sidelong glance. If she sent Jeremiah across the street, then he would be getting in the way of Bella's relationship with David. Now she understood why Sarresh suggested it. Except their parents gestured for her and Jeremiah to hurry along. *Dammit.*

Maybe he shouldn't have gotten so upset the day before, but his skin still crawled when he recalled how David had his hands—and lips—on Bella. And what was up with Amanda? He knew his sister loved him, but she'd been stranger than normal, lately, hovering around him all the time. Now, she huffed past him. What was her deal?

Jeremiah followed after Amanda. He'd surprised himself by getting a present for Bell. She'd been on his mind a lot, even though he'd stayed away. And from what Vick had told him about her relationship with David, the guy seemed to be doing her some good.

"You think Mom's okay?" Amanda asked.

"Please. The woman is a rock. She's carried six of us and shopped like this every single time, I'm sure." Pregnancy seemed to agree with their mom, Jeremiah thought.

Amanda adjusted the straps of the baby backpack she used as a purse on road trips. "I suppose that's true."

"Are you really worried about Mom? Or me?"

"I care about you both, however you are the needier of the two."

"What am I going to do with you, sis?" Jeremiah hooked an arm around her neck, balled up his hand and knuckled his fist against her head. He grinned and released Amanda.

"Jerk. You messed up my hair."

"Come on. Who're you trying to look pretty for? Unless your secret boyfriend magically appeared while I wasn't looking."

Amanda playfully shoved Jeremiah. "Shut up."

"You know, I'll find out who this guy is sometime soon, right?"

"Yeah, well, today is not that day." Amanda poked her tongue out at her brother and stalked ahead.

He laughed. Then his pocket vibrated. Jeremiah dug out his phone and blinked at the name that flashed across the screen: Bell. He eased a few paces behind his family. "Hello?"

Bell's scream pierced Jeremiah's ear. "Bell? Bell!? Are you okay!? Talk to me!"

He heard only heavy breathing in response, Jeremiah ran past his siblings. "Dad! Bell's in trouble!"

"What are you talking about?"

"I don't know. She called me and screamed. I can't get her to respond to me."

"Keep trying to get her to say something." His father pulled his own phone from his pocket and dialed a number.

Jeremiah pressed his cell tight against his ear. What if he couldn't get through to her? What if he was too late like last time? "Bell? Can you hear me?"

"I'll be a good girl." Bell whimpered and the line went dead.

David rushed to Bella's side. "Hey, hey. You're safe."

"Please, please, I'll be a good girl."

"Bella ... it's just me. Come on, Bella. Open your eyes." Carefully, David pried her arms from her face.

Blinking, she whipped her head back and forth and looked from one open end of the alleyway to the other. Her gaze landed on David and tears streamed down her cheeks. She threw her arms around his neck, nearly collapsing as she sobbed.

David wrapped one arm around her neck and slid the other beneath her knees. He scooped her legs up and held her to his chest. She weighed hardly anything. Calmly, he comforted her, reassuring her over and over that she was safe. Slowly, her shaking eased and her tears halted.

"You okay?"

Bella nodded.

He planted a feathery kiss in her hair. If he continued asking questions, at some point she'd respond. This was the worst panic attack he'd seen. What had been going on in that head of hers?

"Can you talk?"

"What happened to my ice cream?"

David laughed and pressed another kiss in her hair. "I tossed our cones when I saw you freaking out. I'll get replacements. Do you think you can stand?"

"Yes."

"I'm going to set you down." Gently, he set her on her feet.

Bella wiped at her face, then bent down and picked up what remained of her phone. The face of the window was cracked and the back was split in half. "I must've stepped on it."

"Come on." He took her hand in his own, and they walked back down the alleyway toward the ice cream parlor.

Once she was seated at a table outside the ice cream place, her eyes dropped to the object in her hand. "What about my phone?"

"We'll go by a store tomorrow and get another one. Okay?"

"Okay."

"You going to be all right by yourself for a minute?" David brushed a hand over her head and down her hair. She appeared to have returned to normal. But he couldn't take the chance she'd break down again. He'd get her the ice cream he promised and take her home.

"Yeah."

The trip was supposed to be a good thing. A place that couldn't trigger another episode with her. How'd the episode been initiated anyway? The alleyway had to be the problem. She avoided them back home. Why would she freely walk down one in Roswell? Something pulled her down that alleyway and instigated the panic attack. His cell phone rang. He checked caller ID and groaned. Of course. "Hi Sarresh."

"Is she okay?"

"She's fine."

"Oh, thank God," Sarresh muttered in relief.

"How'd you know anything happened?"

"My phone got dialed, and I heard her for a second before the line dropped. I kept trying to get hold of her, but she never answered."

Her response seemed simple enough. How come he couldn't trust it was the truth? Because Sarresh had no honest bones in her body, that's why. But he'd go with it for now. "Yeah. Her phone got broken in the midst of a panic attack. I promise she's okay."

"Okay, but bring her home if you have to."

"That's the plan." David hung up. Maybe he had no faith in Sarresh's explanation about what she heard, but he did believe she cared about Bella. That was what mattered most. He ordered their ice cream, headed back to Bella, and set her Oh, Fudge Split in front of her.

"Thank you."

"Do you want to tell me what happened?"

Bella dug into the ice cream. "No."

"Bella—"

"I said I don't want to talk about it."

He could argue with her until he was blue in the face. One thing he'd learned early on about Bella Kynaston, she was as stubborn as a mule. If she refused to discuss something, nothing could change her mind. "Okay. Finish your ice cream and we'll go home."

"Can't we just forget this happened? And stay?"

Taking her home was the best option, he thought. But he didn't want to fight with her either. Maybe if he did as she asked, she'd open up. David nodded. Plan B.

"Yeah, we can do that. What do you want to do next?"

"Are you sure?" Amanda whispered into her cell, as she peered over her shoulder to where her father was talking on the phone to one of his detectives and her brother was pacing. Her brother had flipped out the second that call from Bella dropped. It had been like watching someone kick him in the gut. The worry etched on his face broke her heart.

"Yes, I'm positive."

"Did you talk to her?"

Sarresh smirked. "Oh, yeah, cuz that would be a wise idea. I don't give a rat's ass about lying to David, but I won't do that to B."

"Okay. I'll pass you over." Amanda walked to where her family hovered.

"Call her parents and see if they know where she was going," her father barked into his phone.

"Hey, Dad, someone wants to talk to you."

"Hold on Russell." He took Amanda's cell. "Hello ...? I'm fine, Sarresh, but I hope this is important ... Okay, and ...? You're sure ...? What about her phone ...? How ...? I'll take your word for it ... One more thing. Do you know where she is?"

Amanda took her cell back, then looked up to see that the expression on her father's face as he ended the call on his own phone was not a good one.

He looked her directly in the eye. "Mandy, where is Bella?"

She shouldn't be surprised. He was in cop mode. Always. He interrogated his children like he interrogated suspects. Right now, she was a suspect. Crap. She had to tell them. "Here in Roswell."

"What!?" Jeremiah exclaimed.

"She, uh, kind of came for the light parade too."

Jeremiah glared at his sister. "Please tell me this is some kind of joke."

"No."

"Unbelievable." Her brother clenched his jaw and gave her a death stare.

"Jeremiah, I—"

"Go to hell!"

Not quite the reaction she hoped for. She looked to their father and silently pleaded for him to understand. "I was just trying to help."

fourteen

Luis rolled over to his side and kissed the back of Heather's naked shoulder. "Tell me about your brother."

"You want to know about him, now?"

"The timing is awkward, but I'll be out of communication for a bit. So, yes, now." He and Cristobal had searched one place over the weekend and come up empty-handed. Several places remained, but they had to stay under the radar.

"He's an arrogant, self-absorbed, maddening asshole. Why?"

"Didn't he start dating that girl?"

Heather got out of bed and slipped on her silk bathrobe. "Yes, and he's been a bigger pain in my ass than normal."

"But he watches out for her, correct?"

"You know, ever since we met, you've had this huge interest in Bella. What gives? I'm smarter and better looking than her."

"It isn't like that." Luis crawled out of the bed and yanked his jeans on. He'd never been attracted to Bella. How could he explain to the chick he called his girlfriend why he was truly interested in someone she considered an enemy?

"Then tell me what the hell is so damn intriguing about this bitch."

"My interests in her do not concern you. It's that simple. You don't need to know."

Heather folded her arms over her chest. "Fine. This arrangement is over. You want to know how my brother treats her, go talk to him. He's down the hall."

"Babe, come on. Don't be so dramatic."

"Screw you! That whore has meddled in my life for the last time." She stomped out of the bedroom and slammed the door behind her.

Luis sighed. Story of his life. He pulled his t-shirt on and shoved his feet in his sneakers. The only way he could leave Bella alone was if he believed she would be safe. He left Heather's room and glanced down the hall. Luck must be on his side because her brother stepped out of a room to the right.

"Everything okay with my sister?"

"Mostly, yes. Minor disagreement if you will. You're David, correct?"

"Yeah. And you are? Sorry, I only know you as Heather's boyfriend." David offered a hand.

Good, she had kept his name a secret. "Luis, Luis Hernandez." They shook hands.

"Nice to meet you."

"You, as well. You're dating Bella Kynaston, right?"

"Yeah." David answered hesitantly.

"No worries. I don't wish to encroach on your relationship. We have ... mutual friends, and I just want to make sure she is ... protected."

"I think I've got that covered."

Luis grinned and hoped like hell that was true. "I'm glad to hear that. She deserves to be safe. Would you tell Heather goodnight for me?"

"Um, yeah, I guess. Sure you don't want to tell her yourself?"

"I'm positive my farewell is better handled this way. Thank you." Luis jogged down the stairs and left.

Jeremiah stared at the books in his locker. It had been one hell of a Monday. He'd ignored his sister since Saturday's incident. How could she keep something like that from him? The whole situation tormented his soul. Wasn't the old adage *time healed all wounds*?

Someone stepped up beside him. "Um, can I talk to you?"

Jeremiah turned. *You've got to be kidding me.* He removed a book, tossed it in his backpack, and closed his locker. "What the hell do you want, David?"

"I wanted to apologize. I acted like a jerk Friday after school."

"Why do you even care what I think? I'm the ex, you're the current. Enough said."

"Yeah, but I don't have to be an ass." David dropped his gaze to the floor.

Jeremiah crossed his arms tightly. The guy wasn't here of his own volition. Bell had put him up to this. "So, you were an ass. I expected nothing less. Even though I've stayed out of your way."

"What? You assume because you aren't around physically she doesn't think about you? I'm not an idiot. I apologized. That's all I came by to do."

"Because she made you. Please. Apology not accepted." Jeremiah turned away. He hadn't stayed out of the picture for that douche; he'd done it for Bell.

"You're really going to be a dick about this?"

Hell, why couldn't the guy shut up? Jeremiah spun back around. "What? You expected I'd take your sorry bullshit?"

"No, but I didn't anticipate you being unable to get your head out of your ass. You're the one that left her? Remember? In the end, she chose better."

"You're not better, just the second choice." This conversation ended one way. With all the frustration he'd experienced over the last few weeks, he'd gladly jump at an opportunity to beat the shit out of David. Jeremiah dropped his backpack to the floor.

Ten minutes passed. The apology should've taken less time than that. That he hadn't returned yet, it could only mean trouble. She jogged down the hall and skidded to a stop. In the midst of a forming crowd, both guys had dropped their backpacks and balled up their fists. Bella inserted herself between them and pressed a hand to her boyfriend's chest.

"Walk away, David."

"I can't do that."

"Yes, you can. Getting suspended won't help anything. Just walk away."

"Fine." David grabbed his backpack up from the floor.

Bella pressed a quick kiss to his lips. "I'll meet you at the car."

"Okay." He disappeared into the crowd.

She focused her attention on Miah. "What the hell is wrong with you?"

"Me? Your boyfriend started it."

"Oh, and you had nothing to do with it? You didn't goad him in any way?"

"So what if I did? You couldn't have figured I'd accept his apology. Not when the only reason he did it was you!"

"You could've accepted it, whatever the reason. But, no. You've got to be a *babaca* about it all and shove it back down his throat." She figured Jeremiah'd learned enough Brazilian Portuguese when they were together to know what she meant. She was right.

"I wasn't being an asshole. I simply refuse to accept he actually meant he was sorry. You don't deserve that."

"Oh, and you know exactly what I deserve?"

Miah stepped in close. He leaned down, wrapped his arms around her, and kissed her like he meant it. Then he whispered in her ear. "Better than him."

Oh, my. What just happened? Had he really kissed her? It was completely unlike the too-public kiss David gave her last Friday. Miah had kissed her with an intimacy shared between people who loved each other—not with a possessive passion placed upon a person as a claim.

How was she supposed to react? Shaking the confusion away, Bella yanked her arms from around his neck and pushed Jeremiah back. "David's my boyfriend."

It wasn't much, but it was all she could think of. Without waiting for a response, Bella spun on her heel and walked off through the crowd. *Shit!* What the hell was she going to do about this? News about her and Miah's kiss would be all over school by tomorrow morning. She had to tell David. It was the right thing to do.

Heading out of the doors toward the lot, Bella tenderly rubbed a finger across her lips and tucked the memory of the kiss away. David would be waiting for her in the parking lot. Something had happened last night to worry him, and he called to insist he drive her to school, today. She complied, but hopefully, this new expression of his protectiveness would be short-lived. Being unable to escape from his watchfulness would drive her insane.

"There you are. I was beginning to think I'd have to come find you." David opened the passenger side door for her. "What happened?"

"Nothing. I just yelled at him. Called him an asshole ... and I, um, ... I left."

The lines blurred, and Bella flopped back on her bed. How long had she been trying to read this chapter? Her cell phone dinged. She picked it up and read the text: *Dirty whore.* What? It didn't come from a number she recognized. Whatever. Bella tossed the phone aside and climbed off the bed.

She wandered into the kitchen. "Hey, Mãe, how long before dinner?"

"About ten minutes, my darling. Have you decided on an obstetrician?"

"Um, yeah. I made an appointment for next week." Nothing had been scheduled. She was unprepared for a doctor to sweep in and tell her she had to quit the pills. And doctors like to run tests, so they'd discover what she hid from everyone. Eventually she'd have to contend with the lie, but so many things could happen between now and then.

She opened the refrigerator.

"If you're hungry, go ahead and take something. You're eating for two."

"Right." Bella grabbed an apple and headed back toward her room. She sat on her bed and picked up her phone. More messages.

Ugly slut

Two timing bitch

Stupid cheating whore

Ur such a dirty skank. U should kill yourself!

What the hell? Why would people anonymously send these to her? The people in the crowd from earlier. They hadn't dispersed when David walked away. They must have seen the kiss with Jeremiah. Didn't she have enough on her plate? Why'd he have to kiss her? And like that?

Her phone dinged again. *Ur so selfish. Kill urself already.*

What if she texted him? Asked him about the kiss? No, no, no. That'd lead to a discussion about the investigation, pregnancy, doctors, pills. None of which she wanted to deal with. Her phone dinged twice. What now

Murderer!

Baby killer!

What? She hadn't killed anyone! And abortion was the furthest thing from her mind. She turned off her phone and shoved it into the drawer of her nightstand.

"Bella. Dinner's ready."

Tossing the remnants of the apple in the trash, Bella crossed to the full-length mirror. Yanking off the sheet that covered it, she stared at her reflection. How many days had passed since she'd looked? Her eyes were a little bit warmer, more brown, and some color had returned to her skin. Her midnight black hair had regained some of its gloss, too. When had this happened? When had she begun to look like her old self, again?

"Bella?" Her mother knocked at her door and stuck her head in.

"Sorry. I'm coming."

"You're seeing the glow." The smile her mother gave her was beaming.

"What?"

"The glow of pregnancy. Most women experience it in their first trimester. For some it will continue throughout the entire pregnancy, and for others, the hormone fluctuation, well, it is much more difficult on the body."

"Oh." Blame the pregnancy.

"Do not fret. Your father and I will be here every step of the way."

Bella glanced at her reflection one last time and followed her mother out of her room. The house phone rang just as she approached the dining room table.

Her mother took the call. "Hello? Yes, but we are sitting for dinner ... Very well." She handed Bella the phone. "It's for you."

"Are you okay?"

"Yes, David. I'm fine."

"Heather told me about the rumors that started flying around school, and I wanted to check on you. Why didn't you answer your cell?"

"Sorry. I turned it off. Um ... to study."

"Okay. Listen, there was one other thing. Some people said they saw you and Jeremiah kiss. Is that true?"

Oh, how to answer that? She could lie, but there had been way too many witnesses. And somebody probably had physical proof. *Shit!* "It was nothing. It meant nothing. Okay? That's why I didn't say anything about it. Just let it go."

Amanda glanced at Alex. They were supposed to be watching a movie, but for the last half hour, they'd done nothing, but talk about Bella. Perhaps she shouldn't be surprised. Bella had gotten good at shutting everyone out, herself included.

"I think she still talks to Z and Vick."

"Either way, I don't like this. Something is wrong. She wouldn't even say 'hi' to me today. Do you think she's getting better at all?"

"I don't know. I wish I could say for sure. If Vick knows anything, he isn't saying." Amanda groaned. Her boyfriend had become difficult, to say the least. She couldn't convince him that keeping what he knew to himself was not actually protecting Bella.

"Then there are these new rumors."

"Yeah. I've heard them, too, but I don't want to believe them." Amanda leaned back against her pillows.

"And what about the kiss Bella and your brother shared?" Alex asked.

"I don't know. He won't talk to me. He hasn't forgiven me for the Roswell thing."

"Then maybe it's time we interfere on his behalf." Alex suggested.

"How? Because Vick still doesn't like the idea Z and I came up with to lock them in a room together."

Alex dug her phone out of her back pocket. "If this works, it could convince Vick that locking Bella and Jeremiah in a room is the most logical step."

"What do you have in mind?"

"I recorded the kiss." Alex laid her cell phone out for display.

fifteen

It was Friday afternoon. Bella clutched her books tight as she walked down the hall. Several students murmured as they looked her way. Some spoke loudly enough that she could hear. *Dirty whore. Ugly slut. She's such a dirty skank.* Her cell phone had blown up over the last four days. If only she didn't need to walk these halls and hear all the horrible things people said about her, she could survive another day.

David was waiting at her locker. She forced a smile to prove everything was okay in her world. They exchanged a brief kiss before she opened her locker.

"You all right?"

"Yeah." As good as she could be. Bella focused on gathering the books she needed for the weekend, instead of giving too much attention to her boyfriend.

"You sure? That bug isn't coming back is it?"

"No. It's not coming back." A bug. That's what she'd told him about the episode in Roswell. And it was not going to happen again if she had her way. Trying to reduce the number of pills she was taking had been idiotic. *No way in hell I'm doing that again.*

"Maybe you should just skip your appointment. We could go do something fun. You look like you're a little stressed out."

How observant. Bella smirked at her own unspoken comment. Receiving such cruel messages could do that to a person. She peeked at him and noted the honest concern in his blue eyes. Was she actually going to tell him? "You know when you called on Monday, I told you I turned my phone off to do homework? I lied. I did it because I've been getting these awful texts and calls."

"What? Why didn't you tell me sooner? Have you told the police about them?"

"I didn't want to worry you. And I don't think there's much to tell them. It's just students trying to bully me." Bella closed her locker. David took her hand as they started walking toward the doors to the parking lot.

"Are you sure?"

"I don't want to give them the satisfaction of getting under my skin." But they had. Last night, she'd cried herself to sleep. Again.

Tucking a lock of hair behind her ear, David pressed a tender kiss to her lips. "I understand, babe. Come on. Let's get your appointment over with so I can have time with you."

"Sometimes, I think you're too good to me." Bella laced her fingers through his.

"Nah."

Happily disagreeing, Bella bumped into David, and they both laughed. He was right about one thing: she couldn't wait for the appointment to be over with so they could go to his place. Good food, terrible movies, and great company made her focus on something besides her problems. But as they approached her car, their playfulness ended.

Seven horrid words had been spray-painted in large, white letters on her little black VW. On the driver-side doors, someone had painted, "dirty whore. On the back, "ugly slut." On the front, "baby killer." And on the passenger side, was scrawled, "murderer."

Struggling not to cry, Bella gawked at her car with the crowd gathered nearby. She might've been strong enough to handle it if they hadn't focused all their attention on her as she and David walked up. Unable to contain the tears any longer, she turned and buried her face in David's chest and allowed his arms to wrap tightly around her body.

"Come on. Let's get out of here. You can cancel your appointment." David led her over to his BMW. He held her until she calmed down enough to get in. Then they sped away from the school as he took a firm hold of her hand and lifted it to his lips.

Bella sniffled. "I don't get it. Why would they think I killed my baby? I would never do that."

He answered her question with a question. "Have you gotten away from any of this since it all happened?" He placed a kiss on her fingers and stole a sidelong glance.

"No. There was so much to do with the Fall Harvest Festival, plus my recovery. The trips we made to Carlsbad and Roswell, that's the farthest I've been, recently."

"Then that's what we need to do. We'll go by your place, and you can pack a bag. I'll go by my place, and pack one, too, and then we can go wherever you want to go."

Bella wiped her face. "What're you talking about?"

"We're going to get away from here. You need to escape all this. We can leave for the weekend. Be on a plane in a couple of hours to anywhere you want." David stole a quick peek at Bella.

"Are you for real?"

"Yes! Absolutely!"

Good God! A weekend, in a hotel, with David. No friends, no judgment, no pity, no family, no one who knows me or what's going on in my life, Bella thought. It would be heaven. She gazed at him. "Anywhere?"

"Anywhere."

"A beach?" She was unsure if it would work, but she could dream.

"Okay. We could go out west to California or east to Florida."

Bella covered her mouth. Bile clawed at the back of her throat. "Oh, God. Pull over!"

"What?" David glanced at her, then pulled to the side of the road, stopping just in time for Bella to throw the door open and vomit into the sand.

David swept her hair back from her face. "You okay?"

"Don't look." She lifted her hand to the scar on her neck and tried to hide the hideous thing. Then she was forced to her knees as she threw up a second time. The nauseated sensation settled, and Bella leaned back into David's body.

He scooped her in his arms and carefully returned her to the passenger seat.

"Feeling better?"

"Yeah. Must've been something I ate."

"Or morning sickness. I've heard it goes through all hours of the day."

"Yeah." She'd forgotten that quickly about the baby.

Very sweetly, David buckled her in and closed the door. "You probably—"

"Florida. I want to go to Florida."

He turned to face to her and cupped her chin. "Are you sure?"

"Yes."

"Tampa it is, then. I think you'll like Busch Gardens."

Gervasio sat on his side of the window and picked up the receiver. His *Mamá Gallina* had returned. This looked very bad for the messenger.

"I'm sorry, *papi*. I have some bad news."

"Tell me," he demanded.

"My brother hasn't turned up any leads on my mother. And I can't seem to get a hold of *mi novio*. He's disappeared, too."

That explained how Cristobal earned an early release. Swifty must've arranged the whole thing. This meant the messenger had betrayed him. One person could carry out the sentence he deemed appropriate for the girl's protector: death. As for her, it was time he finished what he started. "Is there a friend who can help?"

"*Sí, papi*. I know who to ask. He is good, strong friend. Very loyal."

"Yes. Tell him, spare no money. Find your *novio*."

"I understand, *papi*." *Mamá Gallina* hung up the phone and left.

Bella tugged on a pair of denim shorts over her midnight blue bikini and stared at herself in the mirror. She didn't look pregnant. But she was. And David had refused to allow her on any of the rides that warned pregnant women of the risks associated with their jarring movements. Bella snatched her t-shirt off the bed and slipped it over her head.

Her cell phone rang. Afraid it was another prank call, she checked caller ID. It was the police station.

"Hello?"

"Hi, Bella. It's Detective Russell."

"Oh, hi. Do you have news on my car?" The police had taken her car the day before. Wisely, she'd explained to her parents it had been vandalized and that, with everything going on, she needed to get away. Of course, she hadn't mentioned all the words spray-painted on her bug—or that "away" meant out of state.

"Not yet. The lab dusted for prints, but they haven't called with an update. I'm touching base with you because we got the paternity test back."

Oh. Bella sat on the bed and prepared herself. "Who ... who is it?"

"Petar Jacobs."

"But I thought ..." No. They'd assumed—and she'd hoped—the baby's DNA would prove Jorge Smith attacked her. If iron-clad evidence existed outside her testimony, then a deal could be offered. And she wouldn't have to get on the stand and testify.

"I know. That's okay. Your testimony and identification are all we need."

That comforted her very little. Truthfully, she feared the trial. Her grip tightened around her phone. "What if I can't testify? I'm not sure I can handle him in the same room."

"I'll be there to support you, and the prosecutor will prepare you. You're stronger than you think."

"Yeah, I guess." Bella wiped the silent tears away. She wasn't strong; she was weak and pathetic.

"A lot of people are behind you. You can do this."

She sniffled. "Sure. Look, I have to go."

"Okay. I'll call you when there's news on your car."

"Thanks." She ended the call and more tears streaked her cheeks. Would her parents support her if she gave the baby up for adoption? She'd do anything not to see its face.

David stood in the doorway. "Babe, you about ready? We need to head out."

"I can't go." Bella stepped around him.

"Babe? What's going on?"

She tucked one of the keycards in her pocket. "Nothing. I just ... I need some air."

"Okay. Well, give me a second, and I'll go with you."

"No. I need to be by myself. I'll be back soon." Bella walked out of their hotel room. She had to do ... something. No help he offered could make a difference. Hell, what could?

She continued down toward the beach. The sinking sun had created a perfect halo of purple, orange, and red. Such a shame the wondrous view was wasted on her. It was as if God was sharing something so beautiful with someone so ugly as a private joke. Why did He hate her so much? Hadn't she praised Him? Spread His Word? Believed in Him? Hadn't she done everything He ever asked of her? Why had *she* been put in this awful situation? Pregnant at sixteen by one of the two men who attacked her. If she hadn't been alone before, she certainly was now. Nothing could wash away the dirt.

She surveyed the area. The place was empty.

She stripped off the t-shirt and shorts she'd thrown on. If she waded in far enough, the tide would carry her away. She'd struggle against the cold water, waves would crash down on her, and in the end, she'd drown. Inevitably, the fight would be over.

"Bella!" David shouted. What the hell? David started into the water. "Bella!"

If she hadn't heard him the first time, she had the second. Bella pivoted in his direction, but didn't move toward him. Salt water splashed at his knees. He was a foot taller than she and had a longer stride. In a matter of seconds, he would be right there with her.

Finally, Bella took a step his way. They met where the water crashed against his thighs and her waist. She muttered two words that melted his heart. "I'm sorry."

"You don't have to apologize." He hugged her tightly, and she wrapped her arms around him and buried her face in his neck. Relief consumed him. What would he have done if she hadn't stopped?

No, that wasn't an option—was it? David couldn't believe Bella would do that to herself or to her unborn child. "Why were you out there?"

She stared at him. "I just ... I figured it'd be a good place to think."

"Okay. Come on. Let's get out of the water. This cold can't be good for the baby." He scooped her up into his arms and carried her back onto the beach.

"Detective Russell called with the paternity results. Petar Jacobs ... he's the father."

"The other rapist." David set her back on her feet and rubbed her arms. She needed to get warm and dry.

"Yeah. The other one. Can we just go back to the hotel? I'm not really feeling the party tonight."

"If that's what you want."

She dropped her gaze to her clothes. "I don't think I can be around happy people right now. Not when my nightmare hasn't ended."

"Sure." His spine tingled. David pressed a kiss to Bella's forehead and breathed in the lavender scent from her hair. No. She'd never do … that. If she truly suffered, she'd talk to someone: him, her parents, her therapist, someone. Bella would never do anything to jeopardize her life.

Sarresh parked in the Detrone's driveway. "I don't give a shit," she said into her phone.

"Z, I'm serious. Don't do this."

"He needs to know what's been going on. Somebody has to tell him." Sarresh headed up the walkway, knocked on the door, and hung up on Amanda. She loved her cousin, but the chick flaked on way too much.

Jeremiah opened the front door. "What are you doing here?"

"I need to talk to you." Sarresh strode past him. One of the bedroom doors opened, and Amanda stepped into the hallway. Her cousin should've told Jeremiah.

"When are you going to get off your ass and fix things with Bella?"

"Excuse me? I don't see how what happens between me and Bell is any of your business."

"It is when I believe my best friend is making the stupidest mistake of her life."

"Sarresh, don't." Amanda grabbed hold of her cousin's arm.

"He deserves to know."

Jeremiah looked from his sister to his cousin. "Know what?"

"Bella's in Tampa right now with David," Sarresh blurted before Amanda could shut her up.

"What?"

"You heard about her car, right?"

"Yeah. Dad's got someone looking into it."

"A lot of stuff's happened, and I guess that was just the icing on the cake. Kind of topped off what she could handle, so David suggested a getaway. They flew to Tampa last night."

"Did you know about this?" Jeremiah glared at his sister.

Why did Sarresh have to go and stir the pot? Amanda folded her arms across her chest and sighed. "Yes, but there's a reason I hadn't said anything yet."

"So, you planned to tell me?"

"Yes, especially after I got that picture of you and B kissing."

"What? That rumor's true!?" Sarresh exclaimed.

"I tried to tell you, but you wouldn't let me get a word in edgewise. You just kept going on and on about how Jeremiah needed to know about the drinking." Amanda glowered at her cousin.

"Drinking? Bell's drinking?"

Shit. The words had accidentally tumbled out of her mouth. She had no more control over what she revealed than Sarresh. "Not exactly."

"Explain."

"Yes, please do." Her mother echoed her brother's request.

Amanda spun on her heel. How much had the woman overheard? "Mom!"

"It wasn't all the time, Aunt Christine," Sarresh responded. "Just a few weekends when she stayed with me and Mike."

"The twenty-four-year-old that got you pregnant?" Their mother rested her hands on her round, pregnant belly.

"Yeah."

"And when exactly was the last time she spent the weekend with you?"

Silently, Amanda made the calculations. Bella hadn't visited Sarresh since the weekend before Roswell. Oh, boy. Hopefully, her mother accepted the answer and said nothing more on the subject.

"Three weeks ago, Aunt Christine. I swear she didn't have a whole lot to drink. Like, a glass of wine or two."

"How much had she been drinking before that?"

Sarresh shrugged. "It varied. Sometimes she got plastered, and others, maybe a few glasses."

"And you knew about this?" Amanda's mother's eyes locked on hers.

"Yeah. That's why I suggested you talk to her."

"Except you failed to mention the drinking. Do you know how that can impact an unborn child?"

"What!?" Sarresh and Jeremiah exclaimed simultaneously.

One more secret revealed. Amanda glanced at her brother. He was beyond livid. Too late to jump off the train now. "I didn't want Sarresh or Mike to get in trouble. And Bella hadn't told anyone about the pregnancy. Except for maybe David and I assume her parents."

"Perfect. The three of you are to leave Bella alone. Let the adults handle the situation."

sixteen

Bella popped one last pill in her mouth, drank a bit of water, and swallowed. She couldn't afford to take more than three pills. When Tommy gave her a new bottle a few days ago, there were only thirty pills, which was a lot fewer than usual. Now, after yesterday's episode, which required an extra large dose, she only had twelve left. She turned the hotel faucet on and washed her hands. Her phone rang as she dried them.

She checked caller ID. Then she closed her eyes. Had she imagined it?

Nope. Not imagining it. Bella eyed Miah's face. They hadn't spoken to one another since he kissed her almost a week ago. She declined the call. Her relationship with David was okay. Miah could damage everything she'd worked so hard to get.

Next, she checked her text messages.

Filthy worthless slut

U should do the world a favor & kill urself

Nobody likes u anyway

Who could love a baby killer like you?

Uv got no friends, u r nothing

Bella shut the phone off. Better if she ignored all the horrible things people continued to say to her.

"Babe, I'm back."

She wiped the tears off her face and stepped into the hallway. "Hey. Get everything?"

"Yeah. You okay?" David set a couple cans of soda and a bucket of ice on the table.

"Sure." Bella tucked her phone into the back pocket of her jeans. "Guess I'm just not ready to go home."

"I understand, but we still have a couple more hours before our flight. Want to watch a movie?"

"Sounds good." *No, not really.* With all the mean things people had texted her, she needed something to reaffirm his commitment. Too much had become untouchable with the people she had once called friends. What if the text was right, and David no longer belonged to her either? She'd have nothing left.

David sat on the couch and opened a soda. "Bella, you'd tell me if something was bothering you, right?"

His question offered her the perfect opportunity. She crawled across his lap and straddled him. "Of course, I would."

"You swear? Because I get the feeling something is going on, but you won't let me in." He rested his hands on her thighs.

"I'm sorry if I seem a little distracted. I got an unwanted call before you got back, but it's not a big deal."

"Who called?"

Her plan was working. If she admitted to Miah's phone call, she could test his commitment.

"Miah."

"What?"

"Hey. I didn't answer. I told you. He's not in my life. Right? Just you." Bella wrapped her arms around his neck and pressed a soft kiss to his cheek.

"He leave a message? Say why he called?"

"I don't know. I shut my phone off. Besides, it doesn't matter. I'm with you. Not him."

David hugged her and tenderly kissed her lips. "Right. With me, not him." Then, his lips melded to hers, and slowly the kiss deepened. Hungry for reassurance, their tongues eagerly battled one another.

Jeremiah stared at the picture of Bell on his phone.

"Well? Did you get a hold of her?"

"No." He hadn't said more than a few words to his sister in the last day. But she'd approached him an hour ago and convinced him to reach out to his ex-girlfriend. Amanda's intention had been for him to warn Bell about what she might come home to. Honestly, he was glad she didn't answer. If everything Sarresh and Amanda revealed yesterday was going on, then Bell needed help. Not protection.

"Crap."

"You don't even know if Mom talked to Bell's parents last night."

Amanda sat on the bed next to him. "But what if she did, and Bella has to deal with all that tonight?"

"Then they can get her the help she needs."

"And what? You think an intervention will help?"

"Yes!" Jeremiah walked over to his desk and dug out the photograph he had of Bell and him at the homecoming dance. It had been one of the best nights of his life, even though they'd nearly gotten killed. She'd been so beautiful in her violet dress. Her eyes sparkled like amber. He could see the life in that picture.

"What if they confront her and push her further away? Have you thought about that?"

He lifted his gaze toward his sister for the first time since she entered his room. "I think about that every day. I've pushed her away. So have you and Sarresh and Alex ... by keeping her secrets. How can her parents address a problem they don't know exists?"

"I thought I'd told Mom enough."

"Why didn't you tell me?"

"It wasn't my place. Plus, you've beaten yourself up for way too long over the break-up. I figured if I let you know everything else ... it would only add to your self-hate. I couldn't do that to you." Amanda walked over to him.

"Part of me feels like I should be upset with you, and part of me understands."

"Good. You should be both."

Jeremiah snickered. If he hadn't known better, he'd believe his sister wanted him to be angry with her. "Thanks."

"Welcome." Amanda hugged him and left.

David loosened his grip on Bella's naked back. She was shaking. He brushed a hand through her hair. "Hey. Talk to me. What's going on?"

She rocked back and forth and wrapped her arms across her chest.

"Dammit, Bella." He grabbed her t-shirt and yanked it back on over her head. Another panic attack. He shifted her legs until she curled up against him. How had this happened? One minute they were making out, and the next she'd started shaking.

Tears rolled down Bella's cheeks. She mumbled something under her breath.

He struggled to get her completely covered. Could she have known another attack would occur if they proceeded down the path of less clothes? Not likely. She hadn't had an attack since ... Roswell. "It's okay, Bella. You're safe."

"Nowhere's safe."

"There are a lot of safe places, babe. One of them is right here with me. I'll always keep you safe." Talking was a good sign. He sighed with relief.

"David?"

"Yeah, babe. It's me."

Bella straightened a little in his arms and glanced around. "What happened?"

"You had another attack."

"Oh, God, not again." She buried her face against his t-shirt and sobbed.

"Shh. It's okay."

"How can it be okay that I freaked out?"

David brushed hair from her face. "Because you're dealing with it. Eventually they'll stop happening all together. Just give it time."

"Time's never on my side." She hiccupped as tears streamed down her cheeks.

"Not true. I have a lot of patience. No need to worry."

Bella climbed out of his embrace. "It wasn't supposed to be like this."

"Babe, it happens. Not something you can control right now, but you'll get there."

"I want to believe that, but what if I ... if I'm never the same again?"

"Then we'll figure it out. Listen, it's been a long weekend. Why don't you clean up, and I'll get our bags. We'll just go ahead and leave for the airport. Once you get home, you can get some rest."

"Thank you."

"Hey. I care about you." He wiped away the remnants of her tears and headed toward the bedroom they'd shared. Her emotions had simply gotten the best of her today. That's what it had to be. Nothing else explained her reaction. Just her emotions.

Jamar exited the elevator on the third floor of the precinct. Russell was working the weekend shift, and he'd called Jamar about an hour ago, saying he had something for him. This was why, at seven p.m., the sheriff was headed into the squad room.

"I hope you have something worth me coming out, tonight."

"I do, sir." Russell gestured toward the case board.

Several pinned strings spanned out from one center point: Bella Kynaston. Jamar crossed his arms and followed each little piece of the puzzle. "What am I looking at?"

"A lot. I've been racking my brain over this. So, I went back over everything, and I noticed things we missed before."

"Okay. Explain."

"Luis Smith and Jocelyn Smith. I checked with the warden, and he immediately recognized the phony IDs. He checked the logs. It's the same guard that lets them through every time. Like we thought, Simms's brother-in-law." Russell traced a piece of string from one bogus ID to the other with his finger.

Jamar nodded. "What else?"

"Facial recognition hasn't given us anything on the true identity of Luis or Jocelyn Smith. So, I did a couple of visual comparisons of them myself—and I did notice facial similarities between Luis Smith and Bella Kynaston."

Jamar eyed the string from Luis Smith to Ileana Costa to Juan Castell. There was a big question mark next to Juan Castell. "Proof?"

"I placed a call to New York. Hospital records show Ileana Costa gave birth to a boy on May 14, 1995, and a girl on July 1, 1997. Names and father unlisted."

"Milena said they renamed Bella, but she failed to mention the girl's birth name." Jamar glowered at the board. Their inability to locate what should exist disturbed him.

"I contacted Mrs. Kynaston this afternoon, but she denied again knowing Bella's birth name. I believe her."

"So," Jamar said. "Based on the pictures of Luis and Bella, they appear related. But there's no real proof. But if Luis Smith is in fact Bella Kynaston's sibling, why would he send her rat-infested roses?"

"I questioned that myself. So, I pulled the signatures from his one visit to Jorge Smith. A graphologist said that the signature on the order form does not match the signature on the visitors' log. Nor does it match the handwriting on the note." Russell tapped the string that connected the order form, note, and visitors' log.

"If he didn't order the flowers, who did? And why would they set him up for it?"

"I think it goes back to the visit he had with Jorge. We already believe everything the guy is saying is coded. What if Luis went off script? Could be why Jocelyn Smith has been to see Jorge three times. And I think I've deciphered part of his code."

"Is that why there is a separate string coming from Jorge Smith?"

"Yes. First, Cristobal. The guy wasn't due to be released until the end of next week, but he was let out last Friday, nearly two weeks early. This could be the brother Jorge referenced to Jocelyn Smith in their last conversation—which would mean Jorge Smith is actually Gervasio Rodriguez. Second, there's Roselyn Rodriguez."

"Their mother. What about her?" The woman hadn't been a person of interest. How could she have possibly played into the scenario?

"She's disappeared."

"I thought you knew where your brother hid things." Luis shoved his hand through his midnight black hair. Time was not on their side. How many places had they now searched with nothing to show? Four? Five? He'd lost track.

"Gervasio trusts very few people. I know of these places because I followed him around as a child. But there is only one other place it could be."

"I already told you, we can't go back to your house."

Cristobal dropped on the bed in Luis's bedroom. "The basement is the last place. He loosened a couple of bricks and hid things in the wall."

"The police are watching your house. Unless you know of a way to get in besides the front door, we're never going to find anything if it is hidden there." Luis stepped into the bathroom and scrubbed the grime from under his fingernails. They'd spent the last hour digging for what he considered buried treasure. All they managed to do was get filthy.

Through the open door, Cristobal replied, "Well, there is, but there isn't."

"What do you mean?"

Gervasio's brother walked over to the desk. He flipped open a notebook to a blank page and sketched out a floor plan. "The window to my room doesn't lock. Never has, and it can be accessed from an alleyway behind the convenience store. We just have to climb the fence from the alley, but that way we can sneak in the back."

"Why the hell didn't you mention this before?"

"Since you said the police are watching my house, I figured it would be a last resort."

"Good point." Luis returned to his room and picked up the notebook. The plan could work, except the police still presented a problem.

"It will be best if we wait for the cover of night and are both well-rested."

"And if we have a distraction. I can arrange one, but it'll take me a couple of days to get things in order."

Cristobal stood. "That will give me a chance to speak with my mother. In case for some reason things go wrong."

"Agreed. Go shower and rest. It's been a long day."

Jamar lifted his eyes to his beautiful wife. "Did I wake you?"

"No, the babies did. But something is obviously weighing on your mind. Is it what I told you about Bella?" Christine eased onto the couch beside him.

He rested a hand on her pregnant belly and calmed his unborn with slow circles. "Part of it is, and part of it goes back to the case."

"Can you talk to me about it?"

"Something in my gut tells me there's an issue with the adoption thing."

"But you can't put your finger on it?" She leaned her head against his shoulder and snuggled up to him.

Jamar kissed Christine's forehead. "Yeah. It was a closed adoption. Judge wouldn't grant us access, and neither Milena, nor DeWei agreed to provide a copy of the paperwork. They insisted they'd shared everything we needed to know. But I'm missing something."

"Maybe Russell will figure it out."

"Maybe …"

"But you haven't given him anything?" She covered his hand with one of her own and entwined her fingers with his.

"No. I trust him, but I feel like this is something to leave out of the case for now."

"Okay, but something about the adoption bothers you. Wasn't it all legal?"

"Straight to the point. One of the many things I love about you."

"You do realize the documentation not being accessible doesn't mean anything is illegal."

"Yes, but if it is, the repercussions could destroy Bella. If that's true, could it have been done on purpose?"

"And without the paperwork, you can't really answer that question."

"Exactly."

"Why don't you research the lawyer who filed the documents? Maybe you'll find what you need to convince Milena and DeWei to let you check the adoption records."

With a smile, Jamar hugged the woman he adored. She always had the right answer. "Brilliant as ever."

"That I am. Now, can we go to bed?"

seventeen

Bella tightened her grip on her car keys. She hadn't really spoken to David all day. Mondays at school she was usually busy—and staying busy helped her avoid him after the mishap they'd had with her attempt to take control of her intimacy issues. And here he was.

But she hadn't expected this. "What—?"

He shoved his phone at her. "Apparently, it's been going around school."

Who had snapped a photo of her and Miah kissing last Monday?

David narrowed his eyes. "I thought you said it was nothing."

"It is nothing."

"Yeah. Right. So … why does it look like you're kissing him?"

"I didn't. He kissed me." Maybe that was only partly true. Everything happened so fast. But she may have possibly kissed Miah back. There was no possibly. She was looking at the proof. Her arms had automatically wrapped around Miah and she had returned the kiss.

"Then why lie to me about it?" His dazzling blue eyes darkened. "That's semantic bullshit, and you know it. You're supposed to be my girlfriend. No matter who kissed who, you should've told me. Because it sure as hell isn't nothing. Instead, you keep that shit a secret?"

"I just … I didn't know what to make of it. It made no sense."

"So, you didn't tell me because you wanted to figure out what the hell it meant?

What if it meant he wanted you back? Would you go?"

"Here me loud and clear, David Warren. I don't want anything to do with Jeremiah Detrone. I haven't even talked to him since this … this whole thing happened.

Bella reached a hand out to him, but he backed away. "David—"

"Don't even. Right now, I need some space from you." He pivoted and stormed off.

David stalked back toward the school. If he was lucky, that jackass hadn't left yet. Bella had stopped them from fighting before, but after the picture he'd had the displeasure of seeing, it was time he finished what he'd started.

And there was Jeremiah, coming down the walkway. David's temper flared at the sight of him. The guy had no idea who he was messing with. He needed to understand he was playing with fire. David dropped his backpack and ran at Jeremiah, tackling him to the ground and getting in an elbow as he straddled him.

"Stay the hell away from my girlfriend."

"Afraid she likes me better?" David's elbow had busted Jeremiah's lip and it was already swelling.

The image of that kiss surfaced in his mind, and David threw a punch at Jeremiah's head, but he moved and David's fist landed hard on the sidewalk. As Jeremiah scrambled to his feet, David dragged himself up, too, knuckles bleeding, and kneed Bella's ex in the gut. Jeremiah grunted and threw a right hook which failed miserably as David lunged at him and they crashed to the ground again.

With a satisfying smack, David slapped Jeremiah in the face, busting the guy's lip open even more. It should have been over, but Jeremiah answered back slamming the base of his palm in to David's nose. David fell back as blood erupted from his nose. Rage flared in him as he watched Jeremiah jump to his feet. *Who the hell was this guy? Jackie Chan?* He had to get Jeremiah flat on his ass and quick, so David stepped forward ready to swing a punch.

A pair of hands caught his arm as someone else grabbed Jeremiah. The teachers had finally arrived to pull them apart.

Snorting, David bent over and blew the blood out of his nose. His side was sore too and he was sure to have a bruise blossoming along his ribs from when he took Jeremiah down. He glanced at Jeremiah's equally bloody face with satisfaction. Well, at least he could claim the other guy had got it worse than he did, he had gotten in more hits.

"Do you two have anything to say for yourself?" Mr. Mattis, the gym teacher, asked.

"No." He and Jeremiah answered simultaneously.

"Fine. To the principal's office. Now."

This hadn't been David's first fight this year—and, sadly, both had been about Bella. Why did he burn with so much fury when it came to situations in where she was involved? David frowned. Not the kind of thing he wanted to consider about the girl he loved.

Her stereo blared loudly, but offered no comfort. Tears rolled down her cheeks. How had she expected David to respond? He had every right to be upset with her. Hell, he had reasons to be angry he didn't even know about.

Bella stared at the tree outside her window. After the argument with David, she'd driven straight home and crawled into bed. Neither of her parents were home—and being alone in the house, it matched the void deep within her soul. Then again, even when she was around people, the emptiness never disappeared.

She'd faked a smile for long enough. All her hopes had faded into nothingness. Her pretend happiness no longer existed. Her punishment was well deserved. She'd lied to everyone: her family ... friends ... David.

"My Immortal," by Evanescence came on the radio. Funny, she never truly understood the words until now. Miah's presence haunted her, yet she was more alone than she'd ever been in her life. The pain was unbearable. The pills helped numb her out, but only for a short period.

Bella climbed out of bed and stood in front of her mirror. The texts she'd received over the last week were right. *I don't like what I see in the mirror, anymore. I am dirty. I'm ashamed of being attracted to anyone. No one this filthy deserves a kind touch. No one could love me.* Her pain would never go away. It would stay with her, no matter who was around. Nothing could save her now.

No, there was one thing.

Her mother knocked at her locked bedroom door. "Can you lower the music?" The door knob shook as her mother attempted to turn it. "Bella? Did you hear me?"

"Và embora." *Go away* seemed like an appropriate response.

"Só quero falar."

Talk? The time for talk had passed. Now, it was time to act. Bella turned the volume on her stereo down and wiped her face. She unlocked her door and cracked it open.

"Sorry, Mãe. I'll keep it down."

"Darling, are you well?"

"I'm okay. I just need to be alone."

"Very well. I am here if you need me." Her mother kissed her forehead and disappeared into the kitchen.

She locked her door again and sat at her desk. There were people who deserved a goodbye. A letter for David, for Amanda, for Sarresh, Vick, Alex, her parents. And Miah. *Yes, this is how I can be saved. And I can protect my baby from the cruelty of this world.*

Jeremiah accepted the bag of ice from his sister and pressed it against his right eye. The fight with David had been brutal. At the end, the guy glared at him with a hatred that burned like fire. How far would it have gone if the teachers hadn't interfered?

"Thanks, Mandy."

"I'm just glad those years in karate paid off."

"I wasn't out to hurt him." All he intended to do was knock the guy down and keep him there. That hadn't exactly happened.

"Well, you got a few good blows in."

Their mother stepped into the kitchen. "That isn't something to be proud of."

"You know, I'm not throwing a party. The last thing I wanted to do was get into a free-for-all with Bell's boyfriend."

"And yet you did." His mother, whose pregnancy had extended a week past her due date, wedged herself sideways into the breakfast nook and set her cell on the table.

"Mom, I swear I didn't start anything."

"Mandy, go check on your brothers, please."

"Sure, Mom." Amanda disappeared down the hallway.

His sister understood the position David had placed him in. But his mother did not. Sure, while Jeremiah had defended himself, he might've also provoked the guy a little bit. But David's first punch fueled an emotion Jeremiah'd believed he'd buried weeks ago.

"I get it, Mom. I shouldn't have fought the guy."

"You're damn straight. Jeremiah Allen, if you ever pull a stunt like this again, you'll be more than just grounded. Am I understood?"

"Yes, ma'am." Jeremiah hadn't argued with his punishment. Being grounded for a week was nothing. Suspension from school presented a challenge. Then again, maybe not.

His mother slowly pushed up to her feet. "Good. Go do your homework."

"Okay." But Jeremiah made a detour, and headed into Amanda's room, where she sat doing a puzzle with two of his brothers.

"Mandy, I need your help."

"Well, color me surprised."

Seven letters finished. Seven goodbyes laid with precision on her desk. She hadn't completed them all before dinner, her last opportunity to spend time with her parents. Bella had enjoyed the meal and their company. Then she'd returned to the letters, and a welcome peace had remained with her for the past few hours. Shutting off her phone had helped.

Bella crawled into bed. Something should've happened by now. Maybe she needed to give it more time. After all, she'd run out of the pills she'd purchased from her dealer and had to settle for the leftover painkillers her doctor had prescribed a month ago. The dosage differed from what she got from Tommy. A little bit more time, though, and they'd kick in.

She yawned. Good. The pills had finally started to work their magic. Would dying be like falling asleep? Oh. Ugh. Bile climbed up her parched throat. Nauseated, Bella hopped out of bed and yanked opened her bedroom door. She reached the toilet in time to upchuck part of the meatloaf she'd had for dinner.

After the first wave of nausea, she stopped vomiting long enough to shut the bathroom door. And then another heave. What the hell was coming up, now? Her vomit tinged the water orange. She flushed the toilet.

"Bella? Are you okay?" Her mother knocked on the door.

"I'm fine. Just go away."

"What's going on? Is it the baby?"

Sweat beading on her forehead, Bella curled her head into the crook of the arm laid across the toilet. Her stomach settled a little.

"I'm sure it's just morning sickness."

"Are you certain? Maybe we should go to the emergency room."

"No, it's fine. I'm—" Bella hurled more from dinner into the toilet. Then she eased back and flushed again. Bella pressed her cheek to the cool tile wall. The sensation felt wonderful in contrast to the heat that consumed her body.

"I'm okay, Mãe. If it'll make you feel better, I'll go to the doctor tomorrow."

"If you won't go to the hospital this evening, yes, I'll accept a visit to the doctor."

"Thanks." She struggled to her feet, rinsed out her mouth, and stumbled to the bathroom door.

"Oh, my goodness. Bella, you look awful."

"Doctor tomorrow. Right now, I just want to go to bed."

Her mother crossed her arms. "Very well. Get some rest. Let me know if you need anything."

"'Night." Bella shuffled to her room and closed the door. She crawled into bed and curled around one of her pillows. The pills hadn't worked. Why not?

Oh. Of course. She'd increased her dosage regularly over the last month, and her body had become accustomed to the drug. She simply hadn't had enough left in the prescription from her doctor to kill herself. She reached for her cell phone and texted her dealer. Next time, she'd have what she needed to succeed.

David pressed the bag of ice to his cheek. His girlfriend's ex-boyfriend hit harder than he'd imagined possible. He dialed Bella's cell phone one more time. There was still no answer. It was too late to call her house. Not to mention, her parents really didn't care for him. Where the hell was she? She'd better not be comforting that loser.

"How's the face?"

"Great."

"You know, I'm kind of surprised he even got a good shot in. Losing your edge, perhaps?" Heather laughed and left the kitchen.

He tossed the ice bag onto the kitchen island and stalked after his sister into the foyer. David grabbed her arm and spun her around. "What the hell did you say to me?"

"Did I stutter? Maybe if I posed it a little differently. Would you understand it better if I told you that fat bitch is weighing you down?"

"Don't talk about Bella like that."

"Like what? The truth? We all agree. In fact, we decided to let her know." Heather's lips tugged into that smile that dared him. Her snarky expression said she was beyond proud of herself and her commitment to ruining his life.

"What do you mean? What'd you do?"

"What I should've done a long time ago. I made sure she knew exactly the type of person she is, and so has everyone else at school."

Outraged, David backhanded his sister. "Are you the reason she's been getting those texts? I bet you even had one of your goonies send me that damn picture. Why are you so intent on destroying any bit of happiness I might have?"

"You're a dumbass. I didn't send you that picture, and none of my friends did, either. I'm not doing anything to hurt you. I'm just trying to ensure the Warren reputation is salvageable when that girl dumps you." Heather smirked.

"Wait. What makes you think she's going to break up with me?"

"Come on. That video said everything."

"What video?"

"Oh? So, you haven't seen it?" Heather dug into the pocket of her black bathrobe. She tapped a few buttons, and his cell phone dinged.

eighteen

Luis shoved his hands in his pockets. Everything had been arranged for their plan. He and Cristobal would sneak into the Rodriguez house, and hopefully, this time they turned up something. He'd forfeited his visit with Gervasio two weeks ago. Around the time he'd managed to get the paperwork resolved for Cristobal. If the Grim Reapers hadn't caught on to his betrayal yet, they would soon enough.

His place may have been located in Desemper Ridge, but he had to avoid being spotted by anyone he knew. It was the reason, when lunch had been required, he'd walked down the alley to get to a diner in neighboring Amorte Cliffstone. Now, Luis hugged the wall of the restaurant's building and peered around the corner.

What the hell? The girl under his protective charge ... talking to—

"Thanks, Tommy. I really appreciate you doing this for me."

"I told you. Anytime." Tommy hooked his thumbs into his back pockets.

"I'm certain this will be the last time."

Last time, for what? Luis scanned the sidewalk, then slipped across the parking lot toward the VW Beetle where Tommy and Bella chitchatted. He'd watched her for weeks. How had he missed this connection?

Tommy glanced over his shoulder. "Swifty?"

"Yeah. Hey, man. Long time no see." Luis clapped one of Tommy's hands and squeezed.

"Yeah. Been busy." Tommy turned toward Bella and ushered her to her car door.

"So, I see. Who's your friend?"

"No one you need to know. Besides, she's leaving. Got somewhere to be." Tommy draped a protective arm around Bella's shoulders and opened her driver side door.

Luis narrowed his eyes. This was a guy he used to trust. But the way he wrapped himself around Bella touched nerves he didn't know were in his body. What was with this brotherly concern for the girl.

As Bella slipped into the driver's seat, Luis grabbed Tommy's arm. "We need to talk."

"Now really isn't a good time."

Smiling politely at Bella, who was watching the two of them, Luis said, "I don't want you to think I'm rude, but I need to borrow Tommy, here. You should go ahead and leave."

"Sure, no problem." She started her car.

Without waiting for the squeal of tires, Luis dragged Tommy back toward the alleyway. "Care to tell me what the hell you were doing with her?"

"That's none of your business."

"Wrong answer. Try again." Luis growled. He'd picked up a few tricks from Gervasio.

Tommy swallowed. "Come on, man. I thought we were friends."

"Last chance."

"Screw you! I don't work for Gervasio no more."

"Have it your way." Luis socked him in the gut.

Tommy grunted and doubled over. He wrapped one arm around his waist and reached for the wall with the other. "Customer."

"What did you sell her?"

"Why does it matter?"

Luis refused to answer. He cared about the girl, but hadn't ever been able to explain why he cared quite so much. But none of that was Tommy's business.

"Not important. What did you sell her?"

"Some cotton."

Some opiates were stronger than others. People didn't usually start on cotton.

They worked their way up to it. If Tommy had sold her OxyContin, she had to have been on opiates for a while. Or going through them like candy. Wait a second, hadn't Bella mentioned this being the last time? *Shit!* How the hell was he going to be in two places at once?

"Give me your phone."

"No."

"Give me your damn phone." Luis held his hand out and snarled.

Looking wary, Tommy placed his phone in Luis's hand. "Just be careful with it."

"Sure, I'll do that." Luis pried the cell phone apart and removed the SIM card, as well as the memory card and battery. Then he dropped the thing on the ground and stomped until it was cracked into pieces.

"What the hell, man?"

"You're officially out of business." Luis walked away.

Bella tucked the bottle of pills between two books in her nightstand. She felt a little uneasy. Bella and Tommy had a very simple system. They met for lunch at the same diner in Amorte Cliffstone. She stored cash in the pocket of her jacket; he slipped the bottle in her coat and removed the cash. They always ordered a meal so as to appear to be just two friends hanging out. The last thing Bella had expected was to see one of her church friends at the diner, today. Oh, well. Will probably hadn't thought anything of it. Anyway, it wouldn't matter, after tonight.

Bella glanced over her desk and straightened out the letters she'd written. She had everything she needed. Tonight, she'd finish what she started.

Her cell phone rang. "Hello?"

"Hey, B."

"Vick? What's going on?"

"Listen, I'm stuck at the lake house. Can you come get me?"

"How'd you get stuck?"

Vick groaned, obviously annoyed with the situation. "I came up this morning to decorate for Christmas as a surprise for my mom. Now, my car won't start." Vick and his father pulled some stunt like this every Christmas, Bella knew. But still ...

"And you can't get a hold of anyone else?"

"No one else answered. I tried Dad, but I can't reach him, either."

Okay, Vick was like her brother. She shouldn't mind going to pick him up. Sure, the drive there and back would take a couple of hours, but at least she'd get away from her mother for a bit.

"All right. I'll come get you."

"Thanks. See you soon."

"Yep." Bella tucked her phone into the back pocket of her black shorts. She grabbed her keys and purse and left her bedroom.

"Where are you going?"

Obviously, a quiet escape wasn't possible. "Vick needs me to pick him up from the lake house."

"What happened?"

"His car won't start. That's all." As her mom knew, it could be worse. The Christmas surprises he and his father constructed often fell apart. Last year, they climbed onto the roof to install pre-lit snowmen. His father lost his hold on one of the snowmen, and it crashed onto the porch. The year before that, they built their own snow machine. It had gotten cold, but not enough to snow. Fake snow lasted for about an hour during their annual Christmas Eve party, and then it blew and knocked out a transformer.

"Dear Lord, I hope so. Please be careful, my darling."

Bella nodded and continued for the door. She had to get out of there before her mother decided it would be a good idea if she tagged along. "Be back later."

"So, what're you working on this time?" Bella stepped into the foyer of the lake house. No Christmas tree. She eyed the kitchen and hallway. Both were undecorated.

"Oh, nothing big. It's simple, really. Dad and I thought we'd put lights up on the outside to make the house look like a gingerbread house."

She glanced over her shoulder. No feat had ever been too small for the Hilliard men. Bella smirked. "Sounds real simple."

"Anyway, can I use your phone to try my dad, again? Mine died after I got off with you."

"Sure." Bella dug her phone out and handed it to him.

"Thanks. One more thing?"

She wanted to get home, but for the last time, Bella indulged her brother. "What?"

"Can you go into the basement and bring up the box of white lights, while I try to reach Dad? I'd like to have it out when he and I come back later."

"Sure." She saluted him. A thing she used to do to annoy him. Heading down into the basement, she saw some changes. A loveseat had been added and a couch had been placed center stage. But the large screen TV still hung on the back wall. How many times had they come down here as kids and played video games on that thing?

"You find it?"

"Not yet."

"Should be on one of the shelves."

"Okay." Poking around the basement, Bella felt memories of good times here with Vick and his family arising. But this was no time to get nostalgic. Determined to find the white twinkle lights, she crossed to the other shelving unit, the heels of her black suede ankle boots echoing in the large room.

Then, above her, the door slammed shut. What the hell? Bella marched up the stairs and turned the knob. It wouldn't budge. She pounded on the door. "Vick? What's going on? Why's the door locked?"

"I'm sorry, B," he called through the door. "It's for your own good."

Then she heard another voice. In the basement.

Bell's shriek was not quite the reaction he'd hoped for. Though his face was a mess. Maybe he should've taken his sister up on that make-up suggestion. No, he'd wear the bruises with pride. For however long they lasted.

"I just want to talk."

Bella ignored him. "Victor MacKeefe Hilliard, you let me out of this basement right now!" she shouted.

Jeremiah stifled a laugh. "He's not going to let you out Bell."

"Vick, if you don't let me out right now, I swear I'll tell your mother what you and your dad are planning this year."

Jeremiah heard a snort from the other side of the basement door. "Good thing I lied. Bella, come on. Gingerbread house? Do you not know me? What we've got planned is so much better. Now, I'm leaving. Have fun, and don't kill each other."

"See?" Jeremiah looked at his ex-girlfriend, who was standing at the top of the stairs glaring at the locked door. Even angry, she looked gorgeous. And the outfit she had on stirred emotions he'd buried deep in his soul. Her red cropped sweater accentuated her curves, and her legs glistened. She glowed from the inside out.

Bell stomped down the stairs, heels clunking on every tread. At the bottom, she stepped around Jeremiah. "I despise you both, right now."

"I'm sorry we tricked you, but I didn't think you'd talk to me any other way. At least, not in private." He meant, not without David around, but he thought that was best kept to himself.

"Me? Not talk to you? Can you even explain to me why you were ignoring me for weeks? Hell, why you even broke up with me in the first place?"

Although he'd expected her questions, he wasn't quite sure how he was going to answer them. But he'd trapped her in the basement with him. So, whether he was ready or not, he had to explain himself. "I thought I was doing the right thing."

"What?"

"When you came to see me in the hospital, and I told you about the charges, I suddenly realized that the shooter, Jorge Smith, or whatever his real name is, he wasn't trying to kill you. He was trying to get rid of me. I thought the only way I could protect you was if I backed off."

"How do you figure?" Bell sat on the couch and looked at him intently.

"At the festival, this Jorge guy, he wanted to trade my life for yours. But, really, he only wanted to leave with you. Then there was the message on the Dodge. That was meant for me, not the cops. And that car that almost ran us over at homecoming? The driver was aiming at me, not you. But you were in danger just from being with me."

"That ... that doesn't make any sense."

"Yes, it does. I was seeing you. So, I was in the way. In his way. Which made it more dangerous for you. I know I hurt you, but I was trying to keep you from ... from collateral damage, I guess."

Instead, he'd broken her heart. All the emotions he'd hidden for weeks clawed their way out. Jeremiah rubbed his eyes. He wouldn't cry.

"You're right. You did hurt me. You said awful things to me and shattered me in ways you can't imagine."

The look of pain that crossed her face reminded him of her expression on the day they split up. But the only reason he'd said those things was so she'd stay away. So she'd be safe.

"I didn't mean any of it."

"I know."

Bella stared at the toe of her black suede boot. "I replayed our break-up over and over again in my mind. For days, I couldn't make sense of it. Things were so good between us. Then out of nowhere, you tell me you want to end things and that you never wanted me? It didn't make sense."

"But you believed me."

"At the time, it seemed right. I'm dirty, and I'm broken. How could anyone love me?" Unabashed by the tears that rolled down her cheeks, Bella lifted her gaze. The rape had created holes in her soul. With everything that had happened since the rape, she'd lost more and more pieces of herself. She may have used the word "broken," but what she really felt was ruined.

"You are not broken."

"I'm not the same, either. Even then, you knew that. That's why you used my insecurities against me. It took me a while to realize that, but even when I did, you still weren't talking to me. And when I heard you telling Mandy you should've left sooner because trouble was always around, it just solidified how I felt."

Miah came and sat on the couch beside her. "I didn't mean that the way it sounded. I only meant trouble seemed to show up when we were together. Which, you've got to admit, is true. So, I figured you'd be safer if I wasn't around."

"You're an idiot. Things are going to happen whether we're together or not. That guy, he's after me. God, the letter, the roses, my car ... all that happened while we were apart. So, hearing you say that to Mandy? It just made me think you were right. You were better off without me. And I forced myself to move on."

Bella swiped at her wet face. Miah wasn't the only idiot. She was an idiot, too.

"I thought you were already dating David when that happened."

"No. We'd hung out a few times, but we didn't make it official until a couple weeks later. And only because I thought it would help."

Miah sat beside her. "Help with what?"

"Make me feel normal. Get the rumors at school to stop. I hated hearing them every day. Still do." And of course, they followed her home now, too. But she deemed that information unnecessary to share. The truth was, she'd used David and cared little about how she'd hurt him in the end. Why couldn't she and Miah have talked like this sooner? Oh, right. he'd been purposely ignoring her.

"And ..." she had to say it. "... I just wanted to feel ... something."

"You're right. I'm an idiot. I pushed you away to keep you safe. And I only made things worse."

"No! Any of those things could've happened, even if we'd stayed together."

Miah turned toward her and grabbed one of her hands. "That may be true, but I accept partial responsibility. You needed me, and I bailed. I should've never left your side."

"Is that why you got into that fight with David, yesterday?" It was a loaded question. One that led directly back to the kiss they shared last Monday. But she'd wanted answers for over a week. And the shivers down her spine from his touch encouraged her to ask.

Jeremiah hadn't recalled seeing her among the crowd. Then again, he'd been kind of busy with David. "You know about that?"

"Somebody texted me a video of the whole thing."

"Great."

"Sorry about that." Bell cupped his cheek. "Does it hurt at all?"

"No. And you have nothing to apologize for. David is the one who started it."

"Actually, I think I started it. I didn't tell David everything about the kiss."

"Then how'd he find out?"

"Someone texted him a picture."

"I'm sorry, Bell. I didn't mean to cause any trouble." Jeremiah threaded his fingers together and pressed them against his forehead. Something else to blame himself for. If he hadn't kissed her, then a fight probably wouldn't have ensued.

Bell pulled his hands away from his face. "Yeah, we kissed, but I'm the one who lied to David about it."

"Why didn't you tell him?"

"I didn't know what to think. I needed time to understand what happened."

"What do you mean?" Had she thought as much about the kiss as he had? What had it meant to her?

"Why'd you kiss me?"

For the same reason he yearned to kiss her now. He missed her more than he dared to say. The harsh realities of their relationship frightened him, but being without her tore him to pieces. As empty as he'd been without her by his side, his heart might as well have been ripped out of his chest. For the first time in too long, that organ inside his ribcage beat loudly in his ears. What would he lose if he admitted how much he longed to hold her? To kiss her? To have her in his arms and never let go? "I couldn't help myself."

"Not exactly an answer." Bell bit her bottom lip.

"Maybe I can explain a little. Even though you were yelling at me, you were so beautiful. So alive. I hadn't realized until that moment how much I missed you."

"You missed me?"

A simple yes would work, but he needed her to know how much he cared. Jeremiah wrapped his arms around her. A small smile tugged on her lips. He leaned down and his lips melded to hers. They kissed as if they'd spent lifetimes apart.

nineteen

Cell tucked against her ear, Amanda chuckled. When she'd discussed the idea with her boyfriend the night before, he'd agreed—reluctantly. But deceiving the friend he considered a sister bothered him enough that he'd spent the night blowing up her phone. "Vick, chill out. I haven't heard from them, but I'm sure they're fine."

"And if they aren't?"

"Honey, you're worrying too much. Jeremiah won't screw this up. Not a second time." *At least he better not.* After her brother had come to her for help, she'd concocted this plan with Sarresh, but the timing hadn't been right. Until now.

"Lord, I hope not."

"He knows what's at stake. I think that fight did him more good than any of us could've anticipated."

Vick groaned. "Don't remind me. She's been getting text after text from David. I'm assuming they haven't spoken since the fight, based on the messages."

"Dude, you kept her phone? Crikey, turn it off. You shouldn't be reading her texts. That's her business."

"No worries. I did shut it off. I got tired of the thing going off every two minutes. Unfortunately, I wish it was only messages from David."

"What else." Amanda frowned. There was concern in his voice. What kind of messages was Bella getting?

"You remember when her car got vandalized?"

Oh, this was not good. The words that had covered her car had been cruel—and entirely wrong. If anyone would ever decide to have an abortion, it wouldn't be Bella. That girl would give up her baby before getting rid of it. Amanda sighed. "Please tell me people aren't sending the same awful things to her phone."

"I wish I could."

"Did she ever say anything to you?" Amanda suspected not. Bella hadn't mentioned much of anything to anyone lately.

"No. You?"

"I wish. I knew a lot of what was going on, but not this."

Vick harrumphed. "Sure you aren't just protecting her?"

"Don't be an ass. Keeping something like that inside isn't healthy. Words hurt in ways people can't begin to comprehend."

"You don't think she'd do anything … do you?"

"I don't know. I'd like to think with Jeremiah in the picture, the answer is no." She did worry that Bella may have already tried. Which Amanda knew made it more likely she'd try again.

"Now I really hope this works," Vick said.

Hearing the front door open, Amanda jumped to her feet and peeked out her bedroom door. "Jeremiah's home. I'll text you, later. In the meantime, keep Bella's phone for a couple of days. I'm going to tell my mom. Her parents need to know."

"All right. Talk to you later, babe."

Amanda hung up and stepped into the hall.

Jeremiah was whistling as he headed toward his room. "Hey, Mandy."

"Everything go well?"

"Yeah. I don't think it could've gone better. Bell just dropped me off. Thanks for helping me set that up. I couldn't have done it without you."

"Great. I'm glad it worked out." This was the best news she'd heard all day. "This mean you guys are back together?"

"Not yet. She wants me to give her a couple days to talk to David."

Nothing to worry about. Amanda nodded. "Okay. Well, I've got to go talk to Mom. I'm glad things are going good for you."

"Everything okay, Mandy?"

"Yeah."

"It should be here. Keep checking for the loose brick." Carefully, Cristobal felt along the back wall. It had been years since he'd been down here with his brother. Cristobal knew he and Luis had to be mindful of the time they spent. How long before the cop car returned? If they could remain unnoticed and find Gervasio's ledger, everything would be good.

"I think I've got something."

Cristobal jogged across the basement as Luis eased a brick out of the wall. "You found it!"

Luis shone the flashlight on his cell into the hole. "I see something in there."

Cristobal reached in and patted around. He felt something small and metal. He pulled it out. A small, square tin he'd never seen before. He handed it to Luis and reached back in. This time he removed two notebooks. "Let's get out of here. We can look at these at your place."

"Sounds good to me." Luis pushed the brick back and straightened it.

To Cristobal, it appeared untouched.

They headed up the stairs. Just then, Cristobal heard the floor above them creak. He glanced toward the door. Time had run out. He handed the notebooks to Luis and whispered, "I'll distract them. Take these back to your place. Then do what you need to."

Keeping his voice low, Luis answered, "No. I can't let you do that."

"Once of us has to. It will be in code. I'm not smart enough to decipher it. You are."

Cristobal cracked the door and poked his head into the hallway. He slipped out and checked the bedrooms first. They were empty. Luis had a shot to escape. He glanced back and gestured for Luis.

With a quick nod, Luis slipped past Cristobal.

Continuing down the hall, Cristobal noticed the door to his brother's room was partially open. He peeked through, then pushed on the door. "Gabriella?"

"Christ! Cristobal, you scared the shit out of me. What're you doing here?"

"I should ask you the same thing."

"I'm doing what *papi* asked." She crossed her arms.

That could mean any of about a million things. Gervasio called Gabriella his *Mamá Gallina*. She was in charge of so many of Gervasio's dealings. But if she was here, only one instruction mattered.

"What did he ask you?" He didn't need her to answer. He only asked to stall her.

"You know I can't tell you that."

"Don't suppose you saw if that cop car was back?"

"What cop car?"

The front door slammed open. Cristobal smiled and lifted his hands, prepared to surrender. "That cop car."

Luis stepped out of the bathroom with a towel wrapped around his waist. He'd showered three times and finally started to smell normal. One of the officers had spotted him and given chase. To keep from getting caught, he'd climbed into the dumpster behind the convenience store. How long had he been in that stink-fest? At least an hour had passed before he'd slipped away.

Although he'd gotten home safely, he had yet to hear from his counterpart. Hopefully, Cristobal showed up soon. If he'd been arrested, the police wouldn't be able to hold him long. The kid lived at the house they'd snuck into. You can't hold someone for breaking into their own house.

Luis tugged on a faded pair of jeans and yanked a white wife-beater over his head. It contrasted with his dark skin, like a full moon against the night sky. He dropped into the chair at his desk and opened the small, square tin they'd collected from the hole in the basement wall at the Rodriguez house.

Inside, he found a neat stack of driver's licenses. He flipped through them. There had to be a hundred or more. Some of the dates were expired. How long had Gervasio been at this? Luis paused at one of the more recent additions. *Maylin Nadalia Christabel Kynaston, date of birth: July 1, 1997, expiration: July 1, 2017.* The guy must've stolen the ID's as souvenirs. Luis returned the licenses and replaced the lid.

Next, he opened one of the notebooks and scanned the contents. Each of the first pages contained three columns. They all followed the same pattern: KAF 060826 5. What the hell could that mean? At the middle of the notebook, the column headings changed to JES 050521 120 TD 2. It would take him a while to figure out the code.

Luis grabbed the other notebook and lifted the cover.

"Holy shit."

Four pictures were glued to the first page. Each was of the same mocha-skinned girl: Bella. Beneath the photographs was scribbled, GC 130827 8. Similar to what he'd seen in the other notebook. What could the GC stand for? Initials? No, then it would've read "MNCK." Wait, hadn't she been adopted? And had her name changed? Luis frowned. He'd tried to hack her adoption file once before and failed to gain access. He'd have to attempt it again.

"Good. Call me when Simms and Robinson get back with those kids. See if any of them will talk. I'd like to know how they found out something Bella hadn't openly shared." Jamar pinched the bridge of his nose and propped himself up against the pillows on his bed. A migraine had developed some time in the last hour over these teenagers. Students who attended Jackson Heights with Bella and had vandalized her car. That poor girl had suffered enough for a lifetime. Since the damages had been less than a thousand dollars, the kids would be fined and assigned community service.

"Will do." Russell paused. "Hey, I've got some good news and some bad news. We found Cristobal Rodriguez."

"What's the bad news?"

"He refuses to talk to anyone except you."

Jamar wasn't surprised. The kid had gall. "Is there anything to hold him on?"

"No. We found him at his mother's house, his official residence. He was there with Jocelyn Smith. She's being brought in, too."

"I think you can handle her. What about Cristobal? You think he's ready to talk?" Every time they'd spoken with the kid, he repeated the same story. Had they simply wasted their time? Or was it possible the kid had been threatened into silence?

"I think he's ready to help. The only thing useful he's likely to give up is an ID of Jorge Smith as his brother, Gervasio Rodriguez. But he might also provide some valuable insight on Jocelyn Smith."

Jamar stood and walked to the closet. *Valuable insight, huh?* He glanced at his wife. She'd been due to deliver over a week ago. He'd made it a habit to be at home as much as possible, in case she went into labor.

He brought his mind back to the matter at hand. If Cristobal couldn't provide information that would help convict his brother, maybe this Jocelyn Smith could.

"You find anything out about her?"

"Her driver's license says she's Gabriella Hernandez. Her prints, on the other hand, come back for Gabriella Caprise from Fabrica, Texas. She went missing there—about six months before being a victim of rape here, ten years ago."

"Didn't you tell me the prints in Bella's rape kit matched the prints in that ten-year old case? And the brand?" What if this Jorge, Gervasio, whoever he was had been behind both? Jamar grabbed a pair of jeans. He had to go in and talk to Cristobal.

"Yeah. And I found a few other cases that fit the profile, too, but I couldn't connect any of them, conclusively."

Phone still pressed to his ear, Jamar kissed his wife on the forehead and left their room. "Let's just hope this Jocelyn doesn't lawyer up. If she's visiting Jorge Smith in prison, then she's complicit. Let her sweat it in interrogation. I'm heading over now."

Before he could get out the front door, Jeremiah stopped him. "Hey, Dad, can I talk to you?" His son held out his cell. "I just got off the phone with Will. He sent me these pictures he took of Bella with some guy at a diner near Desemper Ridge. He didn't recognize him, and neither do I."

"Was there something odd about him?" Jamar accepted his son's phone and scanned the pictures.

"Will said Bella had acted extremely weird. She refused to introduce this guy or tell Will anything about him. And she's known Will for a long time."

Jamar handed the phone back to his son. "Did Will try her parents?"

"Yeah, but he said no one answered the house phone. And Vick still has Bell's cell."

"Okay. Forward the pictures to my email. I'll see if we can identify the guy.

And keep an ear out for your mother. If she goes into labor, call me immediately."

Bella stared at the nightstand as she towel-dried her hair. She'd hidden the bottle of pills among the books stuffed in the top drawer. But her plans for the day had changed. Now she questioned the way she'd intended to end her night. Earlier, she'd imagined how she'd swallow the pills and never wake up. At no point had she dreamt she'd have been trapped in a basement with her ex-boyfriend. And she'd never considered he might want her back.

The conversation with Miah had stirred all kinds of familiar emotions. Fury at the way he'd devastated her already broken soul. Confusion at the way he'd ignored her. Desire at the way he'd revived the fire in her belly. Love for how he'd awakened her heart.

Bella tossed the towel over the back of her chair and brushed out her still damp hair. What if he shattered all that remained of her fragile soul? She'd never pick up the pieces. If her day had played out the way it was supposed to, the struggle would have ended, tonight.

But she hadn't fully processed everything that occurred in that basement. They had each said a lot. Yet so much had gone unspoken on both sides. She hadn't mentioned the pills. Nor had she uttered one word about the pregnancy. And there were all the things he failed to say. Like, why had he decided to talk to her now? Had the fight opened his eyes? Or had he noticed the damage before David punched him? And if Miah had seen what his lack of communication had done to her, why had he waited until now?

Bella pushed her hair from her neck and studied her reflection in the mirror. Her fingers lingered over the crisscrossed scythes seared into her skin. Nothing was simple. Pills numbed the pain, but they hadn't done a thing to erase the memories. At night, the blackness often returned and carried her back to that alleyway where one monster held her down, while the other used a cauterizing pen and burned her body.

She stared at the brand. A couple of hours ago, a pair of gentle lips had caressed the marred skin as if the imperfection didn't exist. Miah'd made her feel just as beautiful as he had on their first date.

She dropped the hairbrush on the dresser and sat on the edge of the bed. No matter how she painted the picture, the truth was, neither had said enough. Bella opened the drawer, dug out the bottle, and shook one pill into her hand. For tonight, she'd sleep on the bits of information she'd collected earlier. For now, she'd take life one day at a time.

twenty

Gervasio followed procedure. The hole in the bars allowed for him to be handcuffed before being led down the corridor. As they walked, the guard on his payroll closed the space between them. "MG got arrested," he muttered.

"I not worry. She not talk."

"Sir, she was arrested with your brother."

"Where they found?" Had Bronco not completed his assignment? The man had been charged with three tasks. Locate his brother and finish what he started. Kill the messenger. Kidnap his girl.

"They were arrested at your house, sir."

Shit! Cristobal had knowledge of where he'd hidden his books. If those documents got turned over to the police, they'd have all the evidence they needed to crucify him. This was not good. Gervasio glanced at the guard. "Who is here?"

"It's your lawyer."

"Excellent. I have assignment for you." It benefited him greatly to have both Harrison and his brother-in-law on his payroll. Keeping family under the same umbrella always worked out well for him.

Gervasio silenced his tongue as they approached the first checkpoint. The guard there buzzed the door open, and they continued down the hall. When they were out of earshot, Gervasio said, "Pass message to brother-in-law. New evidence must be hidden."

"Yes, sir. Is there anything else?"

"Tell Bronco, task three, he must complete today."

Jamar pointed to the man in the pictures with Bella. "He's a local drug dealer." Last night, he'd been able to identify him as Tomas Delgado. Then, he'd called the Kynastons, which was why he now sat across from Bella's parents in their living room.

Milena picked up the picture and stared at Jamar. "How is it possible she was seen with him yesterday afternoon? She advised me she had an appointment with Dr. Greenald."

"Did you go with her?"

"I didn't."

"I thought we agreed to attend all of her appointments," her husband said.

"I suggested accompanying her to the doctor's office, but she convinced me she would feel uncomfortable. This pregnancy is difficult enough for her. I didn't want to make things harder."

"If you have the number for the doctor's office, you may want to call and see if she showed up." Jamar hated to point out the hard truth to such good people, but they needed to recognize the depth of the issue. If Bella had lied about where she'd gone, then she'd probably lied about a lot more.

Milena excused herself to call her daughter's OB-GYN.

DeWei said, "Her psychiatrist has continuously stated the possibility of PTSD, but never a drug addiction. Some of the symptoms are similar, but I believed I could see a bit of both. Then Bella started to improve, looked and acted more like her old self. How could I have missed this?" Dr. Kynaston stared at the photograph as if it was all the proof he needed to blame himself for his daughter's problems.

"You can't blame yourself. Some addicts are very good at hiding the truth. You know now, and you can get her the help she needs."

"You're right. I will call the rehabilitation center and see if they have a bed available."

Mrs. Kynaston stepped back into the living room. Disappointment filled her blue eyes. "Dr. Greenald's office has no record of her visit. How could she lie directly to me?"

"Addicts will do anything to hide the truth. I am so sorry, my love. I should have noticed the signs much earlier."

Jamar watched as DeWei Kynaston comforted his wife. The truth in these situations was always difficult to face, not only for the affected family, but for the one with the addiction, as well. He'd hang around until they confronted Bella upon the girl's return.

"I believe my wife may be able to help you both understand what Bella is dealing with, as well as help Bella face her demons."

"How can she assist?" Mrs. Kynaston asked.

"Christine is a rape survivor. She has dealt with some of the same emotions Bella is experiencing."

"It may be good for her to have someone to talk to besides doctors," DeWei said.

"Excuse me." Milena disappeared down the hallway toward the bedrooms.

Jamar arched an eyebrow. Together, the two men stood and followed after Milena, who entered Bella's bedroom. The woman yanked open her daughter's desk drawers, searched the contents, and closed them. Dr. Kynaston joined his wife, checking the nightstand drawers. Jamar leaned against the wall, waiting outside the bedroom, while they searched. He understood how they felt. Neither wanted to believe their daughter could've gotten hooked on drugs. Hell, he hadn't wanted to believe it of her, either.

"I found something." Milena said, pulling out two small, empty bottles from the chest at the foot of Bella's bed and stepping over to hand them to Jamar.

One bottle was labeled and the other was not. "One of these is was prescribed by her doctor. It was filled about six weeks ago. There's no way to tell how long ago she purchased the other pills, or from whom, but I can take this and have forensics check the residue."

"Not necessary. This is all the confirmation we need. I just have to wonder if she has lied on other matters. Is it true her vehicle was vandalized?"

"Yes. We arrested the students responsible for the damage."

"She told us words were spray-painted on her vehicle. Do you recall what they were?" Milena asked as she sat on the edge of the bed.

"I'd like to believe she gave you an accurate account." Learning about Bella's drug addiction had been enough for her parents. Right now, any other discoveries would only add fuel to the fire. Jamar eyed the bottles in his hand. He'd take the unmarked bottle with him after they confronted Bella.

Dr. Kynaston crossed his arms. "Please, sheriff. Repeat the words written upon my daughter's vehicle."

"I'd advise against it, but I can see you're determined to know. She was called a murderer, baby killer, ugly slut, and dirty whore."

"Baby killer? Where would they gain such an awful idea as this?" Bella's mother looked horrified.

DeWei responded before Jamar could speak. "I cannot imagine they selected those particular words without reason."

"You cannot possibly believe she would have an abortion. We raised her to think of the life of the child," Milena retorted.

"We also taught her not to do drugs, and she has dismissed that lesson. I don't wish to believe she would dispose of the baby, but— "

"Whoa, hold on you two. With all the information we've gathered about these students dumping on Bella, I haven't heard a thing about abortion. You have to keep some faith in her because, right now, she needs the two of you more than ever."

"I will do what is necessary for my daughter to be safe. We will address the issue and show her our support," affirmed Milena.

"As will I," said DeWei.

"Good. Why don't the three of us go into the living room? We can make a plan and wait for Bella, there."

Jamar gestured toward the door and sighed. This day couldn't end fast enough.

Bella pulled into the driveway. Hopefully her car would be released soon and she wouldn't be forced to continue to borrow her mother's car. Of course, she didn't know how long she'd be hanging around. The possibility of her relationship with Miah being repaired had made her reconsider her plans—for the time being. But they might not actually be able to fix things between them. The damage might be simply too great to undo.

She also had to consider her relationship with David. Right now, David was still her boyfriend. Or so she believed. She hadn't spoken with him since their argument on Monday. She knew she should call David, but she wasn't quite ready to face him. Besides, Vick still had her cell phone.

Her intestines were twisted into one huge knot. She'd spent hours at the mall trying to decide what to do. Now, Bella gathered her bags and headed up the walkway.

Man, she was hungry. All that shopping had worn her out. If luck was on her side, dinner would be ready, and she could crash after. Bella stepped inside the house and closed the door. "Mãe, I'm home."

"Bella, would you please join us in the living room?"

"Sure, Bàba." Her father was home? She hadn't paid much mind to his car in the driveway. She'd been focused on getting inside and eating. Bella dropped the bags at the entranceway to the living room. Her father sat in the chair, and her mother occupied the couch. The sheriff leaned against the wall. *What now? Had one of her attackers been released?*

Her father laid a plastic bag that contained an unlabeled pill bottle on the coffee table. "Your mother and I would like to discuss this with you."

"Where did you get that?" Probably not the best way to feign innocence, but she was shocked her parents located the empty pill bottle. Then again, they had the sheriff there to help them look.

"We found it hidden in your chest. Can you explain why you have this bottle in your possession?"

Her breath caught in her throat. What could she say? Unprepared to accept defeat, and angered by the invasion of privacy, Bella glowered at her parents. "You went into my bedroom? I thought we were supposed to have this whole trust thing going on."

"Maylin Nadalia Christabel Kynaston, we have every right to go into your bedroom. We are your parents. For months, we have trusted you, accepted every word you spoke as truth, until we learned otherwise."

"I haven't lied about anything." Bella crossed her arms.

Her mother silenced her father with a look and turned toward Bella. "That is a lie within itself. Yesterday, you advised me you had seen Dr. Greenald, but when I contacted the doctor's office today, they found no record of your visit in their system. I offered you my support when you retained the tattoo, but I will not stand by while you lie directly to me and your father. We raised you better than this."

"You called my doctor?" The walls were closing in on her. Soon she'd have nowhere to go. She'd have no choice but to come clean.

"We are worried about you. Your mother and I understand you have an addiction, but we can get you the help you need. There is a rehabilitation—"

"I'm not an addict! I don't have a problem! And I don't need to be locked up!"

"If you do not have a problem with addiction, then why would we find the empty pill bottle?" her father asked.

"Did you ever think maybe it's old? Or I scraped the label off?"

"Bella, if that was true, then you wouldn't have any reason to see a known drug dealer." The sheriff set a photograph down on the coffee table of her and Tommy.

"Are you spying on me?"

"No, but this was brought to our attention," the sheriff said.

Her father stood and came across to where Bella stood. He grabbed her hands and held them in his own. "Please, your mother and I just want to help. Talk to us."

"He … he … he's just a friend. The guy. I don't get anything from him. I'm fine." Bella yanked her hands from her father's grip and stepped back.

Her father reached for her, and she shrunk away him. "I don't believe that is true. You need help so you can face your addiction and the issues that have stemmed from the rape. The first step is admitting there is a problem."

"I don't need help! I get along just fine." Her parents refused to listen, no matter how many times she repeated those same lines. Arguing with them was pointless. Bella turned around and walked out the door.

DeWei chased after his daughter. If he allowed her to leave, nothing would be resolved. For all of their sakes, things had to improve. "Maylin, you cannot run away from this."

"I'm not running, but I'm not staying to listen to any more of your accusations, either!"

"Do you deny their truth?" He'd like to believe his daughter hadn't turned to drugs, that she hadn't tarnished her skin with a tattoo, that she hadn't lied to him and his wife over the last few weeks. With all these lies, how was he supposed to believe she hadn't had an abortion? His daughter had changed and become someone else. How could he even begin to trust her again? DeWei folded his arms across his chest.

"You don't understand what it's been like for me! I want nothing more than to forget everything that monster did to me! That includes this godforsaken baby!"

Appalled by her words, DeWei gasped. While the circumstances weren't preferred, a baby should still be considered a gift. Here, she dismissed the child as if it were nothing. "Maylin Nadalia Christabel Kynaston, I understand the situation is not ideal, but there is a better way to handle your problems."

"You think this baby is the only problem I have? Have you forgotten how you lied to me for the past sixteen years? Or how that monster is only in my life because he thinks I've been promised to him? My problems don't start or even end with this baby."

"Your mother and I did what was best for you. We continue to do what we believe is right. God gave us faith, and we believed that our support was all you needed to face the trauma of the rape. We would like to think you can get well. How can we do that if we don't even know who you are anymore?"

In all her life, she'd never degraded God by being so disrespectful. DeWei stared at his daughter. When had her faith become so tarnished?

"You want to know who I am? I can tell you. Wǒ shì yīgè chǒulòu de huáiyùn jìnǚ."

One ugly pregnant whore? Where had the thought come from? Had she truly believed all those horrid words that had been painted on her vehicle? DeWei shook his head. Although she had made some poor choices, she could never be ugly. She had been and would always be beautiful. "Nǐ hěn piào liang."

"A bit biased, don't you think?"

"I may be your father, but I shall only ever speak the truth to you."

"The truth? You don't know a damn thing about the truth. You know, since I found out you and Mom adopted me, I've been wondering if I'm not more like my real parents than the two of you. But when it comes to lying, guess I'm more like you than I thought." Bella smirked.

DeWei frowned at her language. The curse words had become more a part of her everyday tongue than he'd ever imagined possible. Surely, she was conscious of what she chose to say. No matter, his rebuttal needed to remain positive. "Milena and I raised you. It is expected you would learn many things from us."

"Too bad it wasn't everything. Right, Dad? I mean, I take pills just like she did and I lie just like you do. It all makes perfect sense."

"What does?" Hopefully his question encouraged her to release more regarding her feelings. His daughter had every right to be angry. And her emotions worked in his favor. If only he'd paid better attention.

"That I hate you as much as I hate myself."

The first pop shattered the bay window. Without hesitation, Jamar darted across the couch and knocked Milena to the ground. Keeping his head down, he glanced toward the front door. More pops resounded as guns were continuously fired.

"Bella and DeWei are out there!"

Jamar gestured for Milena to crawl to the wall. "Keep low to the floor. Get to the phone and call 9-1-1."

Once the woman moved toward the kitchen, Jamar crouch-crawled to the door and drew his weapon. The gun fire stopped. Tires squealed. He ran outside to see a dark blue Buick Century peel off. *GR1. GR1. GR1.* Jamar intended to remember those three characters for a long time to come.

He jogged back to Bella and her father and dropped to his knees. *Shit!* Blood seeped through DeWei's shirt.

"DeWei!!" Milena cried, falling to the ground and clutching her husband and sobbing. Jamar glanced at Bella. She'd been shot, too.

Looking back at Milena, he said, "Here, put your hands on his chest and press down. You hear the sirens? That's a good thing. No, keep the pressure. I'm going to check on Bella."

The girl sprawled a few feet from her father. Blood covered her abdomen and her arm. Appeared she'd taken a bullet to the arm. From their respective positions, looked like her father must've protected her from the onslaught of bullets.

Bella moaned and slowly rolled her head side to side. "Ow."

"Don't move. Ambulance is coming, now." Jamar sighed in relief. Best answer to a prayer he'd received in a while. Too many people would suffer if they lost her.

"What if they're too late?" Bella asked. By the grace of God, the only bullet that hit her had gone straight through her arm. The doctors bandaged her up and gave her a sling. Her father, on the other hand, he'd been struck in the chest. Now, he was in surgery. He had to survive. She owed him a huge apology. Of all the things she had to say, she had to utter one of the cruelest things she could've ever said to her father.

Her mother squeezed her hand in response. "Give them time."

"Okay." Patience had flown away an hour ago.

She and her mother were in a hospital room. And she was strapped up to a machine. Because it wasn't only her life and her father's the doctors were concerned with.

Thump, thump. Thump, thump. A sound like nothing she'd heard before filled the room. Bella blinked a couple of tears free from the corners of her eyes. She glanced to her mother. Was that it?

The doctor smiled as she depressed a few buttons on the ultrasound machine. "Everything looks good. I see a healthy baby, here."

"*Graças a Deus!* Thank you, Dr. Greenald."

"I'm not going to hold you captive, but Bella I think it would be best if you stayed for observation."

"No. I don't want to stay. I'll go somewhere and rest, I promise. I just don't want to be here any longer than I have to." She'd had enough of hospitals to last her lifetime. Maybe she'd have to be in the hospital when she delivered, but that was still a little over five months away. For now, she wanted to get the hell out of there. Bella looked from the doctor to her mother.

"I agree with the doctor, my darling. It is safer for you and the baby to remain here."

"No. I can't do it. If I have to, I'll go stay at Miah's. Just don't make me stay here."

Her mother raised an eyebrow. "Perhaps that would not be the wisest idea."

"I'll check on your lab results and give you a few minutes to talk this out." Dr. Greenald handed Bella the ultrasound picture and stepped out of the room.

"Did you not tell us that you and Jeremiah ended your relationship?"

Oh boy. She hadn't discussed the events of the day before with her parents. Not to mention the lab results her doctor planned to return with could start a whole slew of questions she hadn't yet answered. Bella glanced down at the sonogram image. It really looked like a baby. Head, arms, and legs had all formed. She could even see tiny fingers and toes. She lifted her eyes back to her mother. Honesty was key. "Miah and I did break up, but we talked yesterday. I care about him, more than anything. I don't know. We haven't worked everything out, but maybe we could."

"What about the pills?"

"I'll go to rehab if that's what you want. Just, please don't make me stay."

twenty-one

Bella hardly remembered falling asleep, but she must've. Slowly, she gathered her bearings. White walls, posters of Kirk Franklin, Linkin Park, and Toby Mac. Dark blue, snuggly cotton comforter with baby blue sheets that smelled like fresh rain. *I know this room.* With a small smile, she snuggled closer to Miah. She'd really missed him.

Unfortunately, for the third time in her life, her arm was in a sling. She winced as she attempted to get comfortable. If nothing else, at least she could listen to the steady beat of Miah's heart. "Have you heard anything from your dad?"

"I'll check." He reached over to his nightstand and picked up his phone.

"He has to be okay."

"Dad sent me a text. Said your dad got out of surgery around midnight, and he's in ICU. Your mom is going to stay the night."

Bella eyed the clock on his nightstand. That was an hour ago. At least her father survived surgery. Her mother had finally agreed around nine to let her go back to Miah's house. So far everything seemed to be working out. She was okay, the baby was okay ... and her father. He'd make it. He had to live to see his first grandchild. She stared at the blue comforter. *Good Lord.*

It had taken Dr. Greenald so long to find the heartbeat, she'd been afraid she'd managed to kill her baby. She wanted to cry when that sound filled the room. Her baby had a good strong heartbeat. While it was too soon to tell the sex of the baby, the doctor had indicated she was about sixteen weeks pregnant. Bella had tucked the picture of her little one into the scrub pants she'd been given.

Miah tapped on her forehead. "What's going on in that pretty head of yours?"

"I'm just thinking about the baby, mostly."

"Didn't the doctor say everything is okay?"

"She did, but I know it'll be a long road." Both her mother and the doctor insisted she get into the rehabilitation center as soon as possible. With her father's condition so tenuous, Dr. Greenald offered to make the arrangements at the place her parents had already selected. As much as she'd wanted to deny she had a drug problem, hearing the baby's heartbeat placed everything into perspective. The baby was something to lose. She glanced up at Miah's face. Hell, there was more than one thing she could lose.

Miah raised his brows. "See something you like?"

"Yes, I do."

"What do you see?"

"An extremely good-looking guy, who I've missed a hell of a lot." Bella slid backwards from Miah's chest until her head found the pillow. Gently, she turned toward him and pressed her lips to his.

Carefully, Jeremiah deepened the kiss. He'd missed her too. Their time together in Vick's lake house basement hadn't lasted long enough. And then, tonight, while he was at the hospital waiting for his mother to give birth, his father called to tell him about the shooting. He'd listened long enough to find out which floor Bella was on, then started running. Every horrendous scenario played out in his mind as he charged up those three flights, and fear had gripped his heart as he waited for her mother to step out of the room.

Now, she was safe—and here with him.

He scooted toward Bell, slid an arm underneath her ribcage, and eased her closer. Wrapping his other arm around her back, all his sensibility disappeared, and he pressed her chest tight against him. She felt so good. Her skin was soft like silk. Desire pounded in his veins. He plunged a hand into her midnight black tresses.

Bella's wince yanked his mind away from its single focus.

"I'm sorry. Did I hurt you?"

"Forget about it."

"No. We should stop. I don't want you to be in pain."

"Can we just forget about my arm? Please?" Bell's big hazel eyes silently pleaded for him to continue.

But how could he forget? For a moment, he'd had to imagine living in the world without her. Those seconds he'd waited for a word from her mother had paralyzed him. No ache he'd ever experienced compared to the pain that had settled in his chest at that moment.

Jeremiah touched his forehead to hers and closed his eyes.

With the hand that wasn't occupying a sling, Bell cradled Jeremiah's cheek. "Please. I need you. I need to be reminded I'm alive."

"I can't. Not like this. I want it to be special between us. The way it should be."

"Forget it." She rolled out of his grasp.

Jeremiah grabbed her uninjured arm. "Bell, come on. Be reasonable."

"I thought I was."

"By trying to rush something? How is that being reasonable?"

Yes, he desired her in every way possible, but this seemed like the wrong time. The last thing he wanted was to stomp on something that should be memorable for both of them. At that moment, sex only seemed desperate.

Bell climbed out of the bed. "Never mind. Just ... never mind."

"What's going on? Can you please tell me what happened at your house?"

"We got shot at." As if that was all there was to say, she stepped out of Jeremiah's bedroom and marched down the hall.

He chased after her. "I know you were shot. But ... you're okay. And your dad, he's got a good chance, right?"

Her eyes welled with tears. "My dad ... We got into a fight! Okay?"

"Okay ... but—"

Bell padded around the corner into the living room. Jeremiah followed.

"I said the most awful thing," Bell said softly, dropping to the couch.

"I'm sure whatever you said is forgivable." Jeremiah sat down beside her. He placed a finger beneath her chin and turned her face. "Your dad loves you. No matter what you said, I'm positive he can forgive you."

"You don't understand. I said the cruelest thing I could to him." Bella couldn't meet Jeremiah's gaze. Her words hadn't just been cruel; they'd been downright hateful. Even if she'd been speaking the truth, she regretted the words ever left her mouth. What if that ended up being the last thing she ever said to him?

"I told him 'I hated him as much as I hated myself,'" she said in a whisper.

"Your dad knows you don't hate him." Miah tucked a couple of loose strands of her hair behind her ear. "I'm sure he was bothered more by you saying you hate yourself. Why would you say that?"

She didn't know why. But she hardly recognized herself. "I hate who I've become. I'm a broken shell of who I used to be, and I don't think I can ever get her back."

"I've said it before, and I'll say it again. You are not broken. Do you hear me?"

"How do you know?" Bella lifted her gaze to Miah's bright green eyes. He'd always been sweet and considerate of her feelings. Right now, she needed raw honesty.

He met her gaze. "Do you remember the first day we met?"

Heat flushed her cheeks. How could she forget? She'd been dumbfounded the second she saw him. A small smile crept onto her face as the memory bounced around in her brain. The principal had said something, but all she'd been able to think about was how handsome Miah was. Then they wandered to the library, talking. She'd fallen for him right then.

"It was the day you told Heather off. I saw the whole thing—and I knew I had to find out about you, because I'd never seen anyone fight back with such passion."

"I only did that because Vick intended to intercede on my behalf if I did nothing."

"Are you sure about that?"

Bella bit the inside of her cheek. "Maybe. I don't know. I hadn't exactly planned to tell Heather off. It just happened."

"The point is, she said something that forced you into a corner, and you refused to stay there. You fought back."

"Okay." But she didn't see how that made her not broken. She hadn't fought back at all, lately. Except with her father. A brief shiver ran up her spine, but then Jeremiah continued, returning her from her fears for the man.

"How about after the rape? People argued with you, but you held tight to the director's position, and the show was wonderful."

Ashamed of the way he saw her, compared to how she saw herself, Bella looked away. "It allowed me to focus on anything but the black hole that had formed in my soul."

"I don't think you get it. Telling me why you feel you did something doesn't change that you did the thing."

"It should. Doing those things doesn't make me a hero. It just shows how afraid I am of everyone seeing the truth."

"It makes you human." Miah cupped her chin and turned her face toward him.

Tears trickled down her cheeks. "No, it doesn't. It makes me a coward, who can't even deal with her own emotions."

"A lot of people feel like they can't deal with their emotions, Bell. You're not alone." Man, he hated how she saw herself. He'd talked to her mother for a few minutes before he drove Bell back to his house. But even that hadn't prepared him for the despair she was revealing to him, now. How could she be so down on herself?

"Then why do I feel like I'm so alone?"

With his thumbs, Jeremiah wiped her tears. "Because you've pushed away your friends and family. I don't think you meant to, but without their support, you are left feeling like the worst person in the world. When really, you're just dealing with the harsh realities life has dropped on you."

"I don't like feeling this way. Like I have nothing left to offer the world. But I don't ... I don't know how to not feel like this."

"I know, but I promise I'll help any way I can." Jeremiah pressed his forehead against hers and inhaled. She smelled like the first day of spring, with a hint of lavender in the air.

"You won't leave this time? I won't be able to handle it if you do."

He shook his head, solemnly. He needed her to really understand how much he regretted forcing her out of his hospital room a couple of months ago. She had to know that he would remain by her side for as long as he lived—he had to show her.

Pressing his lips to hers with desperation, he poured every emotion he'd buried over the last couple of months into the embrace. His arms wrapped around her and pulled her close. He deepened their kiss to show how much he missed her, how much he regretted walking away, how much he loved her. Heat raced through his veins as he released her.

"I'm not going anywhere. I love you, Bell."

"Really?" Her lips tugged into a warm smile.

Jeremiah placed another tender kiss on Bell's lips. The flecks of green in her hazel eyes sparkled.

"With all my heart."

"I love you too." Bell curled up in his arms. Then she shuddered.

"Are you cold?"

"No." She bit her bottom lip. Then she laced her fingers through his and stared at their interlocked hands. "My mom said she talked to you. Did she tell you what happened?"

"No. She told me not to let you out of my sight. I didn't question her."

"Right, tabs on me makes sense." Bell lifted their hands and kissed his palm.

"Bell, what's going on?"

She smiled up at him. "Do you know how much I like that nickname?"

"You're stalling. Come on. Talk to me. Whatever it is, we can get through it together." They'd discussed the pregnancy. And she had come clean about the drinking. Thankfully, she'd quit. No more alcohol for her, especially with a baby on the way. Jeremiah squeezed her hand. She had to know she could tell him anything without judgment.

"I was in a lot of pain after the ...." Bell paused and swallowed. It took a few moments, but Jeremiah didn't press her. "... the rape. First, it was only physical. That's why the doctor prescribed the pills. Then I went back to school and heard everything people were saying. So, I wondered ... could I take them for emotional stuff? Numb the pain? That night I took more than I was supposed to, and I slept. It wasn't for long, but I actually slept."

She had just started to reveal the ugly truth. He already knew how the story ended, but she didn't know he knew. He'd stay put and listen; he could do that for every wrong he'd ever committed when it came to their relationship. This would be a new beginning for them. "Go on," he said, rubbing her arm.

"I kept taking more than the recommended dose. When I ran out, the doctor lowered my dose to wean me off. By that point, I couldn't function without them. So, I found a dealer."

"Is that who Will saw you with?"

"Yes. And my parents found out. Your dad told them."

His father must have identified the guy. Jeremiah pressed a feather kiss into her hair.

"I need help. I agreed to go to rehab. This baby is a part of me. Even if I hate Petar for what he did to me, and he is the father, I can't take that out on the baby."

Jeremiah breathed in the relief. The steps she had taken in the last several hours amazed him. His girlfriend was perfect. "'Bell' is quite apt for you. You know that?"

"Why do you say that?"

"Since the day I met you, I have always believed you are a beautiful angel. 'Bell' means beautiful." He pressed a soft kiss to her lips.

"I'm just glad I have you. I don't think I could face this alone."

"Well, I'm not going anywhere. Come on. Let's go back to bed."

twenty-two

They'd discussed this several times this morning. The house wasn't off limits. And Bella really had to do this on her own. She hadn't told Jeremiah she was going to call David from the home phone, just that she needed to get fresh clothes. Of course, he argued.

"I just don't like the idea of you by yourself in that house, especially after yesterday."

"I'm only going to shower and change. I won't be an hour. Nothing will happen."

"You're as stubborn as ever. Fine, I give. Call me before you leave." Miah reached across the console, grabbed her hand and squeezed.

"I will. And I'll call from the hospital, too, after I see how my dad is doing and check in with Dr. Greenald."

"How soon do you think they'll want to admit you to the rehab center?"

That was a good question. The doctor had given her something to keep the edge at bay for twenty-four hours. But after that ... she'd be in withdrawal. "Likely today, but I don't know for sure."

"Okay. Well, let me know. I want to see you before you go."

"Maybe they'll let you take me." She'd really like that. The strength she'd once felt from their relationship had started to fill her again. She'd need that over the coming weeks. Careful of her left arm, Bella leaned across the console and tenderly kissed him.

"I love you. Now go, before I don't let you out."

"I love you, too." Bella climbed out of the car and walked up the driveway, ducking under the yellow police tape. She regarded the damage to the house. A board had been placed over the bay window. Evidently, it had shattered. There were holes in the walls, but it looked like the bullets had been collected as evidence. So many bad memories with this house. Would her parents consider moving? Let them all have a fresh start. If her father recovered, that is. No, when he recovered.

Shaking the thought away, Bella unlocked the door, went to the kitchen, and grabbed a bottle of water. Miah had taken her to brunch, which was delicious, and they'd had a really nice time. She was going to have to tell David. It would be so difficult.

Chugging the water, she headed for her bedroom.

Ding dong!

Bella stopped halfway down the hall. *What the hell?* Who could be at the door? Maybe Miah had decided he couldn't leave her by herself, after all. With a tiny shrug, she crossed the foyer and opened the front door. *Holy hell!* "David!"

His name coming out of her mouth was enough to break him in half right on her front step. Had he shocked her with his arrival? He'd been surprised by her arrival, too—in a car that shouldn't have been there. Then the person he despised most had kissed her, before she trotted up the driveway like nothing'd happened. He stormed past Bella.

Shoulders tensed, he said, "Where the hell have you been? Have you been with him for the last three days?"

"Excuse me?"

"Don't play dumb. It doesn't suit you." He hadn't intended to be accusatory, but his veins burned with rage. He glared at Bella.

"In case you haven't noticed, there was a shooting here yesterday."

That he'd figured out. The police tape. Bullet holes in the walls. The broken window. The sling on her arm. "Yesterday? Doesn't tell me where you've been since Monday."

"I came straight home after our fight, but I've seen Miah a couple times over the last few days." Bella closed the door and led the way into the living room.

"Including last night?"

"Yes."

It felt like someone socked him in the gut. He almost wished she'd lied. But she hadn't confirmed his worst suspicions, yet. David stopped in the entranceway and crossed his arms. "Did you spend the night?"

"Yes."

"Are you back together?"

"Yes."

A single word and it burned like a stab in the back. Had their entire relationship been one big joke to her? Had she felt anything? "So, this whole time we've been together, what? You've just been leading me on? Pining away until you could get him back?"

"It wasn't like that. I'm sorry things—"

"Bullshit! If you were sorry, this wouldn't be happening." David gripped the back of his neck. Her words struck a match and lit an inferno in his blood. Pissed off by her insincere apology, he paced from one side of the room to the other. He had to expend the energy or he'd do something he'd truly regret.

Bella took a swig of the water she was holding and tossed the empty bottle onto the couch. "You're a great guy, but things … just aren't going to work out with us."

"How could I be so stupid? I've just been a placeholder for this jackass. He broke your heart, left you alone, and you're still going back to him?"

"It's not that simple."

"I'm not so sure about that." The worst idea ever crept into his brain. All the times they'd been intimate, she'd felt something. Her body responded to his. He had to show her exactly why they shouldn't split up, the reason they belonged together. David closed the distance between them and, grabbing her head, crushed his lips to hers.

Bella shoved him away. "David, stop. You can't change my mind with a kiss."

"Why the hell not? Because it sure as shit seems like he has." Everything changed when Jeremiah'd kissed her at school. And she'd kissed him back. He'd seen the video. That one moment had turned his world upside down.

He growled and punched the wall.

"What is wrong with you!?"

David looked at his knuckles. They'd only just scabbed over from his fight with Jeremiah. Now, they were bleeding again.

He glanced at Bella. "You don't get it, do you? I'm in love with you."

"What?" Her hazel eyes widened, as if she'd never expected those words to fall from his mouth.

"You don't even care about me, do you?" He suddenly got it. "It's always been him. I thought you defended him more than an ex-girlfriend should, and I just played right along. I'm such an idiot."

"I do care—"

David got right in her face. "Don't say that bullshit to me! Not now! Not when you're standing there ripping out my heart!"

"I know this hurts now, but there is a girl out there—"

"You were the girl for me!"

"I've never been the girl for you. One day, you'll look back and realize its truth."

"I don't think so, but you've always been the smart one. Guess you know best." David smirked.

Slowly, Bella inched away as if she were frightened of him. He'd never intended to scare her, but he also hadn't planned to walk away without a fight.

"David ..."

He shook his head. There was nothing left for him to do—except suffer through the hole in his heart. He looked at Bella one more time, then pivoted and stomped out of the living room, slamming the front door on his way out.

Luis rubbed the sleep from his eyes. He'd crashed for a couple of hours. Stretching, he glanced at the computer. The program hadn't finished yet. *Damn.* He'd figured it would've searched all the documents by now.

Last night he'd finally accessed the sealed adoption files for Bella Kynaston. Unfortunately, it hadn't mentioned her birth parents. However, he'd noticed the paperwork filed with courts had been entered as a "final draft." Since then, he'd been combing the web for the original documents.

The final-draft notation hadn't been the only thing that caught his attention. Luis crossed the room and pulled out a worn-looking file. He flipped through the paperwork and located the court-approved documentation regarding his own adoption. The dates matched those on Bella Kynaston's paperwork. If he'd learned one thing, it was that there are no coincidences.

Luis dropped onto the desk chair and eyed his adoption papers. His birth name hadn't been listed either, but he'd discovered the truth. The beauty of the digital age. He shared his birth mother's last name. Ileana Costa had named him Sabio Costa. It suited him quite well. In Portuguese, "Sabio" meant wise man. Unfortunately, he had no idea what traits he'd inherited from her. If he looked like her, he had no clue. He'd never seen her picture.

The computer dinged.

"Finally!"

Luis skimmed through the documentation the system had located. First drafted September 12, 1997. Interesting. Hadn't his mother died a day or two before then? He frowned and continued reading the file. *Blah, blah.* A whole bunch of shit he didn't need to know. He'd long ago learned all he could about the people who'd adopted her.

"Holy shit." Two names screamed at him. How could this be possible? How could he not know? How could his father have hidden this from him? All this time, and he'd been instructed to watch his own sister. At no point, had Juan Castell mentioned the girl he wanted his son to watch was also his daughter.

Luis frowned. Something about a sister ... a memory ...

"Why sissy go?"

His father kneeled down and clasped his hands. "I must separate you two. It is not safe for the two of you to be together. Come now, say goodbye to Giovanna."

"No want to."

"Please, Sabio. Do as I say."

"Okay, papa." He waddled over to the car seat and kissed the baby's forehead. She cooed at him and gripped his finger with her chubby little hand. "Love you, Gigi."

His father stood and looked at the man. "Go now, take her."

"Gigi!" Sabio called after his sister. His father's arms wrapped around him and prevented him from chasing the tall man who carried the baby away.

How could he have forgotten his sister? Dear God. They'd been separated as children, after their mother died. Luis bolted to his feet and stalked across his bedroom to the dresser. He yanked open the drawer where he'd hidden all the photographs his father sent him. Digging under his clothes, he pulled out Bella's picture and studied her features.

Same hazel eyes with green flecks. Same broad smile. Same dark skin. Same midnight black hair. Luis rubbed the back of his head. They looked so much alike, and he'd never noticed. How had he missed all this? It wasn't that he'd forgotten; he'd simply tucked the memory so far away in his mind. He'd been so saddened by the loss.

The system blared and alerted him to an update. Luis jogged over to the computer and sat again. He checked out the blast. "Crap."

"What?" Cristobal stepped into the room.

"Christ! You scared the shit out of me. I thought you got pinched."

Cristobal flopped on the bed. "They didn't have anything to hold me. Now, why crap?"

"Your brother made bail. We need to get the hell out of here."

Bella tugged the green silk razorback blouse over her head. Her arm throbbed, but she ignored it. Digging through her dresser drawer, she found the eye shadow she'd chosen to match the blouse. It was ironic. The day she'd purchased this blouse was the day she'd run into David in the mall and their whole relationship had begun. And now it was over.

She brushed the shadow on each lid and eyed herself in the mirror. A little mascara and some lip gloss, and she'd be ready to face the rest of the day. Whatever it held in store.

Then she heard a click.

Bella poked her head out of the bathroom and glanced down the hallway. Had the front door opened? "Hello?"

With a tiny frown, she walked to the front door. It was closed, but not locked. She must've forgotten to lock it when David left. No need to panic. Inhaling deeply, she returned to her bedroom and quickly swiped lip gloss on her lips.

As she tossed the gloss back on her dresser, the hairs on the nape of her neck prickled. Her eyes lifted to the mirror. Behind her stood a large Hispanic man with dark hair and cold black eyes.

"Scream, and I kill that baby." The guy stepped forward and tapped a knife against her abdomen.

Bella nodded. She swallowed to wet her dry throat. "Who are you?"

"Not important. Sit in chair."

Following his instructions, she sat in the chair by her desk. "What're you going to do to me?" She didn't expect him to answer. Only one answer made sense. This man had shown up to finish what the shooters had started, yesterday.

He removed two pairs of handcuffs from his back pocket and cuffed each wrist to the chair's arms. "I not do anything. It what you do to yourself. Thank you. Make job so easy."

"I don't—" *Oh shit!* He absolutely planned to kill her. By making it look like she overdosed. Deliberately. And her letters would confirm it. Bella scanned her desk. What had she done with them? Had her would-be murderer found them …?

He walked to her closet and collected a couple items—a bottle of vodka and a rather familiar bottle of pills. "Bad to mix these together."

"You'll kill the baby if you kill me. Doesn't Jorge care about his unborn child?" Time. She needed time. Yes, the paternity test had proven Jorge hadn't fathered her baby, but he couldn't know that. Could he?

"He know about baby, and yes he want."

"Then he wouldn't want me dead."

The guy sheathed the knife in his hand. He unscrewed the top to the bottle of vodka and popped open the bottle of pills. "No. He not want you dead. He love you. And that problem."

"I don't understand."

"No talk. Drink." He grabbed her by her hair and yanked her head back. He dropped some pills into her mouth and poured the vodka in behind them.

Goddamn! It burned. Bella tried not to swallow any of the pills, but the liquid carried them down her throat and into her stomach. Ignoring the searing pain in her arm, she struggled against her restraints. The man's grip on her head loosened, and she coughed up some of the vodka. "Please, just let me go. I won't tell anyone about this, as long as you don't kill me or the baby."

"Shut up!" He backhanded her.

Stars flitted in front of her eyes as she blinked back the pain. She had to think. The chair she sat in rolled, and her feet weren't bound. It wasn't much, but it might be the chance she needed. "Please—"

"Drink!"

As he grabbed her head again and poured more pills and vodka into her mouth, Bella dug her heels into the carpet and shoved the chair backwards. His boots kept the chair from going very far—but the maneuver distracted him enough to stop.

She coughed up some of the pills and alcohol and spat them onto the carpet. "Please—"

"Bad girl!" He slapped her again and jerked a drawer open, searching until he found a couple of scarves.

The room spun around her. *Dammit!* Normally, the pills took a little longer to kick in, but with the liquor ... Her dizziness told her one thing: it was now or never. Bella squinted and focused. When the guy kneeled down to tie her legs, she'd have one opportunity. It had to be timed perfectly. She waited for him to get close enough. Taking aim, she kneed him in the nose and pushed herself backwards as he fell. "Help! HELP!!"

"Punta!" Blood dripped down his face. He scrambled to his feet and punched her in the gut.

"Is that everything?" Luis surveyed the mess they'd made in the process of packing.

"Aside from your computer, I think so."

He strode across the room and dropped into the desk chair he'd become accustomed to inhabiting for hours on end. "Don't worry. I can take care of that."

"What will you do?" Cristobal dragged a chair over and sat beside him.

"I have a back-up at the safe house. I'll shoot everything over there and then burn this hard drive, rendering it inaccessible."

"Good. We need time to crack my brother's black books. Nobody else should be hurt over his ... control issues. I just can't believe he got out. After everything I told the— Hey, you paying attention?"

Luis eyed the four little boxes that flashed red at him from one of the monitors.

He'd hacked the camera set-up he'd installed for Gervasio. Now he could watch the girl he had just learned was his sister. And the red indicated motion; nobody should be in that house. Yesterday, it had been cordoned off. He clicked on the box and it came up full screen. "Shit!"

"Whose window is Bronco crawling out of? And why are you monitoring it?"

"Bella's." To Luis, that one word answered both questions.

"Are you insane?"

Ignoring Cristobal, Luis zoomed in and focused inside the room. His sister lay sprawled across her bed, an empty bottle of vodka and a pill bottle next to her. Without a second of hesitation, he whipped out his cell phone and dialed 9-1-1. When the operator's voice asked about his emergency, he blurted out, "I need an ambulance to 1113 Pecado Avenue in Nautica Valley. My friend has overdosed. Looks like she combined vodka with OxyContin. Please hurry!"

"Crap!" Cristobal tapped the monitor.

Luis looked at what had caught the attention of the one Rodriguez he could count on. It was Bronco. Swinging a leg back over the window sill into Bella's bedroom.

He bit his tongue and listened to the question the operator was asking.

"Is she conscious?"

"No."

"Is she breathing?"

"I don't know... I can't tell." The broad-shouldered jackass paused. He must have perked to something, because the guy quickly climbed back out and jogged out of sight.

Had the operator said something else? "What? What was that?"

"Do you know CPR?"

"Shit! No! Just get there ... you have to help her! You have to help Gigi!" Luis splayed his fingers on the screen in front of him as if he could save his sister through the computer.

"Sir, are you with your friend?"

The question busted him. He quickly hung up his pre-paid phone, which couldn't be traced to him. "Okay." He took a deep breath. "We'll wait until we the see the EMT's, then pack up the hard-drives and get the hell out of here."

"Did you see why he went back?"

Luis scanned the room. Something silver gleamed by his sister's desk. He zoomed in. A pair of handcuffs. Good, this was good. He pulled back and enlarged the screen as a paramedic came into view by her window. Luis released a breath, relieved they had found her. "Come on. We need to move fast!"

twenty-three

Jeremiah was worried. Bell had never called to say she was leaving. She must have forgotten. He'd called the Kynaston house several times, but she hadn't answered. He couldn't wait anymore. Jeremiah headed to the hospital, figuring Bell would be with her parents in intensive care. He made it there in record time, then flew up the stairs to the ICU, walked to the fifth door on the right, and peered through the window.

No Bell. He rapped lightly on the window and lifted his hand to her mother. She came out to meet him in the hall.

"Jeremiah, is everything well?"

"How's he doing?"

"Better. He woke up briefly not long ago."

"That's good," Jeremiah said. He knew the man would make it. If only he knew where his girlfriend was at, everything would be right in his world. "Has Bell been by here? It's been a few hours since I saw her last."

"No, though perhaps she is with Dr. Greenald. I believe she was to meet with her around two o'clock." Mrs. Kynaston glanced at her watch.

Relief washed over him. "Okay. Maybe she's still with her."

"I suppose that—"

Jeremiah turned to see a doctor jogging in their direction. His insides knotted, as he prayed the woman was anyone but Bell's doctor.

"Dr. Greenald? Is something wrong?" Mrs. Kynaston asked.

So, it was Bell's doctor. Jeremiah held his breath, waiting for the woman's response.

"Yes. Bella was brought into the emergency room on a suspected overdose. Her stomach is being pumped, now, but the baby has experienced some distress. I need you to come downstairs with me. You may have some hard decisions to make on her behalf."

Jeremiah followed the women as they headed for the elevators. What the doctor said, it made no sense. Last night, Bell admitted she needed help.

As they waited for an elevator, Mrs. Kynaston asked, "When did you speak to her last?"

"A little before noon. I dropped her off at the house. She wanted to shower and change clothes before coming here. She wanted to make sure the baby was taken care of."

"I'm sorry. Who are you?" Dr. Greenald interceded.

"Jeremiah. I'm Bella's boyfriend. And I promise you. No way she purposely overdosed. She planned to get help."

Mrs. Kynaston looked to the doctor. "What kind of decision would I need to make?"

"Any distress on Bella puts distress on the baby. We'll do everything we can to save them both, but in the end, you may need to choose."

Jeremiah rested his head on his outstretched arm as he held Bella's hand. He refused to leave her side and constantly prayed for her to wake up. The door to her hospital room opened. He rubbed his eyes. It was his dad.

"Were you sleeping?"

He shook his head. "No."

His father rested a hand on his shoulder and squeezed. "Have you slept at all?"

"A little. I keep hoping she'll wake up."

"Has the doctor said anything more?"

"Only the same stuff. No change for her or the baby." All the tests confirmed brain activity, but Bella hadn't come to. The longer Bella remained comatose, the more unlikely she'd wake up.

"Who's been by to see her?"

"Her mother. Alex. Amanda and Sarresh will be here later, and Vick left about twenty minutes ago."

Mrs. Kynaston spent most of her time by her husband's side, as he continued to fight for his life. Jeremiah stayed by Bell's. Earlier, he'd asked Mrs. Kynaston why she'd granted permission for everyone to see Bell. The woman answered him honestly and wisely: "Love heals, and I believe the people who care for her the most can carry her back."

"That's good." His father leaned against the wall. He crossed his arms, and his gaze shifted to the ground.

"Dad? Is something wrong?"

"Jorge Smith, who we've officially identified as Gervasio Rodriguez, posted bail two days ago."

Jeremiah gawked at his father. "What? How did that happen?"

"I don't know. All his financials told us he didn't have access to that kind of money. Seems he did."

"That's bullshit. Can't they do anything?" So what if his father chastised him over the language. Bell was in the hospital fighting for her life, and now they had to fret over that animal being on the street. But his father let it go.

"Not unless we find more charges. The prosecutor is going to try and get Bella's statement read in, since we don't know how her condition will … develop."

Jeremiah dropped his forehead against Bell's hand. "But with … him … out there, how is she supposed to be safe?"

"Have a little faith in your old man. I'm posting an officer outside her room and her father's. They'll be fine."

His father squeezed his shoulder once more and then headed over to the door. He paused with his hand on the knob. "One more thing."

"What?"

"There was a letter in the mailbox for you." His father removed an envelope from his inside jacket pocket and handed it to Jeremiah.

He studied the envelope. There was no return address and no stamp. Only the nickname Bell called him had been scribbled in the middle. "This can't be possible."

"What can't be possible?"

"Dad, this is Bell's handwriting. This is the nickname she gave me. This can't ... no, no way she sent that. When did you find that?"

"Today, but the mail hasn't been checked for a few days. I'll take it to the station and have Russell look into it. Okay?" His father tucked the letter back in his pocket and headed for the door.

Holding a small, wrapped box in his hand, Jeremiah kissed Bell's forehead. His mother had been released with the twins two days ago, but with Bell still in a coma, he'd declined to join his family at home.

"Merry Christmas, Bell. I was hoping you'd be able to unwrap this, but you still haven't woken up. This isn't how I expected to spend our first Christmas."

Jeremiah took her hand in his. "I need you to do something for me. I need you to wake up. Then we can celebrate the right way."

He dropped his forehead against her hand. The consistent lack of response weighed heavy on his heart and was slowly chipping away at what small hope he still carried.

"Bell, please, you have to wake up."

How many times had he begged? And still nothing. But while her heart continued to beat and her body kept the baby alive, there was a chance. He hadn't lost faith.

The hospital door opened. "Hey, son."

"Hey, Dad. What are you doing here?"

"Your mother wanted me to check on the two of you. She's hoping you'll come home for Christmas dinner. Your grandmother is there helping Mandy cook."

"I can't. I won't leave her alone." Most everyone was spending the holiday with their family. Not him. If she came out of the coma, he had to be there.

"Has her mother been by?"

"Not since yesterday." Jeremiah wasn't sure his response could be construed as positive. Dr. Greenald had forced Mrs. Kynaston to make a decision. He'd tried to understand her choice, but ...

"I wish I could say I'm surprised."

Suddenly, the comforting sound of Bell's regularly beeping heart monitor squealed. She'd flat-lined. Jeremiah leapt up and dropped the box in his hand. His dad hollered. Nurses and doctors gathered quickly.

Jeremiah shouted, "Come on, Bell! Don't you give up!"

A doctor tugged on him gently. "Son. You have to move so we can get to her."

"I … can't leave her." Forgetting all about the Christmas ornament, he let his father escort him out of the room.

With his father's arm around his shoulder, Jeremiah stared through the window. The doctors and nurses were working to bring her back. He prayed she'd make it. He'd do anything for them to have their chance. His love for her consumed his soul. His beautiful angel and the baby had to survive.

He turned into his father's arms. He couldn't watch. *God, please don't take her away.* She had to come back. She had to. The eerie monotone of her heart giving out continued. *God, please don't take her away. I'll do anything, but please, please don't take Bell from me.*

His father hugged him closely, then Jeremiah pulled back and looked up—just in time to see one of the doctors call for the others to stop.

He turned back to his father, holding his gaze for strength. Jeremiah couldn't look when it happened. In a matter of moments, Bell would be pronounced dead.

Together, he and his father stood, their eyes brimming. Waiting.

Just when he thought she was gone, he heard someone whisper his name.

Miah.

Jeremiah swallowed his fear and looked through the glass. The doctors and nurses still surrounded Bell, but they were no longer trying to revive her.

Miah.

He glanced at his father. He didn't seem to have heard it.

Jeremiah stared through the window, again, focusing his eyes and his ears. Then he heard something else. Something he hadn't imagined he'd ever hear again. It was Bella's heart monitor. Beeping. Normally.

It was nothing short of a miracle. God had returned her to life. Now, she just had to wake up. He placed a hand on the window and promised her right then and there. *I will be with you. I will be here … waiting.*

twenty-four

"They have to arrest Bronco for what he did to … Bella." Luis used the name Cristobal knew the girl by. He'd almost slipped and said, "Gigi," the name he now called her in his head and heart. How was he supposed to tell his one friend the girl they talked about all the time was his sister?

Cristobal paced from one side of the room to the other. "Shit. Can you swear they can't be linked back to you?"

"Yes. And that lets us focus on finding your brother and cracking the rest of his damn code."

"I hate this."

"You aren't the only one," Luis muttered. He'd reviewed the video footage. His decision to send the recordings anonymously to the police hadn't come easily, but he and Cristobal had to follow through. Every morning he checked the hospital records for an update on his sister's condition. Four days ago, she nearly died. Although the doctors revived her, she'd lost the baby. His heart broke in half. None of this would've happened if he'd kept Gervasio away from his family. He refused to let it happen again.

"I need to go for a walk. Clear my head," Gervasio's brother said.

"Yeah, sure. I'll keep working on the black books. Take a walkie."

Cristobal snatched one of the short-wave two-way radios they kept on hand as he walked out the door.

Luis sighed. He had to decode these books and fast. Part of it he'd figured out: initials and dates. But what the hell could the rest of it mean? As for locating Gervasio, as long as the bastard had no way to find them, it was last on his list. Let the police do at least part of their job.

Turning his back on the door, he sat at his desk and scanned the latest report on credit card activity. The system searched for various aliases he knew Gervasio used. Behind him, the door opened and closed.

"That was a short walk."

"Was it? I am surprised you made it to this location without attracting attention."

"I'm smarter than that." Luis spun to the face the man he assumed gave him life, Juan Castell. The man who helped create all his current problems. They hadn't met since he was two years old. The man before him had to be his blood. He saw how similar they looked: hard jaw-line, black hair, and height. So much like his sister, Gigi, too.

"Is that how you greet your father?"

"The way I greet you is to ask what the hell do you want?"

His father locked his hands behind his back and paced around the room. "I came because you have not responded to any of my calls or texts. And there seems to be much going on here."

"I haven't answered you because I've been busy trying to take care of my sister. Oh yeah, bet you thought I'd never figure it out. Never remember Gigi."

"You were quite young when I separated the two of you. Yes, I believed you would not remember. In fact, I counted on it. Your skills, however, I did not fully take into consideration when I assigned you to watch over her. I suspected your skills might be useful under the right circumstances."

"What? You mean like working for you? Well, you can forget that shit. I don't want a damn thing to do with you. As far as I'm concerned, you can leave. When Gigi wakes up, I can take care of her a lot better than you ever did." Luis grabbed a bottle of water from the small refrigerator and turned around to his computers.

"Explain your words."

"What? Your lawyer associate hasn't kept you informed?"

"That was your job. Now, tell me what the hell is going on with my daughter!" His father demanded loudly.

In some small way, Luis was amused. For once, the shoe was on the other foot. His father wanted information he'd withheld. Too bad. The man could've discovered all this weeks ago if he'd bothered to respond when it mattered the most.

Luis spun around and crossed his arms. "She's in a coma."

"How in the hell did that happen? You were supposed to be watching her!"

"Unfortunately, I didn't have all the deets, so I had no clue Gervasio knew who the hell she was until it was too late! So, thanks Dad, for trying to blame this all on me!"

"What?" His father's dark brown eyes widened in absolute disbelief. His hands dropped to his sides.

Luis suddenly got it. How could he have missed the pieces? The solution had been right before his eyes. All the dots connected. "Yeah. His little black book, her picture, and her initials, G.C. Go ahead, tell me whose fault it is, because from what I've found, he did all this to get you out of hiding. After all, he can't really be the leader of the Grim Reapers unless he can prove the old one is dead. Can he?"

"Take care of your sister. As for Gervasio Rodriguez, you leave him to me." His father snarled and stormed out the door.

Milena paused inside the front door of her house. So many good memories, but her mind only focused on the bad. More positive memories could be made; however, nothing would be the same without her husband. She sniffled, wiped the tears from beneath her eyes, and closed the door. Things would be different here for her and her daughter. Bella had to wake up from the coma.

Sighing in a combination of frustration and sorrow, Milena stepped into the kitchen— and gasped. An older Hispanic man stood near the table. "Who are you? What are you doing in my house?"

"It is not important how I got in. As for whom I am, I am the reason you raised my daughter."

"Dear God. You're alive?" Whatever life he'd led over the last sixteen years had darkened this man's soul, and it showed on his face. His features had hardened.

The brown of his eyes had deepened to black. Yet the similarities between him and her daughter were evident.

"I am alive. I have kept myself safe. Yet, you have failed to keep my daughter, who was placed in your care solely for her protection, equally safe."

He couldn't be serious. She and DeWei had done everything they could to keep Bella away from harm. They had been ill-prepared for how dangerous it would be if anyone discovered the identity of her true parents. Milena folded her arms across her chest. "How dare you! DeWei and I did all we possibly could to keep her safe."

"Ah, yes, your husband. My condolences. I suppose I cannot blame the two of you entirely when he has sacrificed—"

"Take your sympathy and get the hell out of my house! You are not welcome here." She spun on her heel and stomped from the kitchen. But before she could get far, the man launched himself at her, grabbed her by the chin, and slammed her back into the wall.

"I do not give a damn whether or not I am welcome! You will shut up and listen! Do you understand?"

"Go ahead. Kill me. Leave Bella with no one to take care of her when she wakes up."

"My daughter will never be alone. She has me and her brother." He released his grip.

Milena rubbed her jaw where his fingers had dug into her skin. "What brother? Ileana had no other children."

"My Ileana and I had a boy two years before Giovanna. He has lived in this county for the same length of time as my daughter."

"Giovanna? Is that ... is that her birth name?" Those phone calls they had received around the Fourth of July. She had always believed the calls meant something, but she'd never known their daughter by any other name than the one they'd chosen.

"Yes. Why do you ask?"

Milena sat in a chair at the kitchen table. Why hadn't she learned all of this sooner? If she had, maybe her husband wouldn't be gone. "A young man called several times seeking a Giovanna. Every time, I told him the same thing. No one by that name lived here."

"How long ago was the first call?" Juan Castell asked through gritted teeth.

"Six months ago."

Bella's father walked over to the kitchen window. "This is worse than I feared. As you are in no condition to take care of my daughter, here is what you will do. You will turn over temporary guardianship to the sheriff and his wife. He is better equipped to handle this situation."

"Excuse me?"

"It is safest for both of you if you are not around her until I can resolve the problem. Temporary guardianship, do you understand?"

Jamar patted his newborn son's back, while his wife burped their daughter. The twins followed normal newborn schedules: eat, burp, sleep, diaper change, eat, burp, sleep ... and so on. He'd spent less time at the precinct the past few days, and helped his wife as often as possible. After a much-needed burp, his son yawned and conked out. Thankfully, his daughter appeared to follow suit. Carefully, he lay his son down to sleep, and Christine put their new daughter beside him. Then, quietly he and his wife backed out of the nursery.

Hearing a knock on the front door, he jogged down the hall before a second rap woke the twins. He opened the door and raised a curious eyebrow at Bella's mother, who stood in the doorway with a variety of files in her arms.

"Hello. I apologize for arriving unannounced, but it was imperative I speak with you and Christine. May I come in?"

"Of course." Jamar stepped aside.

Clutching the files, Bella's mother offered a tiny smile and walked past him.

"Come on. We can talk in the living room."

The woman sat across from the loveseat and placed the files on the coffee table.

His wife joined them. "Milena, I'm glad to see you," Christine said. "How are you?"

"I am holding myself together. There are many things I wish we had better prepared for. I suppose neither one of us ever considered the other would return to the Father so soon."

"Is that what you came to talk about?" Jamar folded his hands in his lap.

Lowering her eyes, Bella's mother inhaled deeply, then focused her gaze on him. "Partially. Before I go into the details, I must request you act solely as Jamar Detrone, the friend of mine and my husband, not as Sheriff Detrone. Is this something you can do?"

"As much as I'd like to separate the two, I may not be able to. If anything you tell me is pertinent to an open case, I can't exactly overlook that." His job wasn't something he could just turn off. Information related to any case had to be documented. Jamar sighed. Maybe she should just talk to his wife.

"Very well. I will keep my request to the facts."

His wife reached across the couch and squeezed the woman's hand. "Milena, you tell us whatever you need to. If I need to kick my husband out for some it, I will."

"Thank you. There is much I need to say, but I am uncertain where to begin."

"Why don't you tell us what's in the files?" Jamar gestured toward the stack she'd set on the coffee table.

"These are court documents that will allow me to appoint those of my choosing as guardians for Bella. I need someone to take care of her in my absence."

That certainly wasn't the answer he expected. "What are you talking about?"

"DeWei is part Chinese. I will fly with him back to China. I have decided to stay for a short period with his mother."

It was Christine who asked the obvious question. "Why wouldn't you return afterward? Bella still needs you."

"If I am not around, then she is the only one who needs to be protected. Too many risks are associated if I stay close. This is why I would like for the two of you to be her guardians."

She loved her daughter with all her heart. There was a great probability that her friends silently questioned the reason behind her demand. Unnerved by their lack of response, Milena played with the ends of her dark brown hair. This was an idiotic idea. Why had she bothered to listen to that man? "I—"

"Honey, can you give us a few minutes?" Christine glanced at her husband.

Jamar nodded, stood, and stepped out of the room.

"Okay, Milena. What is going on?"

Sighing heavily, she eyed the ceiling above Christine's head. How to explain? Her entire world halted the moment her husband lost the battle for his life. There were many things she now had to finish without him.

Finally, Milena found a way to begin. "Two weeks ago, I went to the doctor. I believed I had hit that point in my life where the concern for young children is gone forever. Surely, you can imagine how shocked I was when the doctor announced I was pregnant."

"Oh, my goodness. Milena, why didn't you say anything?"

"With everything going on with Bella, DeWei and I decided to wait until I was past the first trimester before announcing the pregnancy. Now, he is gone, and I'm not positive what my next step should be. How do I raise a child without his support? As well as keep my teenager safe? It was myself who pushed the conviction that she was not an addict."

"You wanted to believe she was okay. We all did." Christine reached forward, grasped her friend's hand, and squeezed.

"I wanted to believe she would never harm herself or her baby. I am terrified for her health, her safety ... as well as my own."

"You're not afraid of her, are you?"

It was an awful question, but she was grateful Christine asked. The door for what she had to reveal opened wide. "No. But I am afraid *for* her. Has Jamar told you who her biological father is?"

"No. Why?"

"All of these horrible tragic events, I believe they are linked to her birth father. As does he. A territorial war has started, and my Bella is at the center because of him."

"Wait. I'm confused. Have you spoken to this guy?" Christine's green eyes narrowed in concern. She tucked a strand of her red hair behind her ear.

"You cannot tell your husband, but, yes. He visited me yesterday. I have spent the night thinking on these issues." Milena plucked a hair tie from her pocket and swept her thick brown locks into a quick ponytail.

"Who is he?"

"He was ... or is—I am not certain which—he is associated with the local gang. Strange as it may sound, I believe leaving Bella under your care, if she should wake up ... it is the wisest course of action."

Christine laced her fingers together and leaned forward on her knees. "I have faith she will wake up. I don't believe God is done with Bella, yet."

"Thank you. I cannot express how much that means to me." Tears prickled the corner of her eyes. She'd struggled to keep them at bay since the start of the conversation. They really had befriended one another. A soft smile formed on her lips.

"I like to believe something good will come out of the bad. Otherwise we might never have a reason to look up. Now, as for the guardianship, I'll discuss it with Jamar, but I don't see any reason why not. You and I just need to sit down and go over what your plans are for when Bella wakes up."

"Thank you, Christine. From the bottom of my heart, thank you."

twenty-five

"Hey Mandy, are you ..." Jeremiah walked right into the empty bedroom. A chemistry book sat open on his sister's desk, bookmarked by an envelope with her name scrawled across it in Bell's handwriting. It looked like the letter his father had brought to him in the hospital. He picked up the envelope and inspected it.

"What're you doing in my room?" Amanda stood in the doorway, hands on her hips.

"I, uh, I came to see if you were going to visit Bell this afternoon." His girlfriend still hadn't woken up—and now her mother had gone to China. He hoped Mandy would pitch in with visits to the hospital to keep Bell company. Even if she was unconscious, he believed she knew her friends were there.

"What's in your hand?"

He held the envelope up. "Have you read it?" He'd never read his. Hell, he wasn't even sure where it had ended up. Someone at the precinct could've read it, but his father never disclosed what it said. And he never asked.

Amanda held out her hand. "Yes. Now give it back to me."

"Why didn't you say anything?"

"None of us thought it was a good idea. You've been pretty adamant Bella would never consider suicide. We figured it was best not to stir the pot."

"We? We, who?" The police were the ones who labeled Bell's situation as a result of a suicide attempt. Jeremiah regarded the letter. It could contain answers, but was he prepared for them? Even if it proved the police were right? Reluctantly he offered the envelope to his sister.

"Me, Alex, Vick, Sarresh ... we each got one."

Shocked, Jeremiah pulled the envelope back. "What?"

"Look, none of us have discussed our letters with one another. We agreed they were highly personal. Whatever Bella had to say, she said it to each of us individually. Now, give me my letter back."

"Tell me what yours says, and I'll let you have it."

"As God as my witness, if you don't give me the damn letter, I'll kick you in the balls!" Amanda glared at her brother and stepped close enough to him that, if she lifted her foot, it would connect in all the wrong places.

He'd never been kicked in the gonads. Truth be told, he wasn't in a hurry to experience the sensation. Jeremiah handed over the envelope. "Why won't you tell me?"

"Because it's none of your damn business. Now, get the hell out of my room and go see your girlfriend."

He reviewed the court documents his wife insisted he take to work with him. How had she convinced him that temporary guardianship of Bella would be good for all parties involved? Jamar sighed. He'd just prepared to reread the information about their responsibilities, when his office door flew open, and Russell thundered in, a laptop in hand.

"You need to see this."

"More bad news?"

"Depends on your perspective." Russell set the laptop on Jamar's desk and hit play.

A little over two weeks ago, Bella attempted to take her life. At least that had been their official ruling. But based on the video in front of him, their ruling was all wrong. Jamar rubbed his chin as the images continued. "When and where?"

"Thumb drive in an unlabeled manila envelope. On my desk when I came in today.

"The guy in the video is Enrique Gutierrez, also known as Bronco. He's the executioner for the Grim Reapers. Has at least eleven unconfirmed kills under his belt."

Russell. He was one of the few under Jamar's charge who had earned his trust. Russell always brought him information. Never once had there been a reason to doubt him—and he appreciated that. With the new year came change and resolutions. Now, Jamar resolved to get the rats out of his precinct. "Take the envelope to Judy. Have her dust for prints. Thumb drive to Ali. Get Robinson to bring in this Enrique guy. I also want you to bring in Rodney Harrison. Make a show of it. I'll have Simms in a conference room. They'll both think the other is a snitch. With a little luck, they both talk."

"Sir?"

"It's about time we cleaned house, don't you think?"

"Yes, sir. I'll also pull the files for you. I know you handed me the lead, but I think it would be wise if you went over those records. See which investigators and officers were in the vicinity. And maybe you can borrow a neighboring team, have the cameras located." Russell closed the laptop and scooped it up.

Jamar studied the man for a moment. "Don't worry," he assured Russell. "I know you're not dirty. Get to work. I've got calls to make."

"She's been in a coma for three weeks, now. Could she still wake up?" Jeremiah asked the doctor the question he'd been wondering and worrying about for days.

"The longer she is comatose, the less likely she'll wake up, but miracles happen all the time. Her vitals are stable, and there is brain activity, but in the end, it's up to her."

Jeremiah rubbed the top of his head. "Is there anything more we can do?"

"No. Sometimes, all you can do is pray and remind her every day there is something worth fighting for."

"Okay." Jeremiah sat. How many days had he occupied this chair? Twenty-two long days. He wrapped Bell's hand in his own. His heart yearned for Bell to wake up—despite everything.

Their friends still visited every day. Unfortunately, none of them appeared to have an easy time. His sister hadn't lied about the letters. Whatever Bell said had rattled them. What would happen when she woke up? Would her friends still be there for her? Or would she have only him by her side?

Then, there was her mother. The woman left for China twelve days ago. She'd called twice—once, to let his parents know she'd arrived safely with her husband's remains, once, to verify their receipt of the guardianship paperwork.

Jeremiah kissed Bell's hand. "I wish I knew how to bring you back, because I need you here. I need you, Bell."

He laid his head against their entwined hands and prayed for another miracle. But at the same time, a small part of him wished her current condition would continue. She'd come back to so much bad, and he'd protect her any way he could, but if ... no, *when* she woke up there'd be no way to stop her having to face it.

His kissed the back of her hand again. But this time, her fingers twitched beneath his lips. His gaze shifted to her face—just as Bell's eyes fluttered.

That voice. I know that voice. Why is he telling me to come back? Where did I go? Wait. I know. I died. No, that isn't right. He wouldn't be telling me to come back if I was dead. I'm not dead. I'm not dead. I'm not dead.

"Come on, Bell. Keep trying. Open your eyes."

I'm trying, but it's so hard.

"I know you can do it. Come on. Come back to me." He squeezed her hand.

That hand. I know that hand. Something wet trickled down her cheeks. The sensation confused her. What happened to her body? *Why is he encouraging me? I know. He needs me. I have to go back to him. I have to. I have to because ... because I love him.*

"Please, Bell. Don't give up. I need you here. Keep trying. Please keep trying."

Bella tried to nod, but she was so tired. Instead, she focused on the struggle to open her eyes. How much time had passed? How long had she worked to see something other than the inside of her eyelids? Partially, she opened her eyes. The light blinded her, and she snapped her eyes shut. Stars flashed. Her eyeballs throbbed. Then the pain eased, and she attempted to open her eyes again. Her eyes didn't fully cooperate until the brightness faded. Then, sight returned and the face of a handsome man came into view. More tears fell. *Miah.*

"God. I thought I'd lost you." Tears formed in his exquisite green eyes, and a loving smile spread across his face.

Bella attempted to speak his name, but something was in her mouth. It was hard and uncomfortable.

"Shh. It's okay. Don't say anything. Let me get a doctor, and see if we can get the tube out."

Her head barely moved. Her body was stiff. Then Miah stood to leave. A strength she had thought forgotten filled her, and she squeezed his hand as if her life depended on his presence. She couldn't let him go.

"Okay, okay. I'll just page a nurse."

That sounded good. Goodness, she was so tired. Her energy flagged. Bella's grip on Miah loosened. Her eyes drifted shut and sleep claimed her.

It was obvious to Amanda. "Mom and Jeremiah should go. Mom, you have experience, and Jeremiah, you offer unconditional love and support. Bella needs those two things most of all right now. "And you've got to tell her *everything*, Mom."

Amanda glanced between her parents. She'd admitted to her father how much she had learned years ago. It only made sense he'd told her mother. Hadn't he?

Her mother padded across the floor and rested her hands on Amanda's shoulders and looked her deeply in the eye. "How much do you know?"

Or maybe not. "Can we please not talk about this?"

"Oh, Mandy." Her mother pulled her into her arms.

Amanda shrugged out of her mother's grip and stepped back. "Mom, this isn't about me. Not now. Please, just focus on Bella." The time would come when they'd need to discuss the past, but not at this moment.

Her mother accepted this. "But we will discuss it, sweetheart," she said. "Soon."

"But you will tell her, right?" Mandy knew having her mother talk about the experiences she and Bella shared would help the girl feel less vulnerable.

At this, her father sighed. "I don't think that's a wise idea."

"Bella needs to know she's not alone."

"I'm not disagreeing with you about that. It's more the timing. She's just woken up. There's a lot for her to deal with. She's lost a lot. I don't think it's best that your mother share her past with Bella. Not now."

Amanda eyed her brother. The events of the last five months had aged him in ways she wished he'd been able to avoid. At least he could be there for Bella, when she learned the truth. Having someone by your side eased the pain. One of the many things she loved about Vick.

"Okay. I get it." Amanda saw his point. "Right. Anyway, I have studying to do."

"And we need to go visit Bella." Her mother touched her brother's shoulder.

Bella closed the novel by Colleen Hoover and wiped the tears from her eyes. Vick had dropped it off a few hours ago. He mentioned schoolwork, but recommended she wait until she had recovered further before diving into make-up work. The book had been a great distraction.

The door to her hospital room opened. "*Nǐhǎo*, Miah. *Nǐhǎo*, Christine."

"Hey, Bell." Miah crossed to her hospital bed, kissed her forehead, and sat in the chair beside her bed.

An apologetic smile tugged at her lips. The Mandarin she'd learned as a child came out so smoothly—but her body still functioned so awkwardly. "Shorry."

"It's okay. Things will return naturally as you recuperate. How are you doing today?" Miah's mother walked to the other side and settled at the end of the bed.

"Okay." She hadn't spoken much to either of Miah's parents since she'd woken up five days ago. "Ish thish about my mom?"

Miah answered. "Yes and no. You know how I told you that your mom has been ... unreachable? Well ..." Miah squeezed Bella's hand and brushed a kiss across her knuckles.

This was bad. Two people weren't necessary to answer questions regarding the whereabouts of her parents. "What'sh going on?"

"I'm sorry Bella. I know we've been pretty tight-lipped, but we were well intentioned. Jamar and I decided it was best we wait until you had some recovery time under your belt." Miah's mother folded her hands in her lap.

"Pleash, jush tell me."

"Has the doctor told you about what happened on Christmas day?"

Bella nodded. The doctor had informed her that her heart had stopped some time on Christmas morning. She'd barraged the doctor with questions about the baby, which had never been answered. Her breath hitched in her lungs, and she swallowed. Had the air in the room been turned off? Goosebumps prickled her arms. She should've realized the truth, then.

"Yesh."

"The baby had been under distress and depended greatly on your body. Dr. Greenald discussed all the possibilities, beforehand. I'm sorry Bella, but the baby didn't make it."

"Shén me? Bú shì!" *What? No!* She ripped her hand out of Miah's. Tears rolled down her cheeks, and sobs racked her body. How had she missed the emptiness?

She hadn't. She'd simply refused to acknowledge the truth. For days, she had prayed to wake up to a different reality. One where she was still pregnant.

"I wish I could tell you I'm done, but that isn't the only thing that happened that day. While you were fighting for your life in one room, your father was fighting for his in another. We thought he'd be okay after the doctors removed the bullets. Especially, when he came around a day later. Then, Christmas morning, a clot lodged in his heart. There was nothing more the doctors could do for him."

"Bàba! Wèishénme? Wèishénme? Wèishénme?" She yelled *why* at the top of her lungs. He couldn't be gone. He just couldn't. How had this happened?

Jeremiah climbed onto the bed and wrapped his arms around his girlfriend. His eyes lifted to his mother. She nodded and left the room. Enough had been dumped on Bell for one day. Eventually, they would let her know her mother had hopped on a plane for China, but that could wait.

Bell clenched his shirt and cried against his chest.

He pulled her close and held her as the tears fell.

"Thish can't ..." Bell hiccupped between sobs. She fisted some of his t-shirt and squeezed her eyes tight. More tears trickled down her face.

"I know. Bell. Shh, take a breath. Just let it out."

In response, Bell wept harder. Her body shook. "I never ..."

"He forgave you Bell. He knew you loved him." It didn't take a rocket scientist to understand where her mind had gone. She'd told him the last words she uttered to her father, just before the shooting. Now, Jeremiah refused to let the guilt eat her. During the only visit he'd made to Bell's father before the man passed, he'd promised him something—and he'd do whatever it took to keep his word.

Bell's body stilled. He glanced at her and brushed tears off her cheek. The tears continued to flow, but Bell stared straight ahead, zombie-like. He was concerned. What could he do?

The door cracked open, and his mother poked her head inside. "You okay?"

"I'm fine."

"Do you need anything?"

"Yeah." He could do what he promised. He didn't plan to share the details of what that entailed, but he could let his mother know how the night would go.

"Maylin, it is time for you to wake."

Bella rolled over. Something tickled her ear.

"Lin Lin."

His nickname for her. Bella opened her eyes and blinked at the figure in front of her.

"¿Bàba?"

"Shì de." *Yes.* Her father stepped closer and sat on the edge of her hospital bed.

Bella sat up and threw her arms around her father, as tears rolled down her cheeks. "They said you were dead."

"My beautiful daughter. *Duìbùq.*" *I am sorry.*

Bella pulled back. Her father appeared alive, but his presence made no sense. Why would Miah and his mother lie about something like that? "*Shén me? Bú shì! Duìbùq!* I don't hate you." *What? No! I am sorry!*

"Méi shì." *Don't worry about it.*

"Bàba, please explain this to me. How are you here?"

Her father brushed his hand down her hair and kissed her forehead. "I cannot stay long. This is your dream. I can see you for a very short time."

"Nǐde yìsi shì shénme?" *What do you mean?*

"I have left the earth. I was called home so that I may tend to your daughter. The important thing is you are safe."

Daughter? She would've had a little girl? She had hoped for a little girl. More tears trickled down Bella's cheeks. "Bàba, wǒ xūyào nǐ." *Dad, I need you.*

"You need Him. I know you have trouble with everything that has occurred, but you survived. You are my daughter and stronger than you think."

"No, I'm not. I'm not strong. I'm weak, and I'm scared."

"You are strong because you are my daughter. No matter what some paper said, you have always been my daughter. I must go now, but remember ... I am with you right here." Her father tapped her chest where her heart beat.

Bella hugged her father and gripped him tightly. "Wǒ ài nǐ." *I love you.*

"Wǒ yě ài nǐ." *I love you, too.* Her father unwrapped her arms from his waist, stood, and faded away.

Bella gasped. Darkness shrouded the room. Had her father really been there? Or had she only dreamed of him?

"Hey. You okay?" Miah rubbed his eyes and propped up on his elbow.

For a moment, she'd forgotten he stayed. Although she hadn't asked him to, she'd been grateful for his presence. Miah calmed her in ways she hardly believed. The idea of being alone in that hospital room with only her thoughts had frightened her. She feared the road it would've led down. God, how had she deserved a guy like him?

"Yeah. Bad dream."

"You want to talk about it?"

"Maybe, but not now. Pleash, go back to sleep."

Miah frowned, but lay back down. "Okay."

Grateful he hadn't forced the issue, Bella curled up to Miah. Someday she would tell him, but right now she refused to be labeled as crazy. Other labels required more attention. Without the people she loved most, it was all she had to keep the urge at bay. Until the day she no longer desired pills to make it through the pain, she'd cling to whatever forced her to think of life first.

twenty-six

Panting, Bella leaned on the walker and paused mid-step. Her physical therapist walked by her side, as they made their second round of the hospital floor.

"I'm sorry. I didn't think I would get ... so tired."

"That's to be expected. Just take it one step at a time. For now, we'll go back to your room. Do you think you can walk the rest of the way? Or would you like the wheelchair?"

Ding! The elevators opened, and Miah hopped off wearing a huge, lop-sided grin. He nodded at her in approval.

All the encouragement she needed. Bella smiled. "I can walk it."

"Okay. Let's keep going."

Miah ran over. "Looking good."

"I almost made two rounds. We're heading back to my room, now. Have you talked to my mom?" She'd learned of her mother's whereabouts two days ago. Detective Russell had popped in for a visit. The man had hoped to jog her memory. Unfortunately, she hadn't helped much with the puzzle the man had apparently solved.

Miah glanced to the therapist, and then turned his attention back to Bella. "Why don't we talk about it when we get to your room?"

Bella stopped again, but not because she was tired. The shift in Miah's tone said it all. She gathered that they had gotten in touch with her mother, but the news wasn't good. She glanced to her therapist. "Do you mind if Miah helps me the rest of the way?"

The therapist frowned. "I can't leave you until we get you back into your room."

"Okay." Bella pushed forward. Only a couple more doors.

Back at her room, Bella hooked the corner and went straight for the bed. With assistance from the therapist, she climbed in and got settled. "Thanks John. Again, after dinner?"

"If you think you're up for it."

"Yes." Recovering from a coma was hard. The road was longer than she anticipated.

Miah closed the door behind the therapist and sat by the bed.

"What is going on with my mom?"

Jeremiah groaned. "I wish you'd talk to my mom. She knows more about it than me."

"I don't care. Tell me. I have a right to know when my mom is coming home."

"How'd you know she isn't here?" Miah arched an eyebrow.

Uh-oh. She promised not to let anyone know Detective Russell had let the news slip. Bella leaned back against the pillows. "Let's just say a little birdie told me she flew to China. I get that she had to take my dad home, but I figured she'd be back by now."

"Look, I don't know all that's going on. My parents haven't exactly gone full throttle on the information. I think she's coming back, but ..."

"What are you talking about?" If her mother didn't return, where would she go? She had no way to take care of herself. She couldn't get emancipated, like Sarresh.

"All I know is that, after rehab and everything, you'll be staying with us."

Oh, hell.

Bella stared at the television, but she had no idea what she was watching. Five days into February. Her mother had arrived two days ago. But hadn't visited. From what she'd heard, her mother only returned for court. No one knew if she'd stay in town.

If nothing else, Bella would've liked for her mother to see how far she'd come. Her speech and movement had returned to normal. The doctor would release her soon, and then, on to rehab. Which she wasn't looking forward to. And she wasn't looking forward to moving in with Miah's family. Unfortunately, the judge approved everything. She had no choice.

The door opened and Miah's mother entered. "Hi. I hope you don't mind a visit."

"Not at all. I was just watching TV."

"Interesting choice."

Bella turned to the television and snickered. *Dora the Explorer.* She lifted the remote and shut the television off. "So, what's up?"

Miah's mother sat beside the bed. "Since the judge agreed to the terms of the informal kinship care, I wanted to talk to you a little about it. Let you know what we have control over. No matter our legal obligations, we will always discuss everything with you. Okay?"

Bella offered up a half-grin. "Okay."

"Good. We're responsible for your education, health, and finances. I know school isn't an option at the moment, so what Jamar and I have discussed with your principal is make-up schoolwork. When you're released from the hospital, we'd like you to go to a drug rehab center. The one your mom and dad chose seems like a good fit. They can help you with the addiction, the rape, and anything else you need. If you're okay with that, then the principal is willing to have you go to school from there. What do you think so far?"

"How will school work with rehab?"

"We'll hire a tutor to take your classes, then come and teach you the work. You'll do your own homework and take your own tests with the tutor as a monitor."

Bella wasn't sure what to say. It didn't sound too terrible. Then she caught a glimpse of her fingernails. The dirt. She had to clean under her nails.

"There is nothing there." Miah's mom rested a hand on her forearm.

"What?"

"There is no dirt. You can't remove something that doesn't exist."

A tear rolled down Bella's cheek. "How do you know?"

"Because I've been there." Miah's mother squeezed her arm.

"I don't understand."

"There is a reason your mother came to us. You and I are one and the same. But I need you to understand, Jeremiah doesn't know about this, and I'd prefer to keep it that way."

"I won't say anything."

"Good." The woman paused before she continued. "I had just gotten my first book deal, and was out with some friends to celebrate. I decided to walk home. I didn't live that far from the bar. I was a couple blocks away, when I was attacked and raped. I've been in your shoes. I survived, and I have faith you can make it, too."

Bella wiped at the tears on her face. For the first time in what seemed like forever, she felt she could be honest about her fears. "How do you get over rape? How am I supposed to accept that it isn't my fault and that I'm not being punished?"

"First, rape is never, *never* your fault. The only people to blame are your rapists. The two men who raped you are at fault, not you. As for punishment, who do you think punished you?"

"God. Like I did something wrong and He punished me for it." Bella studied the hand still on hers. She had only ever said that to two other people. Sarresh had never offered an alternative, and Miah had only questioned her thinking.

"I see. God does not punish His children, but there is a price we all pay for having free will. Just like I freely chose to walk home, the man who attacked me freely chose to rape me. You chose to leave school when you did, and the men who attacked you chose to rape you. We all have a choice, and in some instances our choices will lead us into horrible situations. This does not mean you're being punished, and it doesn't make it your fault. Do you hear me?"

Her words made perfect sense. Yet, Bella couldn't find a way to agree with what the woman believed so wholeheartedly. Maybe the rape hadn't been a punishment, but surely the miscarriage had been. After all, she'd gotten addicted to drugs and suffered the loss because of her own stupidity.

Bella stared Miah's mother in the eyes and lied. "Yes."

"Good. You look like you need to rest, so I'm going to leave you for a bit. I think Jeremiah plans to be here after school. We can talk more, soon."

"Thanks, Mrs. Detrone. I appreciate everything you're doing for me."

"We're happy to help."

Bella looked up at the knock on her door. "Come in."

Miah entered. "Happy Valentine's Day."

"Already?"

"Should I say, Happy Release Day, instead?"

Bella groaned. "I wish they didn't have to be on the same day."

Miah pulled a small, white teddy bear from behind his back. The bear held a heart with "I Got U" embroidered on it.

"Happy Valentine's Release Day."

"This is a great gift, but now I feel bad. I didn't get you anything." Bella accepted the teddy bear and smiled.

"Seeing you smile is enough of a gift for me."

Bella opened her mouth to respond and quickly snapped it shut. She could do better than a smile. Cupping his cheek, she tenderly kissed Miah on the lips. "Thank you."

"Okay, I won't argue with that either. You ready to go?"

"I guess." Bella glanced around the room. It had been her home for the past couple of weeks. After she was stable, they'd moved her from ICU to here for the rest of her recovery. In total, she had spent yet another eight weeks of her life in this hospital, three in a coma and the five during which she'd worked to become a semblance of who she once had been.

"How are you doing?"

"To be honest, I'm not really sure. It's kind of like I can't breathe. Things are so messed up, and I don't know how to fix it, or even if I can."

"Give your mom some time. I'm sure she'll come around."

"And do what? Pray she gets on the next plane from wherever she is and comes home? Truthfully, I don't blame her for dumping me in someone else's lap ..."

Miah started to shush her, but she just held up a hand. "Please, I need to get this out. I know he got shot because of me. He followed me out, and I argued with him. What makes it worse, I think he saved me." The words left her mouth before she could stop them. She hadn't ever mentioned what she recalled about the shooting on Christmas Day when she nearly died. Again.

"What do you mean?"

"He knocked me down. I think he took bullets that were meant for me."

Miah took her hands in his. "He loved you."

"There's something else. The day my heart stopped? When I woke up, I thought …"

"Go on."

"I remember feeling peaceful. Wherever I was, everything was okay. And I saw my dad. He told me I had to go back. I had to find a way to survive and let go of the pain. I had to use my strength to fight back and help others. He told me he loved me … and left. I chased after him, but I didn't get far." Tears rolled down her cheeks.

"Then what happened?"

"Someone called my name. I walked towards it. The closer I got, the louder it was, and I realized it was you. You were yelling at me not to give up. Before I knew it, I was running toward you. I thought it was all a dream … but what if it wasn't?"

Miah hugged her to him. "Miracles happen all the time. I like to believe you coming back to me was one of those. I really thought I'd lost you that day."

"I'm glad you didn't." Bella wrapped her arms around him. The urge to numb the pain lingered, but with him by her side, maybe she could win the battle that raged inside her soul.

He tucked some of her hair behind her ear and kissed her forehead. "Me too, Bell. Me, too."

"I know you have to take me to the rehab center, but do we have time to go by the cemetery?" Her father's body may have been buried in China, but her mother had a memorial for him erected at the cemetery. This way, Bella could say goodbye properly.

"Yeah. We can do that."

The car coasted through the open iron gates. Tombstones lined the grounds.

How had the service gone in China? Had a lot of people attended? She had no idea. Her grandmother had discussed Chinese traditions with her, but Bella recalled little of how death was handled. Not that that knowledge could make the loss of her father better, especially with how things ended between them. Miah had attempted to reassure her about that awful fight, but she still blamed herself. If not for her, he'd be alive.

Miah pulled the car over. "We're here."

"Already?"

Miah reached across the console and gripped her hand. "You don't have to do this."

"Yes, I do." *He's here because of me. It's time I accepted that.* Bella squeezed Miah's hand back, then released it and unbuckled the seatbelt.

He nodded. "I'll show you where it's at, and then give you some space. Okay?"

"Thank you." She preferred to speak with her father alone. Miah always seemed to know exactly what she desired without her having to tell him. It would be awkward enough talking to a headstone. An audience would only make her feel more self-conscious. They climbed out of the car, and Bella scanned the rows of stones.

Miah slipped an arm around her waist. She jumped a little at the touch.

"You sure you should do this today?"

"Yeah. I'm okay. Really."

"All right." He escorted her to a row about twenty feet from a tree line and pointed out a headstone. "I'll stay here."

It seemed ridiculous. Her father wasn't here. Just the marker. But she couldn't fly to China where her he had actually been buried. She walked to what represented her father.

Loving husband and adoring father. Her mother had selected those words.

Slowly, she knelt and placed a hand on the marble. "I'm so sorry, Bàba. I never meant for any of this to happen. I wish you were here with me."

Tears rolled down her cheeks. Truthfully, she wasn't sure she was as strong as they all believed her to be. The yearning for the numbness had seeped in many times since she'd woken from the coma. There were nights she sobbed, in hopes it would turn out to be a nightmare. The whole thing, even her suicide attempt, which no one appeared to know about. The times she accepted it as her reality, those were the worst—more so, since Miah revealed the truth about her father.

The hairs on the nape of her neck prickled. Bella surveyed her immediate surroundings. Miah hadn't moved from his spot several feet away. She looked to the tree line. Was someone hiding there? She shook off the sensation and returned her gaze to her father's headstone. It was probably just another family visiting their loved one. Then she glanced at the trees again. A tall, dark-haired man stood there. Who could it be? Gervasio?

Whoever it was had hidden themselves well. Her eyes narrowed, and she gripped her father's headstone. If that monster was standing there, she hoped he could read lips.

"He took you from me, Bàba. I know he did. If I do nothing else, I will avenge you. Gervasio Rodriguez will pay."

To be continued ...

Who finds Gervasio Rodriguez, first: Juan Castell, Luis (Swifty), or the police? Does Bella find out she has a brother? What did Bella write in her letters? Does Jeremiah ever find out about Bella's actual suicide attempt?

Get all the answers in

avenged

Released May 19, 2018

Check out the prequel,
and see how Bella and Jeremiah's story began in

addicted

Keep reading for a preview of

a v e n g e d

one

Gervasio eyed the papers in his hands. How had he been so blind to the connection that stared him in the face? And how had he so badly misjudged the one person he had ever truly trusted? He should've had the man investigated when they first met. Some of the trouble he currently found himself in would never have occurred. He most certainly would have taken a different approach with his girl.

He would never forget how he and she crossed paths at the Fourth of July party last year. Her features had turned and turned in his mind, until recognition hit. It had been many years, but once he saw the resemblance to her beautiful mother, he knew. He'd been a mere teenager when he'd met Ileana Castell. Not that she ever introduced herself as a Castell. Instead, she spoke of herself as Ileana Costa. That woman was exquisite. A pure gem that shone, even in death.

And Ileana Costa had tasted divine, too. But, despite his relentless torture, she had refused to tell him where she'd hidden her daughter. When he left her, in the center of a scene made to appear as if she had taken her own life, he knew no more of her daughter's whereabouts than when he'd first entered the house. Then, by happy coincidence, years later, he ran into the girl at a Fourth of July party. A sweet, rich aroma radiated from her skin. As beautiful as her mother, the girl tasted even lovelier. If things had ended differently, he wouldn't be in hiding, right now. Instead, he and Giovanna would be married, and she'd be carrying his son. As it should be.

But events had not gone precisely to plan, and now he *was* in hiding. Thankfully, Gervasio had a list of names. It was the reason he sat in a warehouse, concealed from the police, who scoured the city for any clue of his whereabouts. He was also keeping himself out of sight of his enemies—as well as giving himself much-needed time to hatch his plan for revenge. His girl's entire family—including the woman Giovanna now called mother, who had left Rescate County for safety's sake—would pay for keeping them apart. This time, nothing would be left to chance. He'd take everything into his own hands.

Unfortunately, to get to all the names on his hit list, he would have to use every person who remained loyal to him—and there was a diminishing number of those. For starters, his own brother had betrayed him, along with his girl's scheming brother.

Gervasio dragged a finger down the sheet of paper as he scanned the words written clear as day. It seemed that Swifty, Gervasio's former right-hand man, who was also known as Luis Hernandez, had actually been born Sabio Costa. This made him a blood brother to Gervasio's girl, Giovanna Costa, who was now known as Bella Kynaston.

Getting to Swifty would be easy. All Gervasio had to do was grab the guy's baby sister and hold her hostage—which, anyway, fit in with his plans quite nicely. Getting to his own brother, Cristobal, would be slightly more of a challenge. Then again, if the rumors were true, Cristobal had befriended Swifty, meaning chances were good he could entice them to rescue his own sweet Giovanna, now known as Bella, together. Then he could make short work of killing both Cristobal and Swifty, lessening his remaining problems significantly.

Tapping his chin, Gervasio glanced around the abandoned warehouse. It would take time, but he had the capability to properly execute a full-on plan of destruction. He'd consider the sacrifice of this property a small price to pay for the satisfaction.

He rubbed the jagged scar on his face. It served as a reminder of where he'd been—and exactly where he intended to go. He felt himself grinning at the thought of the two plans he'd formulated. What was most pleasing was that both ended the same way: with bodies on the floor.

Jeremiah hefted Bell's suitcase out of the trunk. It was strange to bring her things home to his house without her, but he'd pick her up from the recovery center soon enough. Bella, who had completed the first two levels of treatment in the hospital, was now being seen on an outpatient basis at Luna Hills Recovery. "Intensive therapy," Bell called it—explaining, when he asked, that she'd be doing a lot of talking as doctors got to the root of her addiction.

God, he hated to think of how close he came to losing her forever. During the worst minutes of his life, he had witnessed her heart giving out completely. By God's will, it hadn't been her time to go. The way they had gotten to that moment, though? It left a lot of unanswered questions. There were a number of things he wanted to ask since she started on her journey to recovery. But, on reflection, he wasn't sure he was ready to handle the truth.

Sure, the video had proven Bella hadn't attempted to take her own life, but why were the letters in her handwriting. She must have written them herself, right? If so, when? Then there was the pill bottle, marked with two sets of fingerprints, one of which was Bell's. How had her prints ended up on the bottle? If he hadn't overheard his father mention that her hands had never left the arms of the chair, Jeremiah would've assumed she'd picked up the bottle herself, and taken the pills.

He shuddered. Yeah. He wasn't sure which scared him more, the questions or the answers.

Jeremiah closed the front door and set the suitcase on the floor. Down the hall, he saw his sister standing outside her bedroom, arms crossed. As he headed towards her, he heard their parents offering suggestions to one another from inside Amanda's room.

"I don't think we have a choice. We'll have to take out Mandy's bed and exchange it for a couple of twin beds."

Jeremiah poked his head into the room, just in time to see their mother, Christine, point toward the middle of Amanda's headboard and say, "We can add a nightstand between them." Their father leaned back against the dresser. "Yeah, but that won't give her any place to put her clothes. Unless Amanda cleans out a couple of drawers and slims her closet down."

"How long have they been discussing this?" Jeremiah asked his sister. She hadn't been thrilled with the idea of sharing a room with Bella to begin with. Now, their parents were discussing how to rearrange her bedroom as if she had no say in the matter.

"A few minutes. I tried helping and got pushed aside. God, I can't wait to turn eighteen."

Jeremiah raised an eyebrow at the comment, which Mandy had been making more and more since the first of the year. He wondered, was she planning to jump right up and move out when she turned eighteen in April, even though there'd still be a good month and a half of school before she graduated? He hoped not.

But that was months away. Now, he stepped into Amanda's bedroom and cleared his throat. "Some food for thought. Have you considered how uncomfortable this will make Bella?"

"Of course, we have, but where else can she stay?" His mother made her way across the room and paused, staring into Amanda's packed closet.

Jeremiah sighed. "I don't think rearranging Mandy's room will make things better. Bella won't just feel like she's inconvenienced the family, generally. Now, she's going to worry about the situation Mandy's been put in."

He glanced at Mandy, who rolled her eyes, but didn't say anything.

"Do you have another idea, son?" his father asked.

"She could move into my room. And before you go all parental, hear me out." Jeremiah paused. He'd seen how nervous Bell had been all morning after visiting her father's grave. Then she'd begun twisting the hem of her blouse tighter and tighter the closer they got to the recovery center. So much had happened to her in such a short period of time: Her rapist had left her pregnant; then Bell lost the baby. Her father had been killed and her mother had disappeared. She needed someplace peaceful to stay—somewhere she wouldn't be subjected to the tension of sharing a room with his already restless, on-edge sister.

His mother sat on Amanda's bed. "We're listening."

"If she stays in my room, she'll have her own space, and so will Mandy. You guys just finished the basement, so I can stay down there. The more peace and calm Bell has, the less of a chance she'll relapse. At least that's how I see it."

"You may be right." His mother sighed and glanced around the room.

With his mother's agreement, Jeremiah turned to his father. "Dad?"

His father nodded. "It's a good plan. I'm just concerned for her. No matter where she sleeps, the situation will not be easy on her—especially with Gervasio Rodriguez still out there somewhere."

What? Didn't his father believe the guy had left town? Surely, he couldn't be stupid enough to come after Bell again?

His mother voiced his question. "You think he'll come looking for her?"

"I do. Both of them. We'll have to be more vigilant than ever."

"Both? Both of whom?" Jeremiah hated it when his parents had silent conversations right in front of him. When neither his father nor mother responded, he arched an eyebrow at his sister. Maybe she had some idea of what the hell his parents meant, but the blank look on her face told him she was just as confused as he was.

His mother stood up and patted his shoulder. "Come on. Let's go get your room ready for Bella, then we can get you set up downstairs."

Juan followed the path behind the cabin. The heat and wisps of steam radiating from the fire pit indicated a fire had recently been extinguished. Although neither his son nor his son's companion were in the small building, he assumed at least one of them was close by.

Passing another stand of trees, he confirmed his opinion of the place, which hadn't altered since he'd first found the safe house. It was well isolated, difficult to find without directions. And, once, it had belonged to him. A fact Sabio likely hadn't learned. Still, he had to give his son credit. His boy had grown into a smart young man—even if Juan, himself, had had next to nothing to do with that outcome.

A branch snapped beneath his foot. Juan growled at the noise giving his position away.

Slipping behind a nearby tree, he surveyed his surroundings. No movement caught his eye. It didn't appear his misstep had attracted attention. Satisfied that he remained unnoticed, Juan left the cover of the tree and continued on his way, hoping he would find Sabio soon. With his enemy out there, he certainly did not want to be caught off guard.

Click.

The sound of a pistol being cocked behind him was unmistakable. Without hesitation, Juan lifted his hands into the air. "I am unarmed."

"Dad?"

"*Sí.*" Relieved to hear his son's voice, Juan turned, expecting Sabio to lower the gun. But the weapon remained pointed at him. Inwardly, he groaned. His son's response probably had to do with their last meeting. Unfortunately, it had not gone well.

Sabio's next words affirmed Juan's thought. "What the hell are you doing here? Didn't you get the picture last time? I don't want, nor do I need your help."

"I understand you are upset with me. While you have reason, would you please disengage your weapon?"

His son smirked, returned the safety to its rightful position, and tucked the gun into his waistband. "What? Don't trust my aim?"

"I am quite certain you have learned to fire that weapon appropriately, otherwise you should not carry it."

"No thanks to you, but, yeah, I did. Now, what're you doing here?"

"I have seen your sister and—"

"Are you shitting me? You tell me not to contact her, and you have the balls to go see her? What'd you do? Hold out your hand and say, 'Sorry I disappeared, but I'm your father.'"

Juan pinched the bridge of his nose. Of course, he had not introduced himself to his daughter at all. Nor did he intend to ever do so. The less she knew of his existence, the better her own life would be. "No, my son. I watched her from a distance, as I asked you to do. She was in the cemetery mourning the man she called father. I believe she spotted me, but I suspect she thought I was Gervasio, which is why I am here."

Sabio's face softened somewhat. "Okay. You have my attention, so speak."

"You have access to information that I do not and which I believe can be useful, if we choose to work together."

Raising his eyebrows, Sabio asked, "And why would I do that? It isn't like you've given me any reason to trust you. The one time I needed you most to help my sister, you left me hanging. No response, no call ... nothing. Gigi nearly died because of it." He shoved his hands into his jeans pockets.

Linking his own hands behind his back, Juan nodded. His son made a fair assessment of the situation. Thus far, Sabio had done all the work. He needed to prove his worth to his son. "I apologize. I carefully weighed all the options and concluded you and your sister were safest if I maintained my distance. That included our communications as well. Much time had passed when I realized the error of my decision."

"I take it that you have a plan, then?"

"I do. You are quite apt with computers and other electronic resources. I, on the other hand, am an excellent shooter. If Gervasio has done all this to seek me out, then I should be the one doing the, shall we say, ground work." Juan carefully offered only the essentials of what he deemed important. Although his son was brilliant, he was only eighteen years of age. On the other hand, perhaps his son's youth had caused Juan to underestimate him.

"I fail to see how your ability with a weapon in any way proves I can trust you. And for all the great shot you claim to be, you haven't exactly protected us. Gervasio found Gigi, and now she's dealing with something no one should ever have to—especially not at the age of sixteen."

Juan held back a smile. Ileana would have seen the humor in how much their son took after her. Before Sabio, Ileana had been the only person to ever call him on his crap. Now, their son was filling her shoes. Clearly, only one thing would convince Sabio he could be trusted.

"You are correct. And I must live with the choices I made that allowed for those events to occur in Giovanna's life. The only way I know how to make things right is to do what I should have many years ago. Go to the desk in the bedroom. There is a false bottom in the center drawer. Inside is a file. That should be sufficient evidence for you to trust me in this endeavor."

"You must think I'm a real idiot. I found that file a long time ago. So, yes, I'm fully aware of your skills. The question is, why should I tell you anything about what I learn about Gervasio's whereabouts?"

"Because it is best if I deal with him before your sister makes any attempts at revenge. My hands are already dirty. Taking him out will not wash my sins away, but it will prevent you or your sister from collecting any sins of your own—at least on Gervasio's account. Is not that a good enough reason?" Juan's question came out in a snarl.

Sabio dragged a hand down his face, thought for a moment, then nodded slowly. "I can't argue with that. For now, we'll work together."

Bella rolled over to her side. She opened an eye and glanced at the clock on the nightstand. Midnight. Had she really only been in bed for two hours? She buried her nose into the pillow. Miah's scent lingered. His natural musk should've done the trick. It should've been enough to give her the peace she always felt around him. But tonight nothing quieted the whirlwind in her brain.

It was like a tornado had set up shop in her head and was tossing around everything that had occurred within the last few weeks. The discovery of her father's death, the loss of her baby, her mother taking off—not to mention the court decision that landed her here, in the Detrone house. The Detrones had been really nice, and in particular she was grateful to be allowed to stay in Miah's room, rather than share a room with Amanda. Being alone gave her time to think. But thinking wouldn't help her get a full night's sleep.

She eased out of bed, tiptoed over, and pressed her ear to the door, listening for any noise to indicate someone was still up. She'd give anything, she thought, just to overhear one of the Detrones talking to her mother. The only call to her mother she'd made herself had been declined. Her one consolation had been brief conversations with both of her grandmothers. Thankfully, neither of them knew everything that had occurred. A small blessing in disguise. She smiled a little. Maybe it was one of Alex's silver linings.

Bella cracked Miah's bedroom door. All seemed quiet. She slipped out and padded down the hall toward the kitchen—and the basement door.

What if Miah had already passed out? He looked exhausted at dinner. Not that she'd paid much attention to anything happening at the dinner table. Instead, her earlier conversation with the psychiatrist had consumed most of her thoughts. They'd discussed a plan: no immediate return to school, twenty to twenty-five hours a week at the facility on an outpatient basis, and a lot of freaking therapy. She'd have to talk herself blue if she intended to get better. Not like anyone would actually listen.

Now, having tiptoed down the basements stairs, Bella bit her bottom lip and stared at the back of Miah's head. God, what was she doing? She couldn't run to Miah every time sleep refused to come. She had to learn to depend on herself. She was all she had, really. Without saying a word, she pivoted on her foot and turned back toward the stairs.

"Bell? You okay?"

Damn. Offering the hint of a smile, she faced him. She should probably be honest, but whatever words she might use to describe her feelings failed her at the moment. So, she only said, "Yeah. Go back to sleep. I didn't mean to wake you."

"You didn't." Miah rolled over, lifted the covers, and patted the spot beside him.

It was all the invitation she needed. Crawling into the bed, Bella said, "I'm sorry. I just ... this is ... I don't know ... strange. But when I'm with you ..." Bella propped up on her elbow. "It's you, Miah. Your presence gives me a little bit of peace. You have to know that."

"I do, but I didn't think my parents would go for us sharing a bed. I hoped my room would be enough." Miah reached up and tucked a loose strand of hair behind her ear.

"Don't get me wrong, it helps, and I appreciate it, but...."

He sat up and climbed out of the bed. "Come on. I can't have you sleeping down here."

"Then what do we do?"

"I have an idea." Miah grinned.

Coming Soon ...

burned

BOOK 4 RELEASES SUMMER 2020

With only two months until graduation, David should only be concerned with three things: the soccer championship, who he'll be escorting to prom, and finishing school. Instead, in an attempt to district himself from his own problems, he offers aide to a girl with issues of her own. Someone is chasing after her. He plans to protect her any way he can, even if it means he goes down in a blaze of glory.

Aurora has been on the run for months with only one goal—find her uncle. She hasn't seen him in nearly ten years and all clues have led her to Rescate County. It seemed like the perfect place to escape her past, but no one ever said leaving gang life would be easy. When her ex-boyfriend, leader of her former gang, catches up with her, her rescuer is someone she'd be better off without. But David is intent on helping her and the more she pushes him away, the tighter he holds on. At the rate they're going, if they don't find her uncle soon—her past will burn them both alive.

Is David willing to risk it all for someone who is dangerous for both his health and his heart? Can Aurora escape her past and finally find the family she's been seeking all these years? Or will they both get burned by the flames?

URBAN FANTASY SERIES

Awakened

Released May 2019

Disillusion

Released June 2019

For FREE sneak peeks, giveaways, upcoming events, and more, sign up for Krys Fenner's monthly newsletter.

https://mailchi.mp/ded3a6cb847f/krysfenner

Author Note

Although the characters in this novel are not real, some of the situations they face are very real. While the main character survives her suicide attempt, not all teenagers do. And those that attempt suicide once are ten times more likely to attempt it again.

As of 2014, suicide has become the second leading cause of death among young adults. We can help change this by learning the warning signs. Listen to your friends and family when they talk. Watch for certain behaviors or mood. All warning signs can be found on **http://www.afsp.org/preventing-suicide/ suicide-warning-signs**.

If you think someone you know may attempt suicide, talk to a trusted adult. Try and get that person help. If you're thinking about suicide, or need someone to talk to, call the National Suicide Prevention Lifeline @ **1-800-273-TALK** (8255).

Suicide can be prevented if we take action.
Sometimes, all it takes is a knock on the door.